I0582412

The Displacement Duology

Dangerous to Heal

Negotiated Fate

Also by Rebecca M. Zornow
It's Over Or It's Eden

NEGOTIATED
FATE

Rebecca M. Zornow

Negotiated Fate

First Edition
978-1-7377118-8-9

*For Lydia Marie Zornow
and Jean Ann Dempsey,
who deserved more time*

Prologue

She bit the inside of her cheek to will herself, force herself, to do it. There was no rewriting fate; she was here. Get it over with. Her hands reached out hesitantly, but she would never allow anyone to see the tremors that racked her at night. Under her fingertips, the man's skin felt cold and hairless, the spine, abnormal. Links of vertebrae curved outward, eager to break through the frail, papery skin.

The man was old—older than even one such as Nica could age. He lay on his side, docile save eyes that greedily drank in every small gesture from Nica as she circled him. This was not the first time a Wea Saavian had worked on his body. His salvation would come from her and the endings of many would come from him, but Nica had a job to do.

Nica's hands warmed sharply and her breath caught in

her throat as she tried to steady her own heartbeat. She fought to keep her composure calm, mindful of an audience of the man's attendants and her own captors. She resisted shaking her curly black hair out of her face. It would only fall back, hunched as she was to the work of healing.

A wheeze escaped the man as her hands muffled the crack of a bone. Then another. The stem of Nica's own spinal cord warmed and throbbed at the base of her skull. Sweat broke across her forehead as pain built along the column of her spine, almost as if it were fighting to arch away from her heart.

Another pop, this one much larger. Someone gasped, but they were at the fuzzy edges of Nica's perception. She was running a thousand miles and standing still. Her hands shook and held firm. She was falling.

When her eyes blinked open, Nica considered her body before moving. She wiggled her fingers, stretched her toes, and finally sat up and pushed the heavy comforter off. Sweat had dried, matting her curly black hair, but she was glad to be in the same clothes. She didn't want the hands of attendants on her while she was unconscious. She didn't have a headache—never did—but it felt as if a swarm of insects would pour from her dry throat.

"I'm glad to see you're finally awake, Nica."

Nica startled lightly. Artificial sunlight poured generously from the window panel and lit a slender, well-dressed man from behind. He didn't smile but leaned forward, as if to inquire how she fared after healing the spine of a man so ancient his back contorted.

"Don't you have anything else to do, Savini?" When he didn't respond, she rasped, "Who was that?"

"Jeffers Hoss, once a representee of the planet Yovalia in the Joint Council, now a memory to most. The current Yovalia representatives take orders from him."

Nica cleared her throat. "I've never seen an older being. He had to be what, five hundred years old?"

It hurt Nica to drift into this conversational pattern. Gossip with Savini. Chatter with the enemy. But there was no one else to talk to. Not since Yaniqui was taken from her. Without her daughter, Savini was the only constant in her life.

"Closer to a thousand years old," he confided.

Nica arched a brow in disdain. "A humanoid who lived to see a millennium? Impossible."

"Not with the right connections and resources."

"Someone within the Joint Council would notice. They would never allow the Yovalian representatives to be controlled by the same global political leader for so long."

"He doesn't. He cycles on and off every few decades. No one is around long enough to remember him. No one would believe."

As Savini was clearly not in a rush to get back to the beck and call of Akar Enterprises, Nica slowly swung her legs off the bed. She filled a purple-hued glass at a dispenser and drank the entire thing. She cleared her throat and then drank half a vessel more. It quenched some of her immediate thirst, but she sensed she was tapped at a greater level.

Savini made as if to stand. "You should order some hot tea. Please, allow me."

Nica waved him down and perched on the side of the bed with the rest of the water. If Nica had met Savini in any other corner of the galaxy, he would have been unremarkable. Well-groomed, charming enough but ordinary. It was hard to believe such a common-looking person was the one to execute the terrible orders of a galactic human trafficking corporation.

"So," she started, eager to say the thing that would make him leave, "I'll finish repairing Hoss's spine in sessions. Maybe three. I didn't expect to be overcome like that..." She didn't want to tell Savini it was the most difficult healing she had ever facilitated. She already regretted her words. She couldn't afford for him to think her weak.

His smooth lips constructed a thin frown. Nica watched him carefully as she sipped her water, trying to read him. He wore a version of the same cream suit with dark green accents he always did, the branding colors of her oppressor. His hair was wavy and grew to touch his ears but was perfectly tamed. Savini's eyes flickered to Nica's face. He always caught her when she watched him. As if he cared what she thought.

Anyone who did the work he did couldn't really care about another being.

"The last Wea Saavian that healed him a decade ago had difficulty too—"

"Damn it, Savini. Don't you tell me that. Don't you dare tell me that." She carelessly set her cup on the nightstand. It tipped and water coated the already glossy surface. Savini righted the glass, but she pointed a finger at him. "I don't want to hear a single word about your entitlement toward my people. 'The last Wea Saavian.' You mean one of my kin, ripped from Wea Saa and made to do the bidding of the most heinous leaders of our galaxy."

Savini stood and turned his back to the corner of the room. A security camera loomed in the upper corner.

"Nica." A flush of red spilled across his normally pale cheeks. His eyes darted to the corner and then back to her. "I know firsthand how hard this path is." His voice came soft. "I *want* to help you, Nica. Your owner, a Joint Council member himself, speaks as to who should be healed. It's just another business transaction, one I am forced to fulfill."

It sounded like Savini was trying to make himself out to be as powerless as Nica, but she fought against the thought.

"Your powers grant you a level of privilege," he continued, "but if you were to, say, share what you know about other Wea Saavian survivors, you would be able to commandeer even more autonomy."

Nica swallowed and fought to keep her face blank. She hadn't told Savini or anyone else that there were none. That she and her daughter were the last of Wea Saa. That even if she knew of others, she would succumb to violence before speaking a word of their whereabouts.

Savini approached the bed, his face gentle, the camera still square behind his back. "This spacecraft is not built for long-term holding. Your owner is building a more secure site, one that's centrally located for his purposes. When that happens, you will go there. Life will much be the same, but, if we handle things correctly, if you have information to exchange with Akar…there's a chance I may be permitted to see you from time to time." His eyes shifted away again. "I can make this life easier to bear."

At last Nica understood the offer Savini was spinning. The entitlement was hungrier than she dared fear. It wasn't Akar's. It was his own.

She bit the inside of her cheek against the embarrassment of coercion, the soft contour already ragged. "Visit me?" Her voice was as dead as she could make it.

Neither of them spoke. She forced herself not to glance up at the camera, not to show any emotion until she knew what she could get out of the transaction.

Savini's hands hung at his side and he stretched them suddenly. "Yes. With the right information, I could persuade certain particularities so your final arrangement was favorable for a visit."

Nica licked her lips, trying to mirror the eagerness she saw in his eyes though she was revolted. She didn't want to hear about his plans. How he'd feed information to his superiors and in exchange get to run his hands along her body once a quarter.

"What about Yaniqui? I'm her maemi. Until she's freed, I would never give up any information."

At the mention of her daughter, the spell was broken. Savini brought his hands together in front of his suit. His dark green pocket square and buttons stood out starkly. He cleared his throat. "Months ago, I told you of the auction."

Nica tried to mask her pain. Pretend he was giving her mundane directions not to embarrass herself in front of clients next time.

"She has—" He stopped. "Nica, it may be difficult to believe, but I do not want to hurt you. So, despite what I'm about to say, you must understand it's an extreme abnormality that will soon be rectified."

Nica blinked and pushed her long curls back over her shoulders. "What are you saying?"

"Yaniqui escaped hours before her auction was to take place."

She couldn't help it. A brilliant grin flitted across Nica's face. She couldn't remember a moment where she felt so much light.

Savini frowned. "Let me finish before you grab at conclusions, Nica. We already know where she is. She—" It was clear Savini would not speak her daughter's name. "—is on a small planet, one not even a full member of the Joint Council. Their security is limited at best. My— Akar's—most experienced contractor is en route. Once the bounty hunter is on the ground, they will have her in their possession within forty-eight hours."

Nica's cheeks turned to stone. Just as quickly as the relief had come, it had shattered.

"Savini," her voice broke. She swallowed and tried again. "I would do anything to assure my daughter's freedom."

She knew he was reading the offer in her eyes, considering it. Then a shadow broke over his face. He did not get to where he was, earn the safety of his position, by giving in to impulse and temptation. He shook his head very slightly.

Nica bared her teeth. "Then we have nothing more to discuss. Get out."

And despite the fact that she was slave, he was master, he did exactly what she asked of him.

Chapter 1

Yaniqui (*Yan-i-key*)
New Washington, WI

Yaniqui dabbed scented oil on the inside bend of her arm like her mother did for her when she was little. The dull calm of vanilla was unfamiliar but the sharp scent of citrus made her think of ander fruit from Wea Saa. After a moment, she awkwardly made two dabs along either side of her neck like she saw Loera do with her perfume.

She fluffed her dark curls and assessed herself in the mirror. She had stripped the loose tank top and khaki shorts she'd spent the day in. Loera called the tan summer dress a cop-out when they bought it—it wasn't anywhere near showy enough for Loera's standards—but Yaniqui liked it. She wasn't used to wearing skirts or dresses, but this one was easy to move in and had giant pockets on either side of her hips. It came with a thin rope one was supposed to tie around the waist, but Yaniqui threw that away the moment she hung the new dress in her closet. She had had a decade of wrapping extra fabric around her waist and she was done.

He would be there soon and she wanted to be ready. It was still awkward with him. They got along, but it wasn't as natural as it should be. Yaniqui intended to make things right at dinner that night.

A stack of books littered the floor next to the tiny white couch. Pillows lay rumpled across the bedspread from where she wrote in her journal that morning. It hadn't taken long to make the room feel like her own. Even if it was in someone else's house.

Yaniqui grabbed a thin wallet that housed her temporary ID from an end table littered with pens and makeshift bookmarks of paper scraps and wrappers. The wallet went in one pocket and a phone in the other. Yaniqui got to the hallway before she tracked back and grabbed her journal from the wrinkled bedspread. She shoved the journal under the couch.

A floorboard creaked and she straightened, tugging her dress into place.

Hloban put his hands on the lintel of the doorway and leaned into the room but didn't quite come into her space. He looked utterly comfortable in a thin blue hoodie, zipped open to reveal the black T-shirt underneath. He should be. It was his house.

"You look nice. Hey, did you consider the proposal Cortez's office sent over? They asked me when they could expect an answer."

Yaniqui refused to let the first statement warm her

cheeks.

"I started to read it. Um, yeah, it's long." She cleared her throat. "I don't know about becoming a healer for Earth. It seems…opportunistic." Yaniqui didn't want to say she was nervous about the Earth government's intentions. She was nervous that once she started helping them they would want to control her time and who she offered her services to. Besides, to Yaniqui at least, her gift had a hint of kismet to it. There were so many people to heal that the best way to decide who deserved it was to let fate do it for her. She wanted to trust that the right people would come into her life at the needed time.

"I think the secretary-general is trying to find a place for you here."

"Do I not have a place in your home?"

Hloban dropped his hands. "Of course you do. For as long as you want." His gaze drifted to the side. "I know living together isn't ideal, but I won't ever abandon you."

Yaniqui was wondering if she was the only one who tacked an "again" onto his statement. No, that wasn't fair. They had been separated, solar systems apart. He got married, had a kid, built a great life. He didn't even know she was still alive. And when he learned that his once-betrothed was still out there and in need, he had come to rescue her.

They both heard a door on the main floor open. Loera was home from work. Hloban's wife.

By the time Yaniqui got down to the first floor, Obani had crawled out from under the dining table where his coloring books were stacked. He jumped at his mother's feet until she hugged him. The moment he got what he wanted, Obani wriggled away as if Loera was the one begging for attention.

"Love you too, baby boy," Loera said as he disappeared under the table. Loera placed a hand on the back of Hloban's sweatshirt and kissed him on the cheek. Then she smiled at Yaniqui. "I see you're in your new dress. Are you heading out soon?"

Yaniqui dipped her head to affirm that. "How was your day?"

Loera waved a hand as she pulled a water filter from the fridge. "You didn't miss much."

Yaniqui hovered. In one part of her mind, she saw herself sliding onto a kitchen stool, easily chatting with Loera about her day. Apologizing for turning down her idea to tag along to Loera's lab for a string of meetings. Be two women that anyone would look at and think were friends.

Instead, Yaniqui *had* turned down Loera's generous offer while still in pajamas. Part of it was she really was tired—she hadn't been sleeping well since she arrived on Earth—but mostly she wondered at the motivation. Did Loera not trust Hloban and Yaniqui while Obani was at preschool? Home together all day, alone.

Yaniqui softly bit the inside of her lip as Loera drank her chilled water.

Loera could feel whatever she wanted to feel. She was the wife. But for Yaniqui, every time Hloban walked in a room, she had to push down emotion. To discard her longing for another life. Her embarrassment for how she had tried to persuade Hloban on his spacecraft the *Caneille* that they really did belong together. Even relief that she could let it all go and start new. It jumbled together until she felt vaguely queasy and it was no wonder Yaniqui and Hloban barely spent any time together during the day. Hloban preferred to shut himself away in his office until it was time to pick up Obani.

Loera was still summarizing her day. "I was double-booked for lunch, so I ended up eating half of two different meals so both groups would feel like they were my only lunch."

Hloban smiled and brushed his hair down. They looked funny standing next to each other—Hloban's casual house clothes with Loera's wide-legged pantsuit and crisp cat's-eye liner. Loera had moved on from her usual twist out to an asymmetrical undercut of cornrows.

The phone in Yaniqui's pocket dinged. "That's Adam." Only a few other people had Yaniqui's number, and nearly half of them were in the room with her. "I guess I better get going."

She pulled out her phone to confirm Adam had sent her an automatic proximity alert as their schedules were synced for the evening and he was getting close to her location. She caught the quick look Hloban and Loera shared. It soured her mood. After the new dress and the encouragement all week, she knew they had high hopes for the night.

"Have a fun time, Yani. If you're going to be very late, let us know," Loera said.

"Right. Have fun and definitely don't rush back," Hloban said. "It will be good for you two to talk."

Yaniqui awkwardly stretched her shoulders to cover her cringe.

"I mean," he clarified, "it's a great evening to...discuss things. Get to know Adam. Stay out late."

She cocked her head at the couple. "We spent weeks locked up together on the *Caneille*. I think I have a good idea of who Adam is."

Loera glanced at Hloban, slightly bemused. He scratched the underlayer of his thick black hair. "Sure, I'll admit I learned more than I ever could want to know about Eeriva," he deflected, "but, still, it's a good opportunity to see if things will work out between the two of you."

It was too much. Yaniqui just knew Hloban had told Loera about his plan to get Adam and Yaniqui together. Get her out of the way so she would be out of the house and he and Loera could live happily ever after.

She could feel it coming. For all the many times she imagined Hloban in the darkness, breath hot on her cheek, he was absolutely infuriating. The sneer was just starting to wrinkle her nose when Loera interrupted.

"Yaniqui, have fun. You're an adult. If you want to stay out late, let us know so we don't worry. If you want to come home early, do that. If you don't want to go at all, cancel. And you"—she turned her focus on her husband—"don't pressure her. Go finish up work. I'll make dinner."

But Hloban didn't move until Yaniqui sighed and marched toward the door. She'd prefer to wait outside.

Adam was pulling into the driveway as Yaniqui opened the door. She thought maybe Hloban was going to stick his head out and wave, but she heard a hiss from the kitchen. Yaniqui smiled. Loera was a good person to have in your corner. If only it wasn't filled with webs of the past.

Yaniqui ran to the passenger side door before Adam

could get out. She wanted to minimize interacting with Adam until they were down the road. Who knew if Hloban was peeking through the drapery?

"Hey, Yani, how are you?" He lowered the volume on the radio and reversed the car out of the driveway.

Did the curtain twitch? Yaniqui decidedly turned away from the house and focused on Adam's face. Once he righted the car on the road, he looked back at her and broke into a huge grin.

"Adam, has anyone ever told you that you have an abnormal level of positive energy?"

His smile broke. "Yaniqui, has anyone ever told you that you distrust everything?"

They both laughed. The house was far behind them. Yaniqui could finally relax. She deserved a night to have fun. A humid but pleasantly warm breeze blew through the open windows. Adam kept his hair a bit longer than Hloban's and it ruffled with the wind.

"I thought we could go to a restaurant in the Eighth Ward. That neighborhood's coming back and I've heard only good things about the food."

"Well, the only places I know in the capital are places I've been to with you, so sure." Since Yaniqui arrived on Earth, she'd hung out with Adam and some of his friends. They were weird in a way Yaniqui was discovering was particular to Earthlings. So chatty. So willing to dive right into the personal stuff. And so obsessed with laying out the perfect plan for their life, as if they had to organize every minute of it or they'd become garbage people.

But this was the first night Yaniqui and Adam would be out together by themselves. She'd spent time at his house, but his parents were usually around, even watched a movie with them. She'd purposefully not invited Adam to Hloban and Loera's house since the first time. She had asked him to come over three days after arriving on Earth. It was hard to relax when Hloban was watching their every move.

It struck Yaniqui to wonder if Hloban had a similar conversation with Adam as he did with Yaniqui.

Think about it, please. If there's a soul mate out there, that's not me...I have to believe it would be him. Yaniqui still remembered the anger she felt toward Hloban until he started crying. It was hard on both of them—the life they had expected to live on Wea Saa together would never happen. Their planet was gone. They had been thrown in different directions.

Maemi would have known what to do.

Traffic was easy as most drivers poured the opposite way out of the city to get home for dinner in the smaller districts. The summer sun would hang heavy in the sky until after Obani's bedtime. Adam pointed out sights along the drive into the New Washington, WI neighborhood he had in mind.

"This wasn't always the capital, you know," Adam said.

"You mean the 'New' is literal?"

"Yes, the old capital was near what used to be the coast so now it's underwater." Adam glanced in his back mirror.

"Rising seawater doesn't quite compare to my—our—entire home planet blinking out of existence."

Adam turned wide eyes on her, did a hasty glance at the road, and then back at Yaniqui. Though he was half-

15

Wea Saavian, the solar flare and aftermath was physically and culturally distant for him.

Yaniqui bristled. "Oh my gods, stop it. I'm not going to cry."

Adam snapped his mouth shut and Yaniqui turned her attention to the city lights. He recounted the latest job applications he submitted while they parked in an underground lot and plugged the car in. The artificial lights and massive tons of concrete made the space feel liminal. Yaniqui was relieved when they were above ground again.

As they walked, Adam pointed out a road that led to the building his mother, Amanda, worked in. He pointed at some billboard for a show and recanted what his friend said about it. Yaniqui didn't have much to add. She didn't know anyone Adam didn't know. She spent her days writing, studying for her citizenship test, and doing chores at Loera and Hloban's house.

In the weeks she had been on Earth, she had only been into the downtown district a few times. After the endless farm fields of Agriculture Planet No. 4,278—she always thought each individual digit as in four two seven eight—it was strange how an impossible number of people fit into the relatively small footprint of the city.

And, for all the diversity of Earthlings, the city still had a feeling of sameness. Which was why Yaniqui did a double take inside when two beings exited the elevator they got on. The man had a layer of black-and-white striped fur across the body, the torso a bit shorter than a human's. He had two eyes, a nose, and a mouth but the similarities ended there. The shape of the skull was more elongated. The other biped wore a bright yellow dress made of thick shiny fabric that contrasted pleasantly with her subtly patterned orange-toned skin.

When the elevator doors shut, Yaniqui spoke, "Those are the only animoids I've seen besides Jeb since arriving on Earth."

Adam understood her unspoken question. "The restaurant we're going to is part of a complex at the top of this building that is more tolerant of aliens."

"Is that why your friends aren't with us tonight? You don't think they'd be...tolerant?"

Yaniqui had already pointed out to Adam when one of them used a slur for aliens. It didn't seem like anyone else noticed or thought it was a problem. When Adam drove her home after hanging out that night, she asked if all his friends were Earthlings and he had seemed mildly offended.

Adam shrugged as the elevator hummed. "Honestly? Partly? Most of the immigrants here are humanoids, but yeah, there's more popular spaces for aliens that appeals to both humanoid and animoids. Waquas told me about this place. But I was going to ask you to dinner anyway."

Yaniqui tried to fight letting the question slip out. But she couldn't.

"Why?" she asked.

Adam looked stricken. "Uh, because Hloban told me to. I thought maybe it was because you've been depressed ever since arriving on Earth."

Yaniqui burst out laughing. The elevator dinged open and she snickered again at Adam's bluntness. The hostess sat them at a small table and Yaniqui laughed again.

"What?" he rasped, trying not to call attention to

themselves.

Yaniqui licked her lips and leaned forward. "That's really what Hloban said? That it would be nice if we got dinner and you thought, 'Sure, I'll do that.'"

Adam's brow scrunched. "I'm trying to help you fit in here. You don't know *anybody*. You didn't even know what a banana was!"

Yaniqui chuckled again. "Adam..." she paused, savoring it, "Hloban has this plan. He married Miss Perfect and I'm the discarded goods that unfortunately followed him home. It would be much more convenient for Hloban to think that there was a reason for bringing me to Earth."

She paused and nodded when a server assistant poured her water. They left and she looked at Adam expectantly. When nothing came, she stated it clearly, "And you're that reason."

Adam gaped.

"But we can just have dinner," she said.

A very thin woman with a mole on one check came to take their order in a rush. It was growing loud in the room. Adam had to raise his voice when the server left.

"Yaniqui, I don't believe in that kind of hokey Wea Saavian stuff. What people do here with someone they like is different: boyfriend/girlfriend."

"Betroth—" Yaniqui started.

"No!" Adam said. "Gah, haven't you had enough of that word? When people here want to spend more time together romantically, they just date." Adam shaded part of his forehead with his palm and curved fingers. He looked up. "Dinner was all that I was...planning."

"That's all I'm here for too. I'm only telling you

what's going on in Hloban's head."

"It all sounds like arranged marriage stuff. I couldn't do that."

"Arranged marriage?"

"The tradition is fading, but in some parts of Earth, parents or community members decide who is going to marry who. I could never imagine my parents picking out a partner for me."

"Oh, that's not it at all," Yaniqui said dismissively. "Nobody picks anybody. In Wea Saavian culture, the placement of the stars at birth determines your life partner. Hloban is older than me so he had to wait until I was born to be betrothed, but I was betrothed as a baby."

"That sounds…unique," Adam said. "Anyway, there goes any dreams for repopulation."

Yaniqui couldn't believe he brought that up. With only three full-blooded Wea Saavians, repopulation was a myth. Their planet died; their culture was gone. It was up to each Wea Saavian to carry a piece of what was left, as small as that was. She saw his eyes grow wider the longer she stared at him and decided to give him a pass.

She leaned back in her chair, away from the table, to remove some of the intensity. "I know. It's too much, it's unfair for two people to be expected to save something that is already gone," Yaniqui said. "That was something Maemi never held me to. I think she saw very clearly that we couldn't simply replicate our old lives. Much more than I did at least."

The server had a smile frozen in place when she brought over a small platter of thick fluffy bread and some kind of smooth green dip. Yaniqui thanked her more than was necessary to reassure her they were an easy table.

Yaniqui changed the subject back to Adam's job search and they eventually talked about how Yaniqui could possibly spend her time on Earth. Adam got a little hysterical while suggesting to Yaniqui she should start a video channel about an outsider's view of life on Earth but make it all up. Insist that everyone else in the galaxy is wild about Beethoven because it was included on *Voyager*'s golden record.

When their meals arrived, they went quiet. Yaniqui was eating some kind of layered vegetable bake when Adam said, "It's just, it's kind of like you're my sister."

Yaniqui looked up, mouth full.

"I can see how"—he motioned between the two of them with his fork—"would be good for the future of Wea Saa, but I can't see myself with you, especially in bed."

Yaniqui frowned. She didn't see herself with Adam either but if there was anyone who was losing out here, it was Adam and he should know it. She tried to chew faster to be able to get her rebuttal out.

"I don't want to get wrapped up in some kind of married life arrangement that should be on reality TV."

"Yeah, well," she said, mouth still half-full, "my thoughts exactly."

Adam raised his eyebrows sharply with disbelief. He turned back to his food skeptically.

"You think I'm lying? Adam, you are my friend. You might be the only person in my life right now who doesn't want to control the outcome of where I live or what I turn into."

"Okay, sorry."

She took a smaller bite and chewed thoughtfully. "I can't stop thinking about Maemi, much less what I want for a future. And if I do think of it, it feels like it could evaporate at any minute." She sighed. "Nothing feels settled."

They talked only about neutral things for the rest of their dinner and then declined dessert.

At the entrance to the restaurant, Adam halted and turned to Yaniqui as if he just realized something. "You said what Hloban wanted and what you didn't want, but you never said what you wanted."

Yaniqui swallowed. It was a terrible question because there were multiple things she wanted with every fiber of her being and couldn't have. She settled for saying, "I don't know how it happened, but you're my best friend. I want you to keep being my friend."

Adam smiled at her, then looked up above her shoulder the same moment a warm hand touched her elbow softly.

Yaniqui turned, surprised to find Waquas. On the *Caneille,* he'd worn thick hooded sweatshirts and acid-washed jeans. On Earth, Yaniqui had seen him mostly in random graphic T-shirts and canvas pants, his gardening clothes. Now both were replaced by a pale linen jacket that made his green-toned skin glow. Waquas looked between her and Adam and smiled. Yaniqui felt her stomach light up when they made eye contact.

"Waquas, hey," Adam said.

"So, you took my recommendation," Waquas said.

He seemed looser than normal. Though, Yaniqui supposed she had seen him only after he'd been living on the *Caneille* for months with Hloban, Eeriva, Adam, and

Keyad. She was a little nutty after that too.

Adam said, "It was good food. I never knew this was here."

"It's a great place for a date," Waquas said.

Adam and Yaniqui looked at each other. She kept her smile neutral.

"We were most definitely having dinner as friends," Adam said.

"Excuse me, sir?" It was the bartender for some reason. "Could you double-check this receipt?"

Adam walked to the edge of the bar, out of earshot. The bartender pointed down at the paper screen and Adam glanced at her to confirm, then back at Yaniqui and Waquas.

Waquas closed the space that Adam had left. He was taller than Adam and Yaniqui found herself staring at his chest until he asked what she had ordered. It took her a moment to hear the question and she glanced up, mouth gone dry.

Adam returned. He leaned forward, eager for something. He asked Waquas, "Are you just getting here for dinner?"

"No, I met a friend for a drink. We're finished."

"So, you're leaving?"

"Yes." Waquas looked inquisitively at Adam, waiting for the point.

"Did you drive?"

Yaniqui swallowed, certain she was about to be ditched. Waquas stared at Adam who seemed determined to remain unfazed.

"What I'm getting at," he clarified, "is I have another

invitation. Would you mind driving Yaniqui home?"

Waquas looked at Yaniqui to see what she wanted. His face was impartial as she thought about it.

She shrugged. Adam leaving with the bartender would at least solidify their newfound realization that they both wanted to be friends. And honestly, she shouldn't be surprised. Adam was a snack.

Moments later, she steered Waquas out of the restaurant and toward the elevator. They got in a little awkwardly.

"What are we doing here?" Waquas asked.

Yaniqui panicked. Did she misunderstand him? Didn't he agree to drive her home?

"My car's the other way."

"Oh." Yaniqui gave a strangled laugh.

But the elevator had already been called. A trio of friends filtered in on another level and Yaniqui shifted over to stand in front of Waquas. She turned her back to him and though the elevator was filled with the odd silence of two parties crowding into the same small space, she felt a delicate thrill go up her back that had nothing to do with the elevator lifting off. A memory popped into Yaniqui's head.

When she was on the *Caneille* after finding out Hloban was estranged from her, she had stormed into the dormitory. The only person in there was Waquas in his briefs. She immediately turned and shot away, embarrassed, but she remembered what she had seen more than once.

It was a quiet walk to the car but on the drive home Waquas

shared about the summer season on his farm at Yaniqui's prompting. She remembered it well—besides the Winslow Space-Earth Station, it was the first place on Earth she set foot on. She studied Waquas's face as he drove. Some might say his lips were too full, but Yaniqui decided she liked them. He had only the sparsest of eyebrows, but it didn't look odd within the composition of his features.

He peered at Yaniqui abruptly out of the corner of his eye and she turned to look over the dashboard. He broke the silence that Yaniqui didn't realize had grown by asking what she'd been doing recently.

She held back a sigh. "Trying to figure things out in between filling out paperwork. Loera is incredibly kind. She took me shopping for clothes—"

"It's a nice dress," he interjected.

"—Hloban's busy a lot or trying to be. Obani finally likes me."

She felt Waquas watching her while he drove and she rushed on. "But it's like I have nothing and every single choice I make keeps disappearing into a hole. I don't know what to do and I can hardly think about the future because of Maemi."

He thought a moment. "I don't know what you're going through, but I can understand how hard it is for you."

"How long have you been on Earth?"

"Eight years." He nodded his head slowly. "It's been good. This is a relatively stable place. There's discrimination for off-planet people like me, but this land, these wild spaces especially, Earth doesn't know what they have."

"Did you keep a journal when you first arrived? Is that

why you gave me the notebook?" Yaniqui still remembered how pleased she was when Waquas gave it to her the day after she arrived, especially since she was sure he had a thousand things to do after spending the past few months in space trying to rescue her from Akar.

"I still do. But less and less. Writing isn't something that comes naturally to me, but when there's no one else who can understand, you can trust that you will when you return to those pages."

"What frustrated you about Earth when you first got here?" She hoped her question didn't seem too petty.

He barked a laugh. It surprised her. He was usually so stoic.

"I hated the food for a long time. There *is* good food here—you just have to find it. Um, the arrogance got to me."

"What do you mean?" Yaniqui shifted in her seat as the car turned a corner. She looked at Waquas's hands on the wheel. The subtle pattern on his skin ended at his fingers the way it did his neck. It was almost imperceptible in the dim light of the car. It wasn't freckles or wrinkles and it definitely wasn't a geometric pattern but more like a wash of watercolor, mottled but abstract.

"They don't yet realize how small their planet is, how big everything else is out there. I felt perpetually annoyed for the first year. Then I let it go. I met Hloban and we became friends. I worked hard to find a real home for myself. It's the same place as when I first arrived, but I like it now. I found a different perspective I guess."

Yaniqui blinked hard when she realized they were on Hloban's street. She found herself near speechless at having her private feelings articulated about Earthlings. She appreciated his perspective and kindness. And, oh gods, there was something about the bridge of his nose that made her want to run her finger along it. What an odd thought to have.

Waquas parked the car and Yaniqui turned toward him. In a slow but sure motion, she took the cuff of Waquas's jacket sleeve in both hands and felt it between her fingers. She ran one of her hands up toward his elbow. Yaniqui hadn't even touched Waquas's skin yet but with that sure small movement everything was communicated at once.

She looked up at his face and knew in an instant how wrong everything was. Hers was flushed and tentative. His face was smooth and blank save shock. He pulled back slightly.

It was like that.

"Ah, goodnight!" Yaniqui slammed the car door behind her and rushed to the house. It was only a few paces, but she was breathing hard. *What had she done?*

Yaniqui choked as she played the rejection over and over in her mind. She was used to feeling taken advantage of or overprotected but never unwanted. Especially not when she had only recently realized how very much she wanted him.

She closed the door and leaned back on it, hands around her neck so her fingerbones could cradle the base of her neck.

Gods. She had ruined everything.

Chapter 2

Lozen (*Lo-zen*)
The Catchment

A bead of sweat dripped down Lozen's ribs. She couldn't smell her perspiration over the other many scents of the Catchment but that didn't stop her from feeling grimy. It was the third day of unbelievably hot temperatures and, for some reason, Lozen decided it was the perfect day to patch a hole in her roof. The perfect day being any day she went to fill up her water container and found a potentially useful piece of junk on the way back.

Lozen balanced solidly on a thick white bucket and removed scraps of cardboard, tired from cycling through rain and sun. She tipped her face down quickly to ensure no little flecks landed in the whites of her eyes. When the gap in her roof was wide and waiting, Lozen raised her hands over her head to jimmy a length of tin back and forth, trying to fit it in without prying up the surrounding larger pieces. There was a bent edge that kept the tin sheet propped up so Lozen took it down and hammered it with a rock and when that didn't work, stood on it until it straightened under protest, then wedged it into place again.

She collected the wrinkled, sun-bleached scraps of cardboard and went to toss the litter beyond the tied-back blanket that served as her summer door.

Lozen ducked back in. She peered from the shadow of her doorway.

It was Monte, out in the sunshine. Monte and Jerramy. Lozen's fingers wiggled excitedly of their own accord on behalf of her friend. She crouched a moment longer and then forced herself back to the center of her shack. She wanted to know how Monte's crush was progressing but didn't want to get caught out.

Lozen lifted her dark hair off her shoulders and rubbed the sweat from the back of her neck. She didn't like dresses and didn't want to cut her pants into shorts, so she wore a very baggy pair of faded black sweatpants and a black sports bra she had traded a bag of wild strawberries for. She looked good, even if two of her back teeth were sore.

She sat down on her pallet and trimmed her nails with her dull cooking knife while she waited.

At last, the door blanket twitched. "*Tep tep*? Hey, Lozen."

"*Tep*. Hey, Monte, how's it going?"

Her friend brightened, even in the windowless room. They broke into whispers so Jerramy or his family wouldn't hear them next door.

"I think he's finally interested. We're meeting up

tonight."

"Of course he's interested. What else would that mean?"

Monte shrugged self-consciously, an unfamiliar look on her. "I don't know. What if he meant meet up with friends?"

Lozen rolled her eyes and brushed her fingers across her lip, feeling the smooth ridges without actually noticing them. "That's not going to happen."

"I'll tell you how everything goes in the morning." Monte licked her lips and scratched her shoulder, just below her short hair. "I actually don't have much time. Charla sent me."

Lozen's stomach dropped. "I don't have any updates."

Monte's glow from chatting with Jerramy was gone. She wouldn't meet Lozen's eye.

"Then you'll have to tell Charla that. And..." she paused awkwardly. "I wouldn't expect another chance to join the Karmas."

"What?"

Monte shrugged.

Lozen went silent. Her hand crept up to her lips and covered them. She was always covering her mouth when she felt bad. Or when she smiled. Or when her oldest friend was either fighting to be indifferent or really did not care that Lozen was going to fail at joining the only thing that mattered in the Catchment.

"Charla gave you months for your initiation."

"It's hard to find a fucking terrorist, go figure—"

"Keep your voice down," Monte hissed.

They glowered at each other. The fact that her friend

thought she'd give the secret society away combined with the fact that Lozen actually did raise her voice made her all the more defensive.

"Shit, bro." Lozen stood to have something to do. She looked up at the newly repaired ceiling, thoughts tumbling through her mind. She wasn't entirely surprised Charla's patience had run out, but she didn't want to lose her chance at joining the community she desperately wanted. She said simply, "I found him."

Monte's head swung up, her short hair in disarray. A huge smile broke out on her face and she jumped up.

"You did? We need to go tell Charla."

Lozen busied herself with flattening the meager cloth rug over her dirt floor. She shook her head. She did not want to have this conversation. Had been putting it off for weeks, as things grew more and more strained between her and Monte. She took a breath.

"Monte...how much do you really know about Charla?"

Something flickered in Monte's face. She wasn't avoiding eye contact now. She was staring at her friend, practically trying to peer into her soul. "What do you mean? The Karmas? It's like family. We know everything. I know everything."

Lozen shook her head. "That's what I want to believe. But the, uh, person, that everyone thinks bombed the handout station isn't. Wasn't them."

Monte folded her arms and stuck a hip to the side. "Lozen, none of this is your call. Your initiation was about finding information, showing Charla and the Karmas what you're capable of. Give them what you know and they'll take out the fucker who's terrorizing all of us. It wasn't only the handout station that burned."

Lozen leaned in as she spoke her whispers, "You don't get it. This whole thing is fucked. Charla's been tricked, Lin's been tricked, the goddamn GIA's been tricked—"

Monte cocked her head. "You know what the Galactic Intelligence Agency is thinking?" she asked sarcastically.

"An agent approached me."

"What the hell, Lozen?"

Lozen jerked back from her friend. She lowered her voice to remind Monte to do the same. "You don't know what they promised me. Life in the capital, most of all—" If only her friend knew about the surgery the GIA had promised in return for her cooperation, Monte would understand.

"I don't know what you've gotten wrapped up in," Monte fought for words she could scream because she sure as hell wasn't going to whisper, "but your loyalties are way the fuck off."

"What about me?" Lozen yelled back. "I'm your oldest friend, Monte, you're going to let, let, let some—" *Oh flip. What could she yell that wouldn't tip anyone off?* "You're going to stop being my friend because I don't drink coffee?"

Monte bared her teeth. With her short hair and heart-shaped face, she resembled an angry pixie. "You have *betrayed* coffee. You're not good enough for coffee!" Monte looked around in terror. Her voice dropped. "I can't be here."

Monte made to push the hanging blanket out of Lozen's doorway when Lozen grabbed her arm.

"Monte, please, we have to talk about this. You don't know what you're getting into."

"No, *you* don't. With your…with your fucking energy drinks. You should have stuck with coffee."

Monte barreled out, got tangled, and ripped away from the blanket.

Lozen stood alone in her shack, staring at the now off-kilter blanket that separated her from the world.

She stumbled out, still shocked at how quickly life had changed. Today was supposed to be a slow summer day. Not the end of a friendship.

Monte was already two shacks down. She called after her, "Don't do this, Monte, don't do this for coffee."

Monte spun around, but her feet kept moving backward, taking her farther and farther away. "You know how much I hate energy drinks. How much *everyone* hates energy drinks!"

One of the lane's grannies watched out a roughly cut window. A group of tiny kids stifled giggles. Lozen knew she and Monte were making a spectacle of themselves, but she couldn't let her friend go.

"Monte, you don't know the first thing about what energy drinks have put me through. You don't understand because you're so *pigheaded*!"

Oh shit. That was definitely not the right thing to say.

Indeed, Monte continued to storm away. Lozen took a big breath and wiped her hands over her face. Monte didn't understand what she was asking Lozen to give up. Her whole life she had wished the mangled split of her top lip would simply disappear. With the GIA promising new life and surgery for her cleft palate, it actually could.

Lozen lowered her hands and noticed Mama Teresa, notorious for beating on anyone who disrupted her blackouts, staring at her. Even though it was warm outside, she wore the same red sweater she always did, oil stains up the left sleeve.

Then Jerramy was next to her. Tall and lanky, he put an elbow on her shoulder and leaned. "I doubt you two will be speaking for a while, but if you do, let Monte know I'm all about coffee."

The scraggly fence around the Catchment posed little threat. Lozen had been slipping through its holes and gaps since her aunt showed her the guards' blind spots as a child. The regulators didn't care if you left, but they preferred it not be flaunted in front of them. The fence was just a physical symbol of the real nature of entrapment. Lozen could walk away from the Catchment, but without the right paperwork, she'd be picked up by Capital Police and returned eventually. Even if she evaded them, there was no fancy job waiting for her, no way to start fresh. The Catchment started as a place to dump the homeless, then a place to store refugees, and then a place to confine aliens. Lozen didn't understand why Earth welcomed alien refugees in the first place. It didn't seem like they were any more wanted here than wherever they came from.

And now, Lozen would be wanted even less. *Traitor.*

After Monte left, Lozen unearthed the small stash of coins and foodstuff she had hidden in a canister, threw a long flannel over her sports bra, put her extra clothes in a bag, and left her house as casually as she could. Monte was going to tell Charla that Lozen had been helping the

Galactic Intelligence Agency. It was only a matter of time until the rest of the Karmas found out, and who knew who they would tell or what any of them would do. She would never be forgiven for working with the same law enforcement agency that had made all their lives so hard.

The fact that Lozen never wanted to work for them in the first place wouldn't matter. She *did* pass on information. And with what she saw Agent Velazquez doing…cooperating with Leggs to illegally move supplies…it didn't matter that Agent Tril was squeaky clean, Lozen wouldn't dare trust them again.

Which left one option.

Lozen stepped through. Bare dirt ran in a circumference around the fence, battered by running children and foraging adults. Lozen hitched her bag on her shoulder and headed for the tree line. Layers of green leaves made a stark contrast to the rust and concrete structures of the Catchment.

At the first tree, Lozen looked back at her home. The sun glinted harshly off a tin roof and a trickle of smoke rose from a cook fire. It was no nice place, but it was hers.

Lozen turned and walked on. She stooped low when she saw amaranth leaves and picked some for her bag. She chewed on a leaf as she hiked. It was nutty in flavor. That didn't mean *he'd* like them, but she wasn't likely to forage nuts this time of year and her winter stores were depleted.

The shadowed woods made her jumpy though her eyes and ears told her she wasn't being followed. Inspiration struck her and she darted under a tree and looked up at the sky. She searched the pockets of blue through the branches until she was certain no GIA drone spied on her. She couldn't imagine she'd be worthy of a satellite.

After most of the morning had passed, Lozen reached the cliff line and turned to follow it in the direction of the shore. She remembered the first time she came out here, at night, and turned the opposite direction to meet with the Karmas. There, Charla set her initiation task to find out who bombed the handout station, the first of three incidents. Joining the secret society was a chance to make the Catchment safer. It was a chance at family.

When Lozen made her choice to protect another, everything else faded away.

Lozen hiked her way up and through a jagged part of cliff. There, low to the ground, under an overhang of limestone, was a crevice just bigger than Lozen. She patted her cheeks and ducked down in a squat. How the fuck was this the best idea she could come up with?

She'd never been able to whistle so she snapped her fingers.

Of course, there was no answer. Well, he couldn't be anywhere else so Lozen chucked her bag down the hole and then gingerly slid in backward on her belly, one foot through the gap at a time. Lozen wondered at how he was able to squeeze in—and then the rock fell away generously. One foot down. One hand. A few inches more. Her arms and calves burned.

"Don't freak out," she grunted. "It's me. Lozen." She knew he had trouble distinguishing between human voices.

Something stirred behind her and the hairs on the back of her neck rose. She hoped he couldn't smell fear like a horse. Or if he did, he'd attribute it to this death-defying climb and not that she was about to attack.

Lozen's left foot slid off the rock face. To counterbalance, her fingers automatically dug into her handhold. It wasn't enough.

She lost her grip altogether and slid belly against rock for one terrifying moment before someone huge plucked her out of the air and set her down undignified on all fours. So, she had almost made it to the bottom this time.

"What's up?" She bounced upright.

The bulky figure denied a response and shambled backward. There was enough of a glow from the opening to see the bag she had dropped in.

"You food."

"I *brought* food," Lozen said.

"Good."

"No, I'm saying 'I brought food.' That's how you say it. 'Brought.' Or, uh, 'bring,' I guess."

There was silence.

She sighed. "I did bring a little food."

She opened her bag and felt for a candle and her lighter. The amber flicker felt paltry and slight in the dark recess of the cave, but Lozen wanted to get a better sense of the layout. And to see him.

D-68's immense frame, already rust-colored, appeared a deep tawny-brown in the dim light. Shells covered his limbs and torso. Platelets he had called them. He struck Lozen as more buglike than sea creature. Stubby bristles stood out on his shoulders and knees. His dark eyes peered intelligently at her from under a sheltered brow. His nose, ribbed and patterned like a brain, used to give Lozen the heebie-jeebies, but she got used to it. It was his size that did it. He had to be the biggest animoid on the planet Earth.

And here he was. Underground. A wanted creature.

"Why you come?"

Lozen's eyes darted away, assessing the cave. For the most part it was rough and natural-looking with stark claw marks in some areas. She wondered where he took the excess rock.

"I had to get away from the Catchment. I've got trouble, which means *we've* got trouble. I'm going to have to stay here for a while."

His face was blank. Then, once he processed her words, his nose scrunched. "No. No. Ten and one nos."

He turned his shoulder on her and Lozen almost reached out to push him back to face her. She thought better of it and pivoted around him.

"Dude, I don't want to be here either. But the ones I told you about, the Karmas, who I thought would maybe help us clear your name with the GIA, well, they're, uh, not going to."

D-68 made some kind of slight gesture with one of his hands, something Lozen interpreted as dismissive. So, he already knew she was a fuckup.

"Here's the plan." She'd never called him by the number he was given. Tried not to address him at all, in fact. "Let me stay here two nights, I'll find you another food source and I'll get us exactly what we need."

"Need what?"

"We need at least one goddamn person to help us."

Chapter 3

Adam (*A-dam*)
New Washington, WI

Theoretically, late-night dinners, adult sleepovers, and lazy mornings were the key to happiness. But as Adam's key fob automatically unlocked his parents' front door, he wondered why he was dreading another day being unemployed. An unfulfilled work ethic? Internalized capitalism? Boredom?

He took his time entering the foyer and cleared his throat. It was the same house he grew up in, but it stopped feeling like his at some point during college. Most likely the point where he came home one night and walked in on his parents having sex in the living room.

But no one was there today. The glass windows of the

small foyer amplified the heat of the day. Adam slipped his shoes off and dumped his keys in a dish that his dad always moved his keys to when Adam left them on the kitchen table prompting him to say, "Now where are my keys?" But he got it now.

Adam put a leftover taco in the fridge and marked the food on the electronic board as his. His mom would eat it guilt-free unless the fridge labeled it. He had slept in in accordance with the late night and Cassie's—the bartender's—schedule. They got up and ate lunch out instead of breakfast. It was a good night but lunch had shown them both it wouldn't be more than a one-time thing. Adam paid for lunch as if wishing her a good life.

"Hello?" Adam's dad's voice carried from his studio.

In the back of the house, little more than a mudroom, was Keyad's art studio. His mom, Amanda, had often prompted Keyad to claim a bigger space, but he said if he needed more space, he'd sit outside.

Keyad had newspapers all around him. He paid extra for print versions that he was currently clipping apart with the hearty green scissors Adam associated with elementary school projects.

"Uh, are you working?" Adam asked.

"It's historical documentation and archival time. Take a look at those, Adam."

Adam picked up the pile of clippings and sat on the worn couch that usually served to hold stacks of art supplies.

"Mom saved my newspapers while we were gone. I'm looking for anything about our trip. This may have been my last voyage to space. It will be neat for your kids to have someday. Or just you, no pressure."

Adam paged through the clippings. One had a large photo of Hloban, the "alien refugee of unique origin." An article from sometime around the midpoint of their trip quoted Adam's mom, "No, we haven't heard from them, but I'd appreciate it if you stepped off my lawn." There was a picture of Yaniqui at the Winslow Space-Earth Station, Adam looking grimy and disorientated in the background.

"Dad, why did you leave Wea Saa?"

Keyad continued his painstaking cutting and didn't look up.

"I mean, I'm glad you did, otherwise we wouldn't be here, but why would you leave your home? From what Yaniqui said, it is—was—a pretty singular community."

"That's right," Keyad said, hesitating, "but it wasn't for me. I was born into a very stable family. You know my mother was an activist and community organizer—homogenous or not we had our issues—and my father was an artist, like me." One of the few things Keyad brought from Wea Saa that survived over the years was a weaving by Adam's grandfather. It hung in the hallway upstairs. "Your grandmother helped pass the vote to open our doors to trade.

"They were betrothed and then partnered and had me. They were very happy together. When I was born, my parents looked for my match. When there was none, it was assumed that she wasn't born yet. They waited and it didn't happen and then it was me who waited. I grew older and older and one day it occurred to me that it wasn't coming."

Adam broke in, "How could that not happen? I thought it was, like, a guaranteed thing." He set the clippings down.

Keyad smiled. "I thought you didn't believe in this stuff."

Adam cleared this throat. "I obviously don't. I mean for the sake of argument."

"Well, it didn't. I don't know why, but it changed my perspective. I began to wonder if it was my home as much as those around me. I came to the hard decision that I had to leave Wea Saa and leaving was near unheard-of. We were an isolationist state. However, I felt..." Keyad searched for the words, "as if I didn't belong. The entire Wea Saavian society is set up on two foundations: self-healing and betrothals, and I was missing half of it.

"I left and eventually came here and met your mother. So, to me, it seems as if I did the right thing."

Adam wasn't sure if he should ask or if he wanted to know, but he couldn't help himself. "Do you think I have a match? Someone I'm inexplicably bound to?"

Keyad shook out a column of words and added them to the stack.

"I recorded the placement of the stars at your birth, in case you wanted it someday, but we won't ever know because to have a match you need two sets of records. And, all those records, all of Wea Saa, whoever you would have matched with, is gone. Whether or not you had a match, you get to choose your future now."

Adam nodded. "I'm not sure betrothal is a good thing. I think Yaniqui and Hloban are still fixated on each other."

"Oh, they most definitely are," Keyad said, which surprised Adam. He didn't think his dad was as emotionally savvy as his mom, but then again, he would know how two Wea Saavians thought.

Keyad saw Adam's question. "I don't think it's going to be a long-term problem. I think the reality of Earth has cooled both of them off. I'm more concerned about the repercussions of what's already been done in passion."

Adam felt his cheeks redden. Why would his dad phrase it that exact way? Still, he asked, "What do you mean?"

Adam's dad stacked the newspapers he was finished with. "I knew there would be a problem when Hloban brought that cloaking device onboard."

Oh, the black box. Not a night of passion.

"Why? It helped us get close to Yaniqui."

"Sure, but those things are incredibly expensive."

"Hloban traded his blood."

"And even that would be nowhere near enough to pay. His blood can't heal. Only a research lab would find value in it. Hloban either promised Onlo something he does not have or is in their debt. At some point, they're going to come seeking payment."

"Huh." Adam sat for a moment while Keyad lined the various papers in his binder.

"So, are you asking about all this because you went to dinner with Yaniqui last night? And never came home?"

"Oh, we decided just to be friends."

Keyad carefully kept his glance down. "And you decided that last night or this morning?"

Adam grimaced. "We talked about it at dinner. She's fine, she's great actually, but we're only ever going to be friends. I spent the night with someone else." Once he heard his words in the air he added, "A consensual night with someone who is not my soul mate or betrothed and is totally fine with that but with whom I have no plans to see again."

"Oh. Bummer."

Adam brushed his hair back and stared at the unfinished painting on the easel. The underpainting built up large swaths of blobs of something that Adam knew would look fantastic someday. Generally uninterested in realism, Keyad's 2-D artwork invariably looked terrible until about ten minutes before they were finished but always turned out fine. Or great.

"So, what are you doing today?"

Adam turned back to his dad. "Filling out more applications, I guess."

It still felt sore, moving back in with his parents. He'd gotten a job in the service industry easily, but the leap into an actual career had stalled.

"You know, when my agent approaches a new gallery, she usually sets up a time to show the gallery owner my portfolio, but some places need a different approach."

Adam straightened. "What do you mean?"

"Sometimes we have to do something different to stand out. I remember a long time ago, I painted a picture of the gallery building before we approached them. I thought it'd be a nice gift, but it didn't work out. In hindsight, I can see it's because I don't specialize in architectural paintings and the first thing I showed them wasn't representative of my work."

"Okay, but what did work?"

Keyad thought. He set the binder on his desk face open and started folding newspapers.

"I have an artist friend who sent puzzles of her work.

She told me later the interns loved them." His eyes brightened. "I once offered to paint a mural in Aunah's gallery for free. We weren't yet friends, but she loved it and couldn't help but represent my work after that. I had coffee with Aunah the last time I was in the area. The mural is still up."

Adam stood, racking his brain. "So not only do I have to be a college graduate, do three different internships, graduate with honors, and send out countless resumés, I also have to find a way to stand out?"

"I guess so." Keyad shook his head. "If that's what it calls for. But you don't have to get a job in space. You don't have to be passionate about your work. Get something that gives you the schedule and lifestyle you want and you might find that's enough. Or bridge things until the right timing opens up."

"You get to do what you want."

"I'm fifty-five Earth years old."

"And an alien. What Earth gallery wouldn't want your art? There's got to be like less than a hundred ex-solar artists on the planet?" He licked his lips. "I think I might have an idea." Adam turned on his foot and went out the door.

"Adam," his dad called after him. "Don't go that route! Anyone who would only want to hire you because you're half-Wea Saavian is someone you don't want to work for."

Adam often went back to company websites months after he interviewed and was summarily rejected to see who they eventually hired. Sometimes Adam figured it was a toss-up. He had a stellar education, but so did the new hire. The company genuinely had a slew of great applicants and Adam just happened to be the one they didn't pick. Again.

But sometimes the rabbit hole led him to the realization that the person who got the job instead of him was the company CFO's great niece. Or it happened that their parents brought them up in a world where membership to an exclusive country club was the norm and, hey, look at that, the top tier of company leaders went there too.

Adam wasn't a nepo baby. But there was a way to stand out and compete.

He watched a few how-to videos and then purchased a domain name and started typing.

By the time Keyad checked on him in the late afternoon, he had a bone-like structure of the story of Yaniqui's partial rescue (she would insist the dŏsvengar rescued her, Hloban would insist she would have perished on that asteroid if he hadn't showed up…which was actually Adam's idea).

It was more than a rescue mission. It was a face-off against the most powerful corporation in the galaxy. You see, I'm half-Wea Saavian. Wea Saa was an isolated planet for millennium. My people developed the ability to regenerate healthy cells and essentially heal ourselves. If I get cut, if I break a bone, I can heal it.

But Wea Saavian women are truly extraordinary. They can not only heal themselves but heal others through physical contact. That's why Akar wanted Yaniqui so badly. They wanted to sell her. And they'd get a lot of money for her. What medical company wouldn't want to study her? What mercenary troupe wouldn't want a leg up against the competition? In fact, *you* probably want her right now—

Adam startled when he realized his dad was reading over his shoulder. He bent to pick up the notebook he had dropped and found himself tongue-tied. "It's a website. I'm starting one. I figure if I can get a lot of readers, maybe the job offers will come on their own."

Keyad looked warily at Adam. "Using Yaniqui's story? Doesn't it seem a bit crass?"

"It's not Yaniqui's story—it's mine. I went to space. I had the idea for how to locate her."

Keyad sat on Adam's single bed. "Is that really how you want to get a job? And how would that make a spacefaring company take note of you anyway?" His son didn't respond so he went on. "People will read this; of course people are curious about Yaniqui and us. You'll put this story out there and people will gawk, but it's not going to make your readers your friends or future employers. They will take everything free and ask for more, but that doesn't mean they'll give you something in return."

Adam slid down in his chair until his butt was at the edge, shoulders and feet pressed firmly to hold him in place. He lay his arms across his stomach and stared at the computer screen.

"I thought this would be a way of jumping the line. But, yeah, I can see what you mean."

"I'm not trying to get down on you. It'd be different if you've always wanted to write a memoir. I'm concerned because you'd be putting yourself out there only in hopes of it getting you a job. That's not a good reason, and likely wouldn't even hold your interest long enough to make it work. Do you really want to write three blog posts a week and hire someone for, uh, better graphics?" Keyad asked, gesturing to an awkwardly designed banner Adam made with a free art generator.

Adam sighed. Then he laughed. "No, I guess I figured I'd go viral this weekend and have a job offer by next Thursday."

Keyad chuckled. "I'm not saying you shouldn't invest your time in a project, but do it for the right reasons and do it for something you really enjoy."

Adam spent the evening cooking with his mom and eating dinner on the patio, which his father preferred whenever the Wisconsin weather permitted. His parents went for a walk in the summer evening—though why they'd want to walk around their cul-de-sac, Adam did not know—and Adam returned to his room. He looked at the hastily scribbled notes that lay next to his computer. His dad was right. He didn't want to write essays about being a Wea Saavian. It felt too personal. And people would read it, sure, but that didn't mean they'd take care of him. It wouldn't make people lean in any deeper than surface-level gawking.

Then he knew. He knew what exactly what he should write about. There was something that would make people his age sit up and listen. Something that would help. And for once it was something he knew all about.

Chapter 4

Hloban (*l-o-ben*)
New Washington, WI

Hloban broke off midsentence. He could tell by the look on his wife's face she didn't want to hear the self-placating justifying. Gods, she was furious. Maybe he should have preemptively called himself names through the explanation.

Loera snapped her fingers, which turned off the television that she had muted when he sat down to talk. Shadows replaced the blue-toned glow on her face. She sat wrapped in a mohair blanket. Hloban stood in front of her, towering over her, not sure if he should sit.

"You kissed Yaniqui?"

"Unfortunately, yes."

"Twice?"

Hloban hesitated. "We kissed when she boarded the *Caneille*. I didn't expect it. Everyone was so caught up in the celebration of finding her and I hadn't yet told her about you or anything. It was kind of like an automatic thing. I'm really sorry."

"And the other time?"

This was painful. "It was, I don't know how long, within a day or two of picking her up. She knew about you and was furious." Loera let out a hiss and Hloban sped ahead, trying to get to the end of all this mess. "I was sleeping in the dorm and she came in. She kissed me and...I kissed her back. And I'm really sorry."

Loera shifted her body to peer directly at Hloban's face. "Who stopped?"

"What?"

"In the bed, you said you didn't have sex. Who stopped?"

"Gods, Loera, I did!" He jerked back and something sharp bit into his foot. He stumbled, almost caught himself, and then fell hard against the wall, dislodging a photograph.

"Look out!"

Hloban barely heard his wife when a framed photograph fell on his head. His eyes automatically shut and the sound of glass crackled around him. He opened them carefully to see the alarmed look on his wife's face, standing, hovering over him, uncertain how to help without stepping on the glass around him. He glanced at the sharp plastic toy that was his downfall. Both of them glanced upward at the ceiling and held their breath, waiting for

Obani to stir.

When the preschooler didn't, Hloban waved her back. He was having trouble deciding whether he should clean the mess or finish what he was saying. He carefully pulled his feet under him and said slowly, "I stopped. She thought we were still supposed to be together. She thought I would just forget about you. I told her it wasn't right."

Loera groaned and put her face in her hands. "And now she's living here. What a mess."

Hloban stepped out of the halo of glass and felt another bite on his foot. His right knee went weak instantly to take pressure off the foot and he collapsed heavily on the couch next to Loera who scooted away, unwilling to be in proximity to him. He propped his foot on his left knee. A half inch of red marked his sole. He sighed. "But you know I'm trying to fix it. I think Yaniqui and Adam belong together. It would be good for them. It would solve everything."

It was quiet for a moment. "Then why are you bringing this up? I obviously want to know, but why did you wait and why are you bringing this up now?"

"She's my responsibility. I'm the only family she has left. I wanted to—Loera, I'm sorry—"

"Yes, I know, just say it."

Hloban wiped the blood away. The cut was already nearly knit together. He held his soiled hand away from the couch. "I wanted to get things settled here, allow you to judge her based on who she is, before telling you. Yani made a mistake, but her entire world and outlook on life was crashing and I didn't want us to judge her based on what she did in the forty-eight hours after being rescued from a human trafficking operation. I wanted to give you the opportunity to get to know her first, unbiased."

"It was fucking dishonest!"

"Yes," Hloban said slowly. "It was."

Something stirred above them. Through the ceiling came Obani's relentless monotone. "Water. Water. Water. Waaaaater. Water."

Loera looked pointedly at Hloban as though he was the one who woke the four-year-old.

Hloban stood and retrieved a cup of water from the kitchen.

After a tense night's sleep and a breakfast where no one wanted to talk except Obani, Emmett, the secretary-general's assistant, lead Hloban through the strangely quiet halls of the United Nations headquarters. The security check-in had been as busy as ever, but back here, in the administrative offices, the normal buzz of conversation and phones was missing.

"Where is everyone?"

"They're at my birthday party."

Hloban staggered forward to look Emmett in the face. "Your birthday? Shouldn't you, you know, be there?"

Emmett shrugged his broad shoulders and adjusted one of his cuffed sleeves. "You think Cortez knows it's my birthday? Anyway, I told them I don't eat cake."

"All right, well, happy birthday, Emmett."

"Thanks, Hloban."

Hloban blinked and smiled. "Wow, that was pretty good." Most Earthlings mixed up the pronunciation of his name. The "Hl" sounded like a "Th" made in the cheeks.

"What kind of assistant would I be if I let the secretary-general mispronounce the names of important people?"

They neared the end of the open office space. A row of plastic tubs filled with program flyers lined one wall.

"I'm a consultant. I wouldn't classify that as an important person."

Emmett turned his head and smiled. "Today," he said, "you're an important person. Try not to mess it up."

After going down two more halls, they arrived at the doors of the secretary-general's office. A huge wall of windows dominated the room. He had been in Secretary-General Cortez's personal office only a handful of times and it never failed to impress. Lake Michigan lay blue and placid, though up close it was anything but, and Hloban spied the new White House building (not even white) and the mass of skyscrapers in the commercial district.

"Good morning, Secretary-General."

"Mr. Milson. How I enjoyed your debrief of the exciting retrieval of Yaniqui Daful. Aren't you glad you brought Eeriva along?" Cortez waved him to the upholstered chair.

"Eeriva was greatly…helpful," he finished awkwardly. He remembered Eeriva elbowing him in the chest in a dire moment on Akar Evion, scolding him often, and completely causing Yaniqui to wig out when she told her about Loera within minutes of boarding. "I'm sorry Patrick died under our watch."

"I didn't know him well, honestly, but these things happen to men of a certain age." Cortez sat elegantly opposite him. Her cherry-brown suit was a hair out of style for Hloban, but he knew she didn't care about things like that. Some assistant with a degree in economics probably set it out for her that morning.

"And Yaniqui's settling into Earth life?"

Hloban considered. Yaniqui learned how to take the bus and had a cell phone and even met a few friends through Adam. She was excited to learn to drive and loved all manner of Earth breakfast foods. But it was a lot to take in after such a traumatic experience and he said as much.

Cortez nodded sagely. She glanced at Emmett and he retrieved a tablet. "I'm sure her mother could help her if she was here."

That startled Hloban. "Nica is nowhere to be found. We tried before we returned to Earth."

Cortez took the tablet from Emmett and glanced at it before handing it to Hloban. "Mr. Milson, I speak with dozens of global leaders every day. Some of them are working in direct opposition to my own goals but most of them want to make me happy." She gave a pointed look at Hloban. "Either way, I can deal with them. What I don't like is unknown factors. As of yet, Yaniqui has not accepted our offer to heal the very population that financed her voyage to safety."

Hloban couldn't maintain eye contact. He glanced down at the tablet.

"Which is why I'm sharing this information with you first. Once again, I have a delicate matter in front of me. One that can benefit Earth, or—if I get the wrong person involved, someone who has not yet determined *her* alliances—it could bring all of us harm."

It was a photo of a woman with a mess of dark, ringed locks. The hair lay askew, and dark bags marked her eyes.

Her skin looked sallow and her mouth was set. "Nica," Hloban breathed. He glanced up and found Cortez watching him in her calculated way, eyes narrowed, one hand resting under her lower lip.

The dossier had basic information on who Nica was and detailed her relationship to Yaniqui and her own disappearance. Hloban read aloud, "Nica Daful has been confirmed to be legal property of Joint Council Member Rezario Kilberg. You've got to be kidding me."

"Unfortunately, I paid very dearly for that information. I wanted background information on Kilberg to help along our negotiations regarding Earth's full Joint Council membership. It's not what I expected to find. And I'm in the uncomfortable position of knowing and not being able to do much."

"Is she okay? Do you know what they're using her for?"

Cortez grimaced. "The best we can tell, she's being treated humanely. Kilberg purchased her, but she's in Akar's possession until a new location is prepared. Kilberg is using her to fulfill and glean favors from other Joint Council members and Akar facilitates the logistics."

"They're probably"—Hloban swallowed—"overworking her. Taxing her system. We need to get her here."

"I agree. But for now, there's not much that can be done. Our informant was uncertain of the Akarian ship's route."

Heat washed over Hloban's face and his stomach went sour. He hoped he wasn't going to throw up on the nice off-white chair. He tried to focus on the single positive. She was alive. And Kilberg, like it or not, was a savvy politician. He would protect his investment.

Cortez smiled. "I once told you to rescue Yaniqui and you did it. Now I'd like to bring Nica to Earth."

"Are you going to cut it out or what?"

Hloban let out a quiet gasp and looked up. Over him towered a white-haired woman, with an equally elderly friend with papers of some sort in her hand.

"I beg your pardon?" Hloban looked around the busy coffee shop. All the tables were taken and there was a line halfway across the store.

"I said, 'Are you finished with the table?'" The woman paused, uncertain in the wake of Hloban's own confusion. "Only it looked like you finished your coffee and your bag is packed up so neatly."

Hloban shook his head. He had misheard her. And it was true, his drink was gone and somehow he had put everything away without realizing it.

"Yes." He swallowed. "Of course, the table is yours to do with as you like."

The friend giggled and Hloban stood to leave. He had hoped a few moments with a hot mug would turn the past twenty-four hours around, but he still had no idea how to fix everything. Save everyone.

Just across the street from the café, Hloban's phone rang, displaying an off-planet code. As it did every time his phone rang since Yaniqui came to live with him, his thoughts swam. Who would be calling him? His paperwork was up-to-date. Was it a reporter about Yani? Did Akar make mundane phone calls?

He wouldn't answer the phone, he decided. No call could be a good call for him. He didn't want to have to make any promises, answer any questions, or even let someone know he knew that they had tried to make contact with him. Hloban was still partly buried under his thoughts, but he tried to shake them away.

Too late he realized he was, in fact expecting a call. A counterpart on another planet was going to reach out so they could talk about how to make sure the Earthlings and the Hassenians could come to terms on the trade they wanted to make. The Hassenians didn't understand why they should write their names on a lifeless contract when their words and a sip of tea should be good enough to secure their intentions.

Hloban's phone rang again.

"Hello?" Hloban ducked into a parklet between two shops.

"Hello, Fra Milson," a smooth voice said. "This is Fra Benton from Onlo. I trust your most recent ventures have gone well."

Hloban brushed his fingertips against his forehead. It wasn't that he wasn't expecting it. He just felt foolish for not expecting it sooner. And for not dashing his phone against the sidewalk when he could have.

"Hi, yes, I'm well. Thank you." Hloban straightened his back. He needed to sound put together on this awful day.

"We need to make arrangement for payment of the Wipeout Con, the craft camouflage, and the list of smaller supplies your crew required. I trust you're finding everything useful." The voice cleared its throat.

"They were all satisfactory. I wouldn't want to have traded my valuable blood to an organization that dealt in poor quality supplies."

"The blood sample and your first payment—thank you for making that early—will cover the supplies. So, it's simply a matter of the craft camouflage and the Con."

"Now wait a minute"—he could feel his temper loosening—"I didn't let you draw my blood in trade for dried mushrooms and vitamin water packets."

There was a pause. "You were in quite the hurry. We never exactly decided how much the vial was worth. Let's talk about the water holdings. If your gift is big enough, perhaps that will cover the Con as well as the camouflage."

Hloban was glad he was in another star system altogether. He wasn't a coward, but he hated losing face.

And he was about to lose face. Why had it seemed like a good idea to give Onlo the impression that he had water holdings on Earth to trade? He would have to be a trillionaire to control such resources on Earth.

But it had been an emergency and Hloban had vowed to save Yaniqui no matter what.

"It's true, we didn't sign a contract. Perhaps you misunderstood me. I don't have any water holdings on Earth, salt or fresh. I *would* be willing to set up a meeting between your representatives and the Earthlings who do, Fra Benton."

Hloban stretched his neck, waiting for the angry response. Would the Fra curse at him? Make threats? Declare he was coming to Earth himself?

Fra Benton laughed. The hair on Hloban's neck prickled.

"That makes things much easier for me, Fra Milson. We were nearly certain you didn't own water on that planet. Your forfeit of our agreement, a handshake agreement let's say"—Hloban heard the man smile through his voice—"means that we can take an alternative route."

"What do you mean?"

"Shipping costs are high right now for anything and even more for large machinery. Then, moving water off planets itself is tedious business. We're looking to move into…a sector with higher profit margins. Information. I advocated to the board that we do this in the first place, but there are a few more ethical members that didn't feel comfortable doing so. That is, until you demonstrated that you didn't intend payment."

His location. They know what planet he lived on. And that would lead them to Obani and Yaniqui and Keyad and Adam. How could he be such a damn fool?

"Akar always pays a fair price for information."

"That's not necessary," Hloban said as calmly as he could. "Now that I understand, we can come to an agreement. I'll get the money or I'll negotiate the trade of water. I can do either. Which do you prefer?"

"No," Fra Benton said again. "I think I prefer selling your location to Akar. Our thanks to you."

Chapter 5

Ippa *(E-pa)*
Earth's Troposphere

Ippa was mentally tallying all the books she had read at Shou University when a jolt ran through the whole spacecraft. She groaned. Weeks of life on the hard metal floor had taken its toll. Her back decided it had given up and wasn't going to do its job anymore. Then came another jolt. Ippa heard the muffled voices of her captors above. She sat up straighter and sniffed. Forget *Philosophical Differences of Galactic Religions* and *The Universal Constants of Biological Evolution*. Something was burning.

She grasped the thin blanket around her shoulders and stood. The heavy manacle on her right foot clinked as she shuffled forward.

"Hey!" She strained her voice to be heard above. "I think something's burning." No response except another lurch that made her stumble. The manacle twisted at her ankle. "Ouch. Hey, what's going on up there?"

Ippa's heart sped as she tried to deduce what exactly was going on. She definitely smelled smoke, and possibly fumes or an electrical fire. Either the vessel was damaged and they would soon know the icy death of space or someone burned breakfast. She rubbed her hands together and peered upward, listening for any further clues.

A dash of footsteps rained. The hatch flung open. The wiry younger woman slid down the ladder. "We're crashing. I'm here to get you strapped in above. Don't try me, understand? We don't have time."

"Crashing? You mean we're crashing?" Ippa babbled as the woman unlocked her chains and pushed her half up the ladder. Ippa recovered herself and climbed the rest of the way. It had been days—possibly even weeks—since she had boarded this crisping spacecraft. The two women obviously weren't ambassadors. They were bounty hunters and Ippa was a side stop along the way to something bigger.

The woman flung Ippa into a seat—the one she had originally sat in when she left the Jupiter Station. The urgency of the woman and the tight look on her face made Ippa wonder what could be so bad that it would put her in that state. The view out the porthole was sheer gray.

Crashing. It finally struck Ippa. To crash they needed to be at a planet. *Crisp.* Ippa hoped it was a habitable planet. With a rescue force of some kind.

Ippa could hear Matts ahead, voice furious in the cockpit. The entire craft vibrated as if it were part of a percussion ensemble. A whine crept out of her. Not only was she going to burn and die on a remote alien planet, she was never going to redeem herself after being expelled from Shou University. Her obituary wouldn't even list her as a graduate.

Ippa's hands tightened around her straps and buckles. No crisping way was she going to let Matts screw things up for her. Until her degree was secured, death was unacceptable. She unbuckled and staggered toward the cockpit. It was a commercial spacecraft so the passenger section was a good distance from the captain's cockpit.

Matts looked up, their sharp face tense but more neutral than their counterpart's. "You really should be strapped in."

"Strap yourself in. What do you know about physics?"

Ippa's mind sped. What were the dangers of crashing beyond the blunt impact? How could one minimize damage? "Dump the fuel. We need to be as light as possible upon landing and we don't want to explode."

Matts did a double take at Ippa. "Do it," they commanded the copilot.

"Aim for the horizon. We don't want to spiral down. We want a long tail of descension."

"I am," Matts growled. "We've also raised the extended flaps."

"To make us less aerodynamic. Good. What planet are we on?"

"Earth."

Ippa shook with more than adrenaline. All those

months trying to reach Earth. She was here.

A sudden force slammed Ippa into the wall. Her left arm flamed with pain. She righted herself and crawled back toward her seat. She called behind her, "Keep us in the air as long as possible. And empty your pockets! You don't want anything sharp on your body if there's an impact."

Now that she was out of sight, her face scrunched up and she started crying. Oh gods, she was going to die. She was never going to see her family again. They might never find out what happened to her. Ippa would never write a book! She strapped herself into her seat and shivered and shook and at some point passed out.

Ippa woke to the smell of smoke. She choked a cough out and realized that her body's instinctual desire for oxygen must have woken her. The cabin vibrated harshly and Ippa grabbed at the straps nestled around her shoulders in an absurd attempt to calm herself. She glanced across the cabin and spied through the porthole a brilliant blue sky and carpet of green. She wasn't a survivor—she was still in the air!

Ippa screamed.

A huge tearing noise came from one side of the cabin. The craft whipped sideways in the same direction and Ippa's body strained against the harness. Ippa screamed again and the entire craft was submersed in the sound of breaking and tearing. Ippa put her hands and arms around her cranium to protect it. The craft bounded up and then down hard. Ippa's teeth knocked together and she couldn't have opened her eyes if she wanted to. She was flung forward against her seat buckle and could hardly groan in response to the pain. The pain. It was all-encompassing and it took Ippa a moment to realize the noise was gone. The craft rolled softly back and forth as it adjusted to whatever it landed on.

Her neck and shoulders were rocks and Ippa shook uncontrollably. She fought to bring her hands to her sides but could only lay still for a moment as the jitters worked their way out of her body. Adrenaline. Shock. A small corner of Ippa's brain took clinical stock of what was happening but, even as she willed herself to action, her physical nature would not be forced to respond.

Eventually her hand came to her mouth and the coolness brought her to her senses. Ippa forced a deep breath and looked around the cabin of the craft. It was in shambles. Doors that were supposed to stay locked upon impact hung by their hinges. The lights flickered and Ippa definitely smelled fumes this time. She had to get out.

She racked her nails against the buckle and the moment it released pain shot across her hips. She put her hands on the armrests and tried to stand but fell backward. *Was her spine…?* She didn't want to think it.

Ippa pulled her tunic up gently as thick anxiety welled in her throat.

A red stripe of burst skin and blood vessels followed the track of the belt. Her skin was already bruising where the largest buckle sat. She guessed she'd have similar marks on her thighs and neck.

Ippa couldn't stay any longer, the smoke and chemical fumes were so overpowering she feared she'd pass out before she could escape. She stood and had trouble moving her body. She lurched toward the emergency door and came face-to-face with Matts.

Matts looked in better shape than Ippa. They were at least standing straight, but they had an entirely different expression than Ippa had seen since she'd been kidnapped from the Jupiter Station. The confidence was gone and replaced with stubborn dread.

"Good, you're up."

"May a grundar crawl up your rectum." Ippa coughed. The words cost her more than she expected.

Matts, however, ignored her and the vulnerable look on their face was gone. They put their hands—their greedy, crisping, immoral hands—on a red bar and the door flew open.

Ippa hadn't noticed the angle they had landed at, hunched as she was, but even without the horizon, she knew they weren't yet steady. Smoke and dust poured out of the doorway, prompting a fresh coughing fit from Ippa. A needle stabbed her pelvis and she instinctively clutched at the spot with a gasp.

"Climb out," Matts commanded. "If this place doesn't burn down in the next hour, we'll come back for supplies."

Matts pushed Ippa harshly out the door. She lost her footing. No, in fact, there was no footing. There was no ramp or stairs or any kind of device to make the four-foot drop any easier.

Ippa screamed. Her entire body protested being slammed against the ground but especially her pelvis. A great shuddering sob racked Ippa's body. Matts grabbed her by the arm and hip. They heaved and balanced Ippa over their shoulders like a sack.

Ippa rasped, "Put me down."

Matts didn't hear her. She could barely hear herself.

The smoke cleared as they advanced. Ippa looked back and could make out only the shape of the burning spacecraft, the smallest craft she'd ever been on, the one she boarded with two supreme dignitaries and was now leaving in the hands of a bounty hunter though there was no bounty on Ippa's head.

Matts lowered Ippa to the ground slowly. She shoved them away the moment she found footing.

Matts sucked on their teeth and tsked, as if Ippa should be ashamed of her behavior. "I saved you, you know."

"You're the whole reason *I'm here*. Why are you doing this to me?"

Matts didn't respond to her outburst but instead said, "Tamra, she's dead."

Ippa didn't ask what exactly happened to the other bounty hunter, assistant bounty hunter, hecking intern, whatever she was. She refused to be sad that someone who kidnapped her had died.

She fought for a clear breath and looked up.

It wasn't just hot because of the burning Earth ambassador craft. A canopy of trees lay a heavy, humid warmth over them. Everything was different shades of green. Tall slender trees rose into the air, vines of a parasitic plant wrapped tightly around their trunks so they could push their own leaves into the sunlight. Ferns covered the floor in a dense layer. And the sky, what Ippa could make out of the sky through the canopy, was a shockingly brilliant blue that matched Ippa's hair.

She sucked in a breath. "So, this is Earth."

The planet she'd studied before being expelled from

The Shou. The subject of the very presentation that caused Professor Jinu to kick her out. Ippa didn't know if she wanted to cry in gratitude to be on flat ground, or if another crash was coming.

Matts interrupted her thoughts. "Okay, Ippo—"

"It's Ippa."

"I know. Ippo is a nickname."

"How is that a nickname? It's just my name but wrong."

"Do you not understand what a nickname is? Anyway, Ippo," they continued, "There's nothing worth going back into that fiery inferno for." A series of sharp pops came from the burning hull. "We're heading north."

Ippa looked at the crackling fire, the scent of melting plastic and burning metals in the air. "I don't think a wildfire is likely. Look how green and well-watered everything is. We should stay here. Authorities are sure to come."

"Exactly." Matts smiled sarcastically.

The pain across Ippa's body had settled in her left hip. It was a brutal march through the forest. Every step stabbed into the front of her left ilium. She really shouldn't be walking, but she had no choice. She'd already tried defying Matts. She'd laid on the ground in peaceful protest, but Matts twisted her ear until it felt like it would rip off. She tried running into the maze of trees but a few of Matts's long strides made Ippa feel slower than a toddler.

So, she was following her captor through the forest.

In the distance, a whoop trilled its way through the trees. Matts barely looked up, but Ippa stopped in her tracks. Chills broke out across her arms. It was the sound of an Earthling primate, she was sure of it.

Ippa was so foggy-headed, she had barely noticed her surroundings. Survival mode had narrowed her window of perception. Not survival mode. Sheer panic and fear. Survival was still up in the air.

She licked her lips and forced herself to breathe deeply. Tendrils of humid rot filtered through the air, half life, half decay. Sweat gathered and trickled down her sides. It was nothing like the climate-controlled biblioplaza or recycled spacecraft air. It wasn't even like the air on her home planet. This was something different altogether. A hot, humid mess of life. They had to be in one of Earth's rain forests.

A hand fell heavily on Ippa's shoulder and spun her around.

"Ippa, you're not thinking of running again—"

"We're in an Earth jungle!" Ippa had no one to share this news with except her deranged captor, but it was exciting news all the same. "It's likely that from where we're standing that we're looking at dozens of species of trees. And each tree could have a hundred different species of insects, birds, and amphibians." Ippa crouched down, leaning heavily on her right leg to take the pressure off her left hip. She grabbed a handful of compost. "You can actually see how nutritious this underlayer is. The texture is astonishing. An Earthling rain forest is a beautiful example of a finely tuned natural system at work. I read about this at the biblioplaza but being here…"

Matts squatted down. They managed to convey a look of distant bemusement mingled with frustration. "I'm here for a paycheck, Ippa." They gave a long stare. "I get that this dirt is interesting to a nerd like you, but I have work to do. And, honestly, if we're going to survive, we need to keep moving."

Ippa stood grudgingly. It was clear Matts was a philistine.

Matts turned their back on Ippa once it was clear she was going to follow.

"It's nothing more than the humanoid hierarchy of needs," Matts called over their shoulder.

Ippa sighed. She wasn't going to give Matts any bonus credit for knowing some basic psychology.

She took a few larger steps to catch up. "Why did you even take me from the Jupiter Station? You could have just told me to crisp off."

"I did, in fact, do just that. But you're a persistent little weed and when the fates bring fresh meat into my path, I don't say no." Matts gave a toothy grin Ippa tried not to draw back from. "But..." they drew out the word in pleasure, "it was your mention of a specific person of interest that hooked me. There's a very valuable Wea Saavian on this planet and I intend to be the one who turns her over to Akar."

Ippa's upper lip drew up in disgust. "First of all, I don't even know the race of the woman staying with, um, the person I know here. Second, that's deplorable. The Joint Council—"

"—has given every provision to Akar Enterprises. It's an aboveboard business."

It was true. The work and sales of Akar Enterprises were protected by the Joint Council. Ippa stepped over a log and checked for snakes before she set her foot down. "There are provisions for beings who enter into indentured labor of their own free will. Like if someone has a lot of debt and chooses to be purchased in exchange for their owner entity paying their debt down."

Matts looked at Ippa out of the corner of their eye to see if she saw the irony.

"I'm *not saying* it makes any sense, but what you're doing especially isn't allowed. You can't go to a planet you've never been to before, pluck someone off the street, and sell them to Akar. There are bureaus that check up on these kinds of things. You need paperwork."

"Which is always a pleasure to falsify."

Ippa, who had studied her whole life to be accepted to Shou University where she researched and wrote essay upon essay, relying on the validity of primary sources to draw conclusions and build data sets, took this personally. "That's lying. You can't make up paperwork. That's immoral. And what you plan to do to the girl is too. It's totally immoral!" Ippa felt her vocabulary shrinking in the light of such news.

The buzz and click of insects and the tree of chattering birds to the right went quiet.

Matts turned to look at Ippa, then gazed at the sky. The pristine blue atmosphere they had hurtled through earlier was turning peach and auburn. Without noticing it, the shadows around them had lengthened and, if an evening cool wasn't coming on, at the very least the sun didn't beat down on the crown of Ippa's azure head.

"Night is falling," Matts said. "We're on a strange planet"—Ippa almost protested at the judgmental terminology but thought better of it—"we have no food, no supplies, and I'm sure there's something in this forest of infinite species that is hungry." Matts looked Ippa in the eyes to make sure she was listening. "I plan to stay alive until morning. And if you want to as well, I suggest you focus on our most immediate problem instead of philosophy."

Matts spun on the heel of their thick worn boot and marched on, without checking if Ippa was coming.

Ippa rubbed her hands along her forearms and surveyed the jungle. Dappled sunlight fell on the thick vegetation. Already Matts was nearly obscured by greenery. Could Ippa run for it?

An earsplitting, eerie animal shriek made Ippa bolt, chest thundering as if she were a three-hearted tarnieo as she raced to catch up to her captor.

Chapter 6

D-68
The Forest

The human lies still, ragged fabric shrouded around her body, a thin, bald arm curled up under her head. The night passed easier than D-68 expected. He had planned to simmer in a half sleep, to better observe what the woman intended but, once it was clear she was under the immobilizing world of sleep, his own eyes quickly followed suit.

Languid morning shadows cloak rocky walls made of brittle limestone. It is a difficult stone to work with. It has a tendency to split along fissures in less than aesthetically pleasing ways, but he has made do and the thick stone allows himself to feel if not safe, at least able to take a breath in peace.

He is hesitant to move about, make the noise that will wake the human. Part of it is that it's rude. The other part, he resists thinking. He senses in some abstract way, deep within his cranium, that when she wakes, everything will change. He was captured long ago, so long that the reality of his home planet, of his partner and their coming young ones, the kits, is nearly gone. He cannot hold on to the past. His kind do not have the ability.

Running is his new reality. Running is his life. When the Earthling wakes, that will come to a close. He will have to face and act. Either free himself from Earth, or die trying—

"What's good?" The human hasn't moved position but peers at him sleepily.

D-68 can't flush or respond in any physiological way that the human would understand to indicate embarrassment, but he still averts his eyes, caught while playing out his deepest thoughts.

"Am good," he replies.

She sits up and rubs at her eyes with her hands and bends her neck from side to side in a way that is impossible for D-68 and makes him feel queasy watching those important bones flex as if they'll pop.

"So, I guess we have to figure out what to do today."

"Fly ship."

"Whoa, buddy." She puts her hands up. "We're about twelve steps away from getting you on a ship home. Either twelve or fifty-four, somewhere in there." She stands and rolls up her fibrous sheet. "Today, we have two things to do. We need to find food for both of us and then we need to figure out who we can trust. You and I can't do this alone."

The human—Lozen—talks quickly. It takes D-68 a moment to catalog and understand the intention of her words before he can respond.

"Water know I. Food. None."

Lozen looks at him with an expression he does not understand. "Yeah, water good. It's not as if we can get water from the well in the Catchment." She walks over to the wall. "As for food, I might have a couple of ideas for you. The important thing will be keeping you out of sight. These woods are often deserted, but it only takes one being…"

D-68 knows that. That is why he has gone out only at night. He is apprehensive to leave his hole in the dawn light. He decides that if they are caught, he will climb a tree and leave the humanoid on the ground. Escape while she serves as a distraction.

The Earthling tries to heft herself up the side of the rock wall to reach the opening.

It is painfully evident that humans have little propensity for climbing. She slips and limestone dust, thick with calcium, settles to the ground. He climbs around the woman. His thick upper body was built for cliffs a thousand times more treacherous than these. Horned talons, unkept in a way they never would have been in civilized life among his communal hamlet, hardly need to dig into the rock. Rather, he places the tips of the talons strategically on minute handholds.

He is up and out of the cave as quickly as he started. He hears the grunts and heavy breathing of the woman but leaves that behind him to step into the sun. It is mild compared to the tireless glare of his own star, but it is bright and he is pleased at the warmth in the air. Since he arrived on Earth, the cold and snow and then the mud and rain impacted his ability to move about.

Now, the trees bloom with green life. The brittle bark he once tried to eat stands healthy. It is a growing season.

A thud comes from behind, but he does not turn. Lozen is finally upside at least. She coughs and staggers.

"No problem," she wheezes. She stands next to him and he can see her arms shake with fatigue. "I totally dominated that. This way." She staggers in one direction before veering the opposite way.

D-68 follows. He is slower than ever before in his life. The leg missing its platelet aches when he walks too far. More than that, he is hungry for nutrients he cannot find on Earth. Even when his four stomachs are full, a dull hunger lingers in his center.

They drink at the stream. Lozen disappears behind a grove of trees and comes back smelling slightly like ammonia, which makes D-68 uncomfortable. She sneezes when they walk into the sunlight after a shadowed trail. It is faintly revolting being so close to this wet, smelly creature, but D-68 reminds himself of his goal of getting home. He cannot continue working with Leggs who D-68 thinks does not want him to leave Earth.

She pulls strand after leaf after twig of vegetation for him to sniff. Only once does he take a nibble.

"You have to eat something. There won't be any more acorns or nuts until fall. Which is a *long* time from now," she clarifies.

74

"Don't 'have eat something.' Food here built bad."

She nods her head, black fibers called hair nodding in the breeze. She tries to hand him a small red fruit and he wrinkles his soft nasal pads in disgust. He tried that once and much regretted it.

Finally, she digs into the soft loam of her planet and hands D-68 a root. It crunches harshly between his teeth and is woodier than he would like, but it might work.

He struggles to pick remains from his broad teeth as she investigates another plant.

"What about this?"

It smells good. Strange and earthy, but he is surprised to find himself eager to try it. He bites the white part but leaves the leaves. It crunches satisfyingly between his teeth. It's not too hard but has a more chewable texture than their limp lettuces.

"What is?"

"It's a leek. They grow on their own through the forest but, like most edible things here, they're overharvested this close to the Catchment." She hands him another.

She sits on the ground and leans against a tree while he eats. He envies how comfortable she is in this wild space. Her body was designed to live and thrive here. His was decidedly not.

"I fought with my, uh, friend. I messed things up with the one person I thought would help us."

D-68 looks at her sharply.

"We're going to have to figure out who else can help us. I can't go home until it's clear we didn't do anything wrong."

She is only a human. The human who knows much

about her environment but has such little capacity for high
intelligence. Her kind has been given great technology and
uses it maliciously, but she has no basis for the higher
critical thinking of his people. It is up to him to find the
way forward.

He decides. "Kill Many Legged One."

Lozen sputters and gapes at him.

"Necessary," he says simply.

"Get down," she orders, suddenly panicked. She
flattens herself to the ground and points in the direction of
the meadow.

He smells the scent of wet human flesh on the
breeze—not hers, he is already used to hers—but a
stranger's. Two strangers. He digs into the tree bark and
hoists himself up to the top branches. He arranges himself
so the russet of his armor is covered by green leaves and
thin spindly branches. A voice carries, but he has enough
trouble deciphering their language when they are close. He
knows not what they say.

And yet he knows they must not be seen. He takes his
cue from Lozen who has not raised herself from the grasses
but buried herself the best she can under a shrub, her thin
frame curled awkwardly around the base. The forest has
gone silent. No animals chirp at the approach of these
newcomers.

They appear between two trees, women, he thinks.
They move with purpose. One's foot catches slightly on
something and she stumbles briefly. The other turns and
exposes what she holds. D-68's breath stills when he sees
it. A thin metal barrel. Like the type the guard shot at him
with. He didn't find the crack it left in his armor until later,

after he escaped deep underground, after the adrenaline left his body shaking.

He is shocked by a vision of himself stalking them from the treetops. Dropping down and breaking their fragile spines. Bending the barrel.

A pebble hits his shoulder.

He looks down. Lozen beckons him down with a finger pressed to her lips. He hesitates, drawn by an urge to take that weapon and destroy it. Instead, he drops down next to Lozen and follows her in the opposite direction.

After a while, he places himself in front of Lozen, forcing her to stop.

"I recognized one of the women from the Karmas—"

"Go to cave." The humans search for Lozen. He must take care of Leggs on his own. He is strong. It is up to him. "Before home built, broken rock must scrape from it."

Her eyebrows crawl toward each other and she tilts her head in confusion.

"So, you are unsatisfied?" the Many Legged One asks in a series of tsks, as the human kit translates. The kit who is always present. Who has big eyes but no swollen belly like some of the little ones D-68 has spied looking through rubbish for food. D-68 knows why the boy assists such an abominable creature, but this one will never grow up to be a true adult. A shame his life has already spiraled out of his control, so young.

D-68 stands stooped in the little creature's home. Homes of animoids are laid out all around. It is nighttime and D-68 had taken pains to get there unseen, difficult for him to do when he has to maneuver the tight paths between homes and makeshift service centers. He does not enjoy coming into the settlement, the Catchment it is called. It is full of unusual smells and things press closely, even in the dark.

At night, when he sleeps in his cave, he relives the flames coming out of the tower. During the day it is easier to forget, but with the absence of stimuli at night, his mind takes him there again and again. D-68 is not used to reliving any memory, much less a traumatic one. One that was forced upon him by the Many Legged One.

D-68 does not seek to kill others. Not to eat, not for vengeance. He is irate at the presumption of the Many Legged One to use him to kill other beings. He has gone too far.

Plus, although he has done his part, there is no sign of payment. He is no servant. He would not spend what was left of his life lifting heavy things for something he could easily squash.

Lozen was adamant that he not come, but she could not stop him. The human threats are small. He now realizes the real war is waged by the Many Legged One. If he can extinguish the threat, perhaps the humans can be persuaded to let him go home.

"You do not want to help load the ships, move items? Is it you are bored? I could send you to another side of this planet. One with wider open spaces and more room for you to roam. But there, you would have obligations as well, and then I would not seek to help you off this planet if you are moved away from the capital." The boy translates smoothly, as if he knows what his master will say before it is said.

"Betray, you," D-68 says. He may not be fluent in the language or have his own translator, but he will be clear enough. He will not roll away on his belly like a legless sand creature.

The Many Legged One perches on the side of the wall. He takes a moment to crawl up to the ceiling. He hangs easily, his long limbs gripping and thwarting gravity, but D-68 is not impressed. He himself moves and swings and slices through rock effortlessly. He has never seen the Many Legged One outside this structure. It is weak, needing protection. Its legs thin and frail, its oblong buggish head, crushable.

"I betrayed you?" it asks. It quivers.

The boy goes to stand against the wall below his master.

"You give fire. I kill. No want."

There is a hiss even before the boy translates D-68's response.

"I see. I thought I found a kindred spirit in you. Now you tell me you regret the lives you took from our overseers? What about the ones you killed early in your time on Earth, and even before you came here? Your reputation in the animoid prison was well-founded, I thought." The creature holds still, waiting.

"Mistake. I not kill more."

At this, the Many Legged One rears on the back half of his leg sets. The front legs paw at the open air in front of him. The thin stems move agilely. D-68 takes a step back, unnerved at the display. Then, when he reminds himself what he looks at, he snorts and bares his own broad teeth. He will not back down. D-68 is not afraid.

The boy jumps to the ground, falling flat on his face.

A wet spray issues from the mouth of the Many Legged One and hits D-68 in his eyes and nose. His eyes hurt, but it is the shock to the powerful sense pads on his nose that cause him to bellow. His long roar rings through the night. It burns. He thrashes his head back and forth. Instead of wiping his face, he uses the instant after the attack to go on the offensive. He thrusts his hands into the air before him, where the Many Legged One hung moments before and finds the space empty.

A fresh barrage of wet, stringy mess comes at D-68 from the side and hits his ear hole. He throws himself sideways and feels the wall of the structure break. He knows he missed his opponent. If he cannot finish this creature, what use is he?

There are voices outside, some curious, others panicked. Everyone will know of D-68's presence in the settlement. It is only a matter of time before the Earthlings find him.

D-68 rubs his face to get the poison off, but it burns at the beds of his talons instead. Though his skin is thick, he feels his thin face platelets bubble. His ear rings and his nose can't sense anything at all. He peels off what he can of the loose, stringy substance shot at him. Everything around him is dim and blurry.

He doesn't know where the Many Legged One is anymore. He thrashes back and forth and claws at the weak concrete walls around him. It doesn't matter to D-68 if the boy is still in the house, he is going to dismantle it. The sheaths of rock come undone under his talons and dust fills the air—at last he can sense something through his nose, though it's weakly felt.

There are screams and roars outside. D-68 raises himself from the rubble.

He sees motion in the near distance but his bleary eyes cannot discern who it is and whether they too are coming to attack him.

D-68 has no plan for himself, but he is done here. He darts away as fast as he can. For once, he doesn't take care to sneak quietly through the streets. He propels himself off any rock that he senses will be solid enough to hold him and lands on tin and wood, crushing what is beneath him.

D-68 didn't retain memories of how he got to the Many Legged One from the forest. He relies on intuition to lead him to the edge of the settlement. The shouts fade behind him. He sensed that he was chased briefly, but none kept up with him.

He is disgusted by his overconfidence. Instead of a confrontation, he should have smashed the Many Legged One while it was unexpected. Taken his chances and traveled far away by night.

But that's not possible. He has already explored the perimeters of what space is open to him. It took days when he first arrived, but he struggled north and south to the edge of the forest and found rock. Not the strong formations of his homeland, but crushed, powered, and shaped manufactured rock to build structures. He has nowhere to go.

In the forest, the experience falls away and with it, the emotions. D-68 is shaken, but his rage is gone. The right side of his head throbs with strange blisters.

Alone and surrounded by tall trees, D-68 moves much

more slowly. He needs to care for his wounds. He makes his way to the stream where he drinks and sinks to the edge of it.

The poisonous mixture has settled in unreachable places between his platelets. He typically cannot dunk his head for all the water that gets trapped in his platelets, but now that is what he needs.

He moves slowly—never having submerged his head in his life—gets on his hands and knees, and puts his head close to the water. His body screams against this course of action, but he forces himself to set his aching head in the cool water.

Frigidness envelops him and there is a light hum, the sound of water flowing. Water goes in his nose and D-68 thinks of holding himself there, under the water. Ending his life journey and shedding at last the burdens of his experience.

Instead, he comes out coughing, his body fearful and eager for air. He blows wet snot from his nasal pads and tips his shoulders from side to side to let the water trickle down from his ears.

The water has eased the burning. He can see more clearly and sense with his nose again. It is his hearing that is troubled.

D-68 is exhausted. He paws the edge of the water looking for wet weed to eat and comes up with a few pathetic handfuls.

He rests in the darkness.

But he must go to the human woman. She is waiting for him.

Chapter 7

Yaniqui
New Washington, WI

Would you like to have dinner at my house? I hope we'll be able to talk.

No emoji. No "I'm sorry, but I'm confused." No hint as to what he was thinking. After all that happened in the span of twenty seconds between Yaniqui taking Waquas's sleeve in her hands and rushing out of the car, who sends a vague message like that?

Yaniqui turned down his offer for a ride—driving on Earth seemed like a breeze but Loera was adamant she not try until she had an official license—and instead bribed Adam.

When Adam picked her up, she asked, "Adam, did you

know you have only four systems of government on-planet?"

Adam laughed. "I did. We do, in fact, learn that in fourth grade."

"Fourth grade?"

"School when we're about nine years old. There's a song: 'Demo-cracy, Atono-my, that is two you see, but let's get to three. Monar-chy is rare and Auto-cracy are a bear, but we all fare!'"

"How's studying going?"

Yaniqui wrinkled her nose. "It's fine. There is not that much information for the citizenship test, but it's tedious. And some of the terminology is unfamiliar."

"So, why are you going to Waquas's house?"

Yaniqui briefly, and with flushed cheeks, told Adam what happened.

"It was humiliating. He was so disinterested in me."

"Maybe he didn't know you were interested."

"Trust me, he definitely knew." She swallowed.

"He's still inviting you over."

Yaniqui made a face. "But he's so nice. It might only be because he wants to state his boundaries." She sighed, flipped the visor down, and straightened her curls when she saw how chaotic they were. "Do you know how old he is?" she asked.

"He's got to be in his forties. Wouldn't that age difference be weird?" Adam asked. He looked over when she didn't respond. "You're unbelievable. You are seriously worried Waquas doesn't like you? You can heal yourself. You've traveled the galaxy. Yan, you're hot. I hate to be insensitive—"

"No, you don't."

"—but we got you from a sales house. There was going to be a mega bidding war and some of those buyers were willing to pay quite a lot, not just for your abilities, but to add that ability to their line, and I'm sure they were looking forward to that. Yet you think you're not attractive."

"Okay, that is…something entirely separate. You should know that the psychology behind rape is horrific yet complex. It's more about power dynamics than attraction."

"Oh."

"And I know I'm attractive. That's not the only thing people worry about, Adam." She said his name angrily.

"I guess all I meant is you shouldn't feel insecure. You're a beautiful woman that rode a dragon and saved herself from something terrible."

Yaniqui closed her eyes.

Adam tactfully changed the subject. "I'd like to cash in my favor tomorrow. I want you to read something I wrote."

That was a surprise. "Sure. What is it? Giant lizard erotica?"

He barked a laugh. "You are the worst. How do you even know about giant lizard erotica? I guess 4,278 was more cosmopolitan than I knew." He said the planet numbers individually like she did.

They pulled onto a highway and Yaniqui let the conversation stall while she watched the electric cars and self-automated delivery trucks cut each other off. Maybe she wasn't ready to drive.

Adam revisited the topic hesitantly. "Actually, I'm

writing about what we talked about on the *Caneille* before coming home."

Yaniqui resisted the thought of calling Earth *home*, but she let it pass. "What was that?"

"That young people here don't know how the galaxy actually works and what Earth's real standing is. We think we're this big deal, but we're not."

Yaniqui made a thoughtful noise with her throat. "I guess that was one of the first things Maemi taught me when we went into hiding. We were just two small beings, safe only as long as no one saw us." She swallowed back emotion and forced herself to brighten. "Of course I'll review it for you."

The talked as they drove through the countryside and then Adam turned down the long driveway Yaniqui remembered from when she first left with Loera and Hloban—first *met* Loera. They passed an orchard of squat, gnarled trees.

Yaniqui had no idea what was going to happen, but it was going to be defining. Either Waquas was going to nicely tell her off, because he was, if anything, polite, or it was a dinner between friends and he was going to pretend nothing happened. Or, maybe, he was interested.

She tried not to think that last thought again, especially with Adam in the car. She didn't even really know what attracted her to Waquas. Just that there was this sense that he was more than any of them. But also that when he looked at her, he saw her, not the layers that had been added to her throughout her life. And, man, those pecs.

"You're sure he's going to give you a ride back?"

"Ninety percent sure."

"Okay, call me if you need anything."

Yaniqui gave him a genuine smile. "Thanks. I appreciate that. I'll talk to you tomorrow about your paper. Let's get you an A+ educating these Earthling rubes." She slammed the door as Adam opened his mouth in protest.

"Hi, Waquas," Yaniqui said, popping into his view from behind a stone wall.

"Mi oaff!" Waquas threw a seedling and dirt showered her hair. The scent of clean earth permeated everything.

"Sorry, I thought you saw me coming." After knocking on the door of Waquas's quiet house, Yaniqui wandered around to the back and saw him at work.

"No, I'm sorry. I don't know why I threw that tomato plant. I was surprised. I didn't expect to see you until six." He cut off his laugh, shy.

Yaniqui realized that even though they had spent weeks in space together, she rarely heard him laugh. He was often on the outside of things, not really in sync with those around him. Among the green plants—as opposed to a room full of Earthlings—Waquas's lightly colored green skin looked completely natural. He had on dark brown, thick-layered pants and a shirt that said "AI Crunch."

"It's six now."

Yaniqui was delighted her arrival caused such a stir. On the way to the farm Yaniqui wasn't sure if she actually wanted to try this. But suddenly she was.

"What was that language you spoke?"

"My own, Laural." He brushed his hands against each other. He didn't have any gloves on and clumps of rich dark dirt fell to the ground. "I said, well, it translates to 'cursed sky,' but it's only an expression. I guess time slipped by me."

"I didn't take in very much of your farm when we first landed. Now I can see this is so different than where I worked as an ag. laborer with my mother," Yaniqui rushed on, surprised with hard thoughts. "This is much nicer."

"I've heard of some of those places."

"Yeah, poor living conditions. Not a lot to eat despite all the growth."

"I'm sorry you faced that. And the plants. All those artificial methods of squeezing out all that they can out of minerals, water, and sunlight." Waquas bent back down. "I have a few more seedlings to get in the ground, if you don't mind. I like to do a late planting for some of these vegetables. A neighbor tended most of the earlier planting work while we were traveling."

Again, Yaniqui realized how much trouble the travelers went through to get her. Even though it wasn't what she intended for them to do, she felt responsible that they had put their lives on hold.

Yaniqui squatted down on the ground where Waquas carefully packed soil down.

"These plants grow a round red fruit. You know pasta sauce?" Waquas asked.

"Do I ever." Yaniqui reached out and touched the soft fragrant leaves.

"Tomatoes are the main ingredient. But the best way to eat them is fresh with a little bit of salt from our seas."

"You say 'our seas,' but Earth is not your real home." She looked at him curiously.

"It is now." Waquas took another small seedling from

a tray. "I have traveled so far from my home, I know I will never go back. I had lived there for fifteen years when I set out."

"How long is that in Earth years?" Yaniqui asked. Finally, some real information about Waquas's past.

"That's converted—fifteen years."

"How old are you now?"

"I'm not sure. I've traveled through cryogenic sleep and made the great Leap from my galaxy to yours."

Yaniqui raised her eyebrows in shock.

"You may have noticed I look a bit different?" He almost smiled.

Yaniqui nodded.

He continued, "Trying to figure out my age is only guesswork. I'm not important—no one's tracking any data on me. I don't know the full impact of relativity from the Leap. The best I can figure is my physical body has spanned 624 years, but I haven't been conscious for even a tenth of my existence."

Waquas straightened a plant. He was well muscled and agile. He was bright and peaceful. And over six hundred years old. It did not compute.

"But for you, you can heal yourself." He hesitated. "Are you invincible?"

Yaniqui laughed. "That's the stuff of legends. I'm sure it looks that way from the outside, but we still feel pain and that pain can be too great for us to survive. Our organs, however, don't face the same sicknesses as others. Like cancer. That a body would attack itself rather than heal is terrible."

Waquas dug a new hole. The ground parted easily.

"What planet are you from, then?" Yaniqui asked.

She felt Waquas hesitate. "Laur. It's...very far away from Earth, as you can imagine."

Yaniqui got the impression that Waquas didn't want to talk about it, but she made up her mind to look up the planet later and hoped that was okay to do.

He said he had to wash his hands and put away the supplies, but then he would give her a tour and make dinner. Yaniqui sat on a chair outside his house, one made of wide wood slats. It was clearly homemade but surprisingly comfortable.

All things considered, she supposed this was her first time "dropping in on someone," a term she'd heard Loera use.

He came out and walked her through his fields. It was hard to imagine the capital was just a few leagues away. Yaniqui watched Waquas, without looking like she was watching him. His shirt was slightly damp with perspiration. The sun was low in the sky, as Earthlings would say, but the air was still warm.

Like much of what she saw of Earth, there was green everywhere, but Yaniqui especially loved the massive trees, the first thing she noticed when she arrived on-planet. Yaniqui listened to Waquas explain about the orchard and the crops. But she wondered what he was doing, doing all of this on Earth. For someone who was so aged and had traveled so far, how could he be content with this small place?

At beds of herbs, Waquas told her the crops you tend least and pick least go farthest away from where you sleep and eat. The things you grow for daily use, like herbs, go as close to your home as possible. Waquas said it was the same on every planet, in every society, that purposefully grew food. That even with all of humanity's variations, some things were basic logic agreed upon by everyone.

Yaniqui challenged him on that. The crops she took care of on the ag. planet had no rhyme or reason to them. Waquas pointed out that they weren't growing the food for themselves on the ag. planet. It wasn't driven by human intuition but corporate values. They only cared about efficiency when it saved them money.

Finally, he invited her inside his decidedly compact home. It was much smaller than Hloban and Loera's house, so much that they would have looked ridiculous side by side. There was only the loft upstairs and the kitchen, storage room, living room, and bathroom on the first floor. Outside was a small workshop.

Waquas climbed the ladder to change his clothes in the loft.

Yaniqui's thoughts were upstairs, but she looked carefully around the first floor. There was one abstract painting on the widest wall, but no photographs or holos or anything personal or technologically remarkable.

"I'm enjoying the notebook," she called up. "There's…a lot to write down. And thank you once again for coming to help me. You all risked so much to come and save me."

"When you didn't need saving at all."

Yaniqui's face fell. Did he feel like Hloban did? Frustrated to sacrifice so much and not even get to play the hero?

She said, "If you and the rest hadn't come, I could have

died on the asteroid. The dŏsvengar seemed certain that I'd live, but I couldn't see how. Besides, I wouldn't have thought to come to Earth. I would have been too afraid to access the endangered species records with the Joint Council. I never would have been united with the last few of my people."

He descended the ladder and leaned against the back of his couch, facing Yaniqui. Soft knits replaced his work clothes. "It's all right, I understand. We helped, but you didn't need our help escaping. I have to confess though, once I saw the…dŏsvengar, I was all for leaving you behind." Waquas smiled.

"I would have felt the same, I'm sure."

"And yet you went in and released it."

"I had just enough information and was just stupid enough to try. If I had known Hloban was there, I would have gone to find him. But I didn't. The only thing strong enough on the planet to upset Akar's plans was the dŏsvengar. Everyone talked about it endlessly—the guards, the other captives. I heard she was frozen in sleep for a short time, but her metabolizer broke and Akar didn't want to risk their profits disappearing before finalizing a sale, so they woke her and paralyzed her. I had no idea if she'd be strong enough to escape or willing to help me."

"What did you do to convince her?"

"I didn't know what to do. I collapsed in front of her and told her I wanted to help and that I needed help. I was so scared. It was as if it was impossible for me to look into her eyes, even paralyzed as she was. I turned off all the machines, without even knowing what they were." Yaniqui remembered the heat in that room, emanating off the dragon's body. "I blasted as much healing into her as I could and I think she sensed that I meant what I said. But I don't know if words made any difference. She *knows* things."

Yaniqui remembered the enormous body twisting as it roused from slumber. It stretched and rumbled and whipped its thick tail back and forth. Yaniqui was truly terrified but it was different than the terror she felt when she was separated from her mother. Different than when she woke on a slaver's ship.

The terror was sublime—it was the type of terror you wanted to embrace. The dragon was no common animal, no mere creature. If a god was a thing you instantly worshiped, this was it.

Her voice had rasped but spoke a perfect common language. *These little beasts are growing bolder.* She lowered her enormous head and looked at Yaniqui with molten eyes the color of liquid amber. *Long ago, we decided humans should govern their own matters. A mistake.* The dragon flexed her neck. The mass of scar tissue from chains and electric shockers was evident. Dark smoke trickled from her nostrils.

A crash came from outside and her honey eyes rolled. She shivered with anticipation or perhaps the inability to hold herself back any longer, Yaniqui didn't know.

If you want freedom, you must come with me. But only so far, human. I have chaos to spread.

Yaniqui swallowed and her mind reeled as she considered what to do, how to save herself.

Quickly! the dragon snapped.

Yaniqui reached for the neck, the fire demon already

lowering herself. Yaniqui fought to climb on, nearly burning herself on the scales through her thick spacesuit, fighting desperately to hold on as the dragon's body trembled with energy. Once she reached the withers and clung, bewildered tears escaped Yaniqui's eyes, impossible to wipe away because of her helmet. Then it was as if they were one creature. Her body pulsed with another's heartbeat. Her mind stirred in a strange way, dulling itself, yet feeling more endless than she'd ever been.

"Well, it worked," Waquas said, returning her to the present. "And now you're here on Earth. Things are safe. And it's nice that you can be with Adam." He stretched his arms as he made for the tiny kitchen.

Yaniqui felt her face sour. Is that what he thought? "No," she said a bit too loud, "we're not together."

"Oh, Hloban had said—"

"Hloban doesn't decide what I do." Yaniqui pushed her curls back.

"Of course. I was only confused because of something Hloban said." His eyes darted away.

Why did she have to get so heated? She was supposed to be wowing him with how amazing she was.

Yaniqui explained, "I really like Adam. But he's my friend. We know we're not supposed to be together." Yaniqui avoided eye contact and her ears warmed.

Waquas pulled vegetables from bins and loaded an electric machine with slender tips of rice.

Waquas steered the conversation back to neutral territory and she let him. It grew humid in the kitchen and steam clung to the window. Despite her nerves, dinner smelled good. But she couldn't figure him out.

Yaniqui set the table simply and lit the candle in the middle. Waquas's back was to her, but she glanced anyway, straining to read any cue in his broad shoulders, the back of his marbled green neck. Anticipation rose rapidly in her.

Yaniqui cast around for something to say, anything to not make the evening stall. "Hloban says he'll return your holo index soon," but Waquas didn't turn.

"Okay. Good."

She held back a frown. Did he even want her? Was he asexual, or not interested, or elderly?

Yaniqui leaned against the large butcher block that served as a pseudo island. There was a mishmash of cut carrot heads, onion peels, and other leafy green castoffs. She picked up a sliver of yellow pepper and put it in her mouth. It was sweet and crunchy.

"That's done. It can simmer for a moment." Waquas finally turned around. "Let's sit down."

Yaniqui moved toward the chairs at the table.

"No, no, in here." He sat on the pillowed couch, a few strides away from where he ate. A fireplace lay opposite them, still in the summer heat.

Yaniqui sat.

"Yaniqui, let's talk about this before anything else. When we were together last..."

Yaniqui couldn't utter a word.

"I got the sense that you wanted...you wanted maybe to be together?"

"Waquas." What was she supposed to say next? Dear gods, was she brave enough to say it? "Yes. That's what I want. I want to be together."

Waquas picked at his lower lip with two fingers, then said, "Can I ask why? My life, me, I'm so much quieter than anything I would think you would choose."

"I'll tell you, but I'd like to hear your answer to a question first. Why did you come to save me?" Yaniqui looked up through her lashes and breathed in through her mouth. She was sure her face had never been warmer.

Waquas responded immediately and simply. "Because it was the right thing to do." He seemed to be weighing something else out. "I didn't come to this galaxy under the best circumstances. Why would I let someone else get trafficked? There are always more people to help, but we're not often in the position to do so. But with you, I knew trying might make a difference."

So that was it. He understood in a way Adam and Hloban couldn't.

Yaniqui licked her lips. She tried to breathe calmly through her nose even as her heart sped. "Everyone who came to save me had their own motives. Hloban felt possessive, Keyad felt the responsibility of family, and Adam came because he was trying to reach for a life he envisioned. I never met Patrick, but from what Adam said, he had hoped for a last adventure. And Eeriva, she's bound by obligation. You came to save me because I needed help and it was the right thing to do. That's the type of person I want around me."

Waquas sighed and leaned back in his chair. "You don't have to choose one of the people who saved you. And I can still be in your life without being *involved*."

Oh damn, did *he* just blush? His cheeks were dark green. No one could look at those high cheekbones and not know they came from somewhere else altogether.

His eyebrows lifted when Yaniqui laughed. "I met a lot of different people with Akar, and I lived closely with many different races while my maemi and I worked. I know how rare good people are. You're kind and responsible and observant of others. You're diligent and hard-working. Look at all of this around you that you've created. And it's clear you could do more, but you stopped yourself when you had enough. I think one of the reasons it wouldn't have worked out with Adam is because he views life with the perspective of an Earthling. He seems to think everything is malleable. That's good, for him, but I make decisions carefully and follow through. I'm loyal. I think you are too."

Yaniqui felt a little shaky, but she was gaining her stand. There wasn't much encouragement in his face, but he was listening.

"I'm not sure why I'm on Earth. It's not to be with Hloban and it's not to be with Adam. I don't have to be with anyone at all. I have this chance to choose my own life. I've never felt I could really choose before. And I want to choose you. That's what I want."

Waquas finally smiled. "That's what I want too."

Yaniqui's ears hummed, her cheeks warmed even more, her nipples tingled, her heart pounded, her stomach tightened, and she got the most delicious touch of anticipation.

It had been four days since she had dinner with Waquas. Days that felt utterly perfect. Then, Hloban—again watching Yaniqui get ready to be picked up—ruined it.

"I would think you have better things to do than to cling to Waquas."

Yaniqui pressed her lips together. She had figured that Hloban would be jealous. In fact, she was counting on it. But she hadn't expected him to get mean about it.

"It's not clinging if both people want to spend time together."

Hloban sat on the other end of the couch from where she was writing in the notebook Waquas had given her when she first arrived on Earth. How amazing was that? That he knew, before anyone else, before herself, that she'd want a space to process everything.

"You have better things to do." Hloban looked at Yaniqui until she had to look away, his stare too intense.

"I'm relaxing after being on the run for pretty much my entire life."

"Relaxing while other people don't have time left."

Yaniqui swallowed. She was not taking that bait. But she didn't need to.

"Like," Hloban expounded, "people on this planet you could heal. Show Earth you appreciate the safe haven they've given you. Cortez is waiting for your answer." He paused and pursed his lips while he thought. "Or your maemi."

Yaniqui stood bolt upright from the couch, her notebook dropping to the floor. "Are you seriously implying I don't care about *my own maemi*? That if I knew where she was, I wouldn't be on the first spacecraft off-planet?"

Obani peeked around the corner. Yaniqui and Hloban both glanced at his big eyes. She gave him a smile. She had learned soon after arriving that there were no private conversations in the Milton household.

"Hey squirt, why don't you go get yourself a cookie?" Hloban's suggestion was enough incentive for Obani and a moment later, a cupboard door rattled.

She turned squarely to Hloban. "What is your problem?" Yaniqui hadn't expected living with her once-betrothed, his wife, and his child would be fun, but she hadn't realized how prickly of a person Hloban was. When he picked her up off that asteroid, it was the first time they had shared any time together since they were teens. She had been desperate for it. Now, it was turning into too much.

"I don't have a problem. I'm making a suggestion. Trying to help you find your way."

Yaniqui grimaced and decided she should have a fight with Waquas soon to see if all men were so emotionally obtuse.

"Don't roll your eyes at me."

"Young lady," she corrected. "'Don't roll your eyes at me, young lady.'"

"Gods!" Hloban threw up his hands.

After a moment where the only sound was a voracious ripping of plastic and devouring of cookies from the kitchen, Yaniqui turned back to Hloban.

"What the hell is going on?"

Hloban had closed his eyes but batted one open. "Did you learn that from Loera?"

Yaniqui laughed, satisfied to break a little of the tension. "Hell is a fire-place for evildoers and people who eat too much. How embarrassing for Earth."

"I'm not trying to cause a problem," Hloban said. "I've been trying to catch you to talk about this, but you're always gone."

"I am not always gone," she said calmly. "If you want to talk to me, you have to tell me. I can't read your mind."

"Yaniqui, it's like you don't even realize what people gave up to come save you. Don't realize the danger we're in—were put in," he corrected.

She scowled at him. She knew all too well the disruption she had caused. Was still trying to recover from the guilt of it.

He continued, willing her to listen, "Last week, I had a meeting."

The doorbell rang. Yaniqui was there in a flash, but she still didn't beat Obani who had his face pressed against one of the vertical panes of glass that formed a triptych with the door.

Yaniqui peeked through too and then wrenched the door open. She smiled. "Hey."

The summer sun wouldn't set for a couple hours so Waquas stood in a pair of light colored shorts and a faintly rose-colored shirt, both of which contrasted nicely with his skin. Whirls of patterned green ran across his folded forearms. Black sunglasses perched on his bald head. Yaniqui had envisioned running her hand through thick black hair so many times, she was surprised the baldness didn't bother her. It was a trademark of his kind, so of course it just seemed to fit.

She leaned into him and gave a relatively chaste kiss, but Obani didn't seem to appreciate her efforts. He pushed right in.

"Why haven't you brought strawberries?"

Waquas looked down. "They're out of season, little bud. Done growing for the year."

"Damn, I liked those," Yaniqui said.

"But I don't see any box." Obani looked for the brown CSA produce subscription box Waquas always brought when he stopped over.

"I'm not here to deliver vegetables. I'm here to take your auntie out."

Obani sighed. "She's not my *real* aunt. I don't even *have* any real aunts." He threw his hands up and Yaniqui couldn't help but see a mini Hloban.

Yaniqui retrieved her phone and wallet.

"Hloban," Yaniqui called, "I'm going out with Waquas." Maybe it was wrong but after getting her heart broken, she did take a little satisfaction in his discomfort.

Hloban appeared in the doorway. A shadow shifted in his eye before he pasted a slight smile on his face.

Good. Jealous.

"Where are you going?" he asked.

Yaniqui looked to Waquas. She was a recent transplant. The only place she could confidently get to was the taco place Adam liked.

"The art gallery on Seventh is having an opening. The owner, Aunah, is friends with Keyad. You and Obani could come if you like." Waquas turned to Obani. "There's snacks."

"No, that's okay," Hloban said quickly. "I've got some work to do." He opened his mouth to say something else.

"We can talk later," Yaniqui called over, eyes forward on her evening.

Chapter 8

Lozen
The Forest

It was too dark to see well through the trees but Lozen could make out D-68's telltale footsteps—quiet but lumbering. She sat up from the still-warm rocks and instantly knew it hadn't gone well. His energy felt off. There definitely wasn't a celebration coming. She felt bad, but her first thought was gratitude, gratitude that she hadn't gone with D-68 to talk to Leggs, even though she should have questioned him about Agent Velazquez's involvement in his operation.

Lozen gasped when the moon lit D-68's face.

"What happened? Did he have a bunch of animoids beat you?" It was hard to imagine animoids big enough to take on D-68.

"Bad. From mouth of he. Strings of wet."

"Huh? Like venom? Like poison?" Lozen sucked air in through her teeth and hissed. "That fucking bug." She stood from the rocks she had been sitting on staring up at the stars while she waited.

D-68 moved laboriously toward the gap in the stones and lowered himself in without saying any more. Lozen was irked. She had stayed up half the night waiting for her partner, and he barely said a word. How was she supposed to help him—and herself—if he wouldn't talk to her? It wasn't that he didn't know the words for things, he wasn't even effing trying.

And where did this latest encounter leave her? D-68 no longer had any allies, even fake ones, and now they'd be hunting for him too. Lozen no longer had a best friend. She was no longer safe at home. The only place she had to hide was in a strange animoid's cavern. Her world was growing smaller. Soon it would be only D-68 and the cave.

It was the first time since her aunt died that she lived with anyone. First time in over ten years. Not that she was really living with someone at all. How long could she stay in a hole, realistically? A few days? How long until D-68 got hungry enough to try human à la Lozen?

No, she shouldn't think like that. He was a vegetarian. It was much more likely they'd both be captured and eventually shot for being the most useless, ineffectual duo in the galaxy.

There was only one option left. Lozen pulled her flannel more tightly around herself. She could hear D-68's movements in the cave below. Whatever else, he wasn't well and wasn't going to come up with the solution on his own. She'd have to talk to Tril. She really didn't want to. Not only was it dangerous—What if Tril was as corrupt as Velazquez?—but it felt like she'd be betraying her people even more. Monte didn't even like the fact that Lozen had talked with Tril. How would her best friend feel if trucks full of agents came to the Catchment to help Lozen get D-68 back to his planet? Would Monte feel any different if those same agents came to arrest Lozen?

An owl hooted from high in a tree and Lozen shivered. She started the climb into the dark hole. Earlier, she'd brought down wood for a fire, but she decided to just curl up and try to go to sleep.

Neither of them slept comfortably. D-68 was restless, pawing unconsciously at his face through the night. She didn't know if he dreamed, but if he did, they must have been unnerving.

Eventually, morning light filtered through, casting a dim glow about the limestone hollow. Lozen stood, stretched, and sat in the thin shaft of sunlight. She still had her blanket tucked around her. She looked over at D-68. He was already sitting up, facing away from her.

"Morning."

He didn't respond.

Lozen's bladder was bursting, but it seemed rude to run off. Plus, she was only getting up that rocky wall once today. There was no way she was coming back in, and D-68 didn't seem inclined to move.

"How do you feel? Do you want to talk about Leggs? You said last night he poisoned you. Is that what happened to your face?"

Lozen thought D-68 wasn't going to respond. Then he

stood and turned. Her hand flew to cover her mouth, for once not because she was self-conscious about herself.

A dark film lay thickly in one eye. Bubbled skin—if his thin facial platelets could be called that—rimmed harshly around the ruined eye. She stood and the blanket dropped from her shoulders. She was staring but couldn't help it. She was growing used to D-68's otherworldly look, but this was grotesque.

"Fix you?"

"Huh?"

"Heal head my?"

"I'm not that type of Native."

"What?"

She sighed. "Never mind. No, I can't. I have no idea what kind of plant would help or even what kind of medicine to use if we were in a whole store full of stuff."

D-68 dropped to the ground. Gloom hung over him and Lozen didn't blame him. Here he was, some number of light-years from his family, recently brutally attacked by a big bug. Lozen wondered about the logistics of that. It never once occurred to her that Leggs could pose a threat to D-68.

Could Lozen be more empathetic to D-68? Sure. But what his current predicament really did was put her lack of friends into perspective. It was time to do what Agent Tril always told her was in her own best interest: fully cooperate.

She slugged her way over to her canvas bag and opened it. Inside, wrapped in a spare shirt was the GIA device, powered down. Lozen turned it off most of the time because she didn't have a reliable source of electricity. This also made it hard for Tril to contact *her*, which she liked.

Lozen glanced in the corner at D-68. He had lain down and was despondent, taking no notice of her.

If only the Karmas had assigned her a different task for initiation. If only she had been unable to make contact with D-68.

Instead, here she was, living in a cave, putting herself out on a limb for an animoid.

Well, he could look a bit more appreciative. She didn't want to call Tril, but she was doing it for the both of them.

It was a perfect summer day. Not too humid, not blazing. Lozen should be on the beach with Monte, having a sundowner surrounded by friends, an electric thrill in the air. They'd eat piping hot grilled fish and tell stories, like the time Mama Teresa fell off the roof of her house. The last time Lozen had told that story, she was so drunk she forgot to cover her mouth when she smiled, didn't think twice about what Dan or anyone else thought of her cleft lip. In the morning, she swam in the lake and foraged in the forest and met up with Monte to do the night all over again.

Instead, Lozen was waiting in the clearing when Tril's ship touched down. The first time she saw it, she was in utter awe. It shimmered in the air, nearly invisible unless you were looking for it. Tril had let her sit at the console of buttons and screens, and answered all her questions.

No wonder Tril didn't take her seriously. Lozen flushed as she watched the ship settle on the grass, little more than a flicker of greens, yellows, and browns, all the colors you expected to see when you looked at a meadow in the forest. The ship whirled faintly until it cut off. Then, the outline materialized and a door powered down to create a ramp. She was just some dumb kid from the Catchment.

Lozen hefted herself up from the base of the tree as Tril stepped out. Her hair was pulled back in its usual ponytail and her holobadge ran her GIA agent numbers.

"Lozen, I didn't want to tell you over the call," Tril got straight to the point, "but you're going to come with me. Now that you know where D-68 is located, we'll make sure you're in a safe space."

Lozen took an involuntary step back. "What? No, I'm not leaving the Catchment." She couldn't. Wasn't ready. She'd never get to make up with Monte. And what would happen to D-68? She wanted to convince Tril he was innocent—nearly innocent—not run away and leave him to be executed.

Tril paused and scanned the trees. "I know change can be difficult—scary even—but it's time, Lozen. I'll make sure you're set up at the capital."

New Washington, WI. A life of food and electricity for her very own phone and more of that ice cream with the candied strawberries. Most compelling of all, surgery to repair her lip.

Lozen's mouth went dry.

Tril continued, speaking softly as if trying to convince a puppy it was time to come inside. "You did good, Lozen. This was the goal all along. Come on. The best place to have this conversation in full is at HQ."

When in Lozen's life had she ever expected to have to choose between a life of luxury, of freedom and her own apartment with a real roof and doctors, and a stupid, rock-headed animoid? She wanted to bite her tongue off.

"Shit. Agent Tril, I wish it were that easy." Her eyes went wide as she started her rehearsed appeal. "But it's not safe where *you* are. This whole thing is much more than you were told. D-68 is just a scapegoat."

A thin line appeared between Tril's eyebrows. "What are you talking about, Lozen?"

Lozen swallowed. "Your partner…Velazquez." She brought a hand to her forehead. "I saw him in the forest here. He was working with a few different animoids from the Catchment. Animoids that work for Leggs."

Tril wrinkled her nose. Impatience fell across her face. "Lozen, that's ridiculous. Like all of us, Agent Velazquez spent years being vetted by the GIA." She realized she was losing her top informant and her tone turned hard. "I'm sure it's all a misunderstanding. Get in the ship. Let's go sort this out."

Tril reached over to Lozen's shoulder to guide her toward the opening, but Lozen wrenched away. "If you would just listen to me"—Lozen put both her hands up in front of her. Why wasn't Tril *listening* to her?—"you'd realize you have the wrong bad guy. D-68 is being set up by Leggs and Velazquez.

"Leggs was moving drugs, but someone told me he also helped kidnap people from the Catchment."

"Who, Lozen? Who told you that?"

Lozen looked Tril right in the face, steeling herself. "D-68."

Tril got a strange look on her face and it was only pure instinct and a childhood in the Catchment that forced Lozen to dive out of the way of Tril's sudden tackle. Tril made for Lozen's middle but instead clipped her upper thigh. They both scrambled to right themselves. Lozen staggered a step forward and lurched into a flat-out run. She didn't care what direction, she just had to move.

A blinding buzz shot up her leg and her teeth clanged together. A grunt escaped her throat as she fell to the grass in a convulsion. She tried to speak but couldn't get the words out.

Agent Tril approached cautiously and not with an unkind face. She and her buddies at the GIA were probably well versed in the knowledge that you could never really trust the scum of the Catchment. That *those people* never knew what was best for themselves. "Lozen, it's clear you have information on D-68. Taking you in is under GIA judication. I'm sorry we couldn't have done this peacefully. You'll probably regret not taking our offer for the rest of your life."

Lozen's calf muscles stopped twitching. She let out a rush of air. "Fine. Just don't do that to me again. That was freaky as fuck."

Tril holstered the taser and slid thick rings of matte black metal from her belt—handcuffs. Lozen had no choice but to follow her directions to roll onto her stomach, hands behind her. Once Tril was close, Lozen kicked out and knocked Tril to the ground. They wrestled and Lozen knew she was going to lose—Tril's upper body strength was fearsome—when Tril was lifted off her.

D-68 stood, Tril in hand.

"No," shrieked Lozen. "Don't hurt her. She doesn't understand."

D-68 bared his broad teeth. He grabbed the taser and threw it aside. Lozen grabbed, desperate for it, hoping she didn't buzz herself in the process, and D-68 dropped Tril to the ground in a heap. Lozen pulled the phone Tril had given her last spring, smashed the power off button, and chucked it into the ferns. She'd return for it later, even if she couldn't turn it on without being located.

"I'm sorry. Really, I am. But you didn't trust me." Lozen was very close to a panic attack. She had to fight to get the right words out. "If you look into Velazquez, you'll understand."

She pulled the trigger on the taser and ran like fuck, D-68 close beside.

They ran to the tree line, through the forest, climbed a tree like panicked black bears, doubled back, got lost, and finally, the sun high in the sky, made it back to the hideout.

They dropped down into the rocky crevice, Lozen's muscles stiff and unyielding.

She lay panting, then fought to sit up. Resigned, she spoke, "Okay, now we're really without friends."

Chapter 9

Ippa
An Earth Rain Forest

A delicate tickle woke Ippa. She lay prone on a layer of broad green leaves that she built to try to keep the ravenous ants, beetles, and centipedes off her. Her first thought was that it was a bug on her cheek. Ippa deliberately raised her head and tilted the tickled cheek toward the ground to dislodge the being. Instead, a substance ran down her cheek, wet and as warm as she was. Ippa wiped at her face with her sleeved forearm awkwardly because her hands were bound by a strip of ripped cloth—Matts's insistence—and came away with smear of white.

Bird poop. Excellent.

Ippa pushed up to sitting and cleaned her face the best

she could.

The morning sun had crested the horizon, already brighter and livelier than Ippa expected at this time of day. The leaves around her glowed with health. Leaves of that size were needy. When would it rain next? Matts was most concerned about being followed by various unknown authorities, but Ippa knew it was exposure that picked people off with glee.

Matts was still sleeping. They had their back to a rotted log. The remnants of the fire they managed to build lay between them. It had been hard to get the green wood started, even with Matts's lighter, and it smoldered more than burned but the ample smoke was a welcome relief when hordes of mosquitos descended to dine. Matts's face, exposed neck, and forearms were peppered with red welts. A collection of throbs told Ippa her face must look much the same. Neither of them was dressed in what could count as explorer gear. Matts wore black jeans and a thick black shirt with sleeves that stopped at the elbows. Ippa wore one of the tunics she had traded her Shou University uniform for, the one with buttons along the shoulder, linen pants, and a pair of simple, flat slip-on shoes. Already everything was filthy and the shoes were near useless. She couldn't wait to chuck them.

She stood carefully and peered around them. The jungle was full of morning noise made up of insect clicks and buzzes and trees full of birds, but there were no animals in sight. Her stomach growled. Yes, there would be much more of that.

Ippa took a step and Matts's eyes peeled open like a cat's. Ippa fought to pretend she wasn't terrified of them.

She focused intently on assessing their surroundings though she was primarily trying to appear both confident and nonthreatening. Matts hadn't yet spoken.

All right, so, they wouldn't say good morning to each other.

Ippa got right to it. "This forest is unusually well-watered. I'm sure we're in its rainy season, maybe at the end of it based on the lack of clouds."

Matts pushed themselves up much like Ippa did moments ago but had the blessed full-range motion of freed hands. They rubbed unknowingly at the bug bites, then gestured. Ippa came forward, hands out. It took Matts a moment to untie the cloth knot. Ippa stepped away quickly out of arm's reach. Matts paid her no mind and simply rewound the cloth length and tucked it in one of their many pockets.

"Any idea about food sources?"

Ippa hesitated as she combed through her research on Earth. She was versed in its histories and knew books' worth of information on its many ecosystems, but food, well, one wrong decision could kill them. "We should stay away from any kind of fungi. Earth mushrooms can be deadly and I don't know the local species well enough to type them. If we find tree fruit, that's bound to be fine except for maybe some berry types. If we see mammals eating it, we should be fine. But my top priority is fresh water."

"Oh really," Matts leered. "Water is your top priority?" It went unsaid that Ippa—the woman who was kidnapped by an intersolar bounty hunter—wasn't in a position to be making decisions.

Ippa pushed her snarled blue hair back and frowned. "You're the reason I'm in this mess"—Ippa didn't mention that she'd been on her way to halfheartedly signing up as a laborer before they met due to her own poor decision making—"and I suggest you listen. You're not going to survive this environment without me."

Matts cocked their head. "You think your fancy education is going to save you?"

"I think my research on *Earth and its ecosystems* is what's going to save me."

Matts scratched at their forearms and stood. A new wave of assessment scuttled across their face. "You didn't mention that you studied Earth specifically."

Ippa shook her head. "You mean when I was kidnapped and interrogated? Yes, I think I went light on the particulars of my research." She raised an eyebrow, forcing more bravado than she was comfortable with. "That's why I was coming to Earth. To further my work."

If Ippa had been looking for approval, she wasn't going to get it.

"That's why I came to Earth too," Matts said dismissively. "Use the facilities. Stretch out. We leave in three minutes."

Matts insisted on heading north. They said they didn't know exactly where they were on-planet, but they had to pick a direction and walk until they found a city.

Ippa agreed. The continents on Earth were top heavy but she guessed that they were at the equator because of the heat and jungled forest. Though it didn't matter much. It wasn't as if they were going to *walk* to where the woman,

Yaniqui, was. They just had to find humanity. Then maybe Ippa would have a chance at escape.

"So, you came way out here to the boonies, where civilization barely exists, to chase after some bounty?"

Matts led their hike, circling trees and dodgy-looking anthills. "Not some bounty. A career-defining bounty."

Ippa snorted—she didn't know bounty hunters thought about their careers—but Matts ignored her.

"One that I had already captured, delivered, and was paid for. Then she escaped Akar Enterprises." Matts shook their head in disbelief. They looked back and leveled a finger at Ippa, "Once you're in the system, cooperation is key. Remember that. Things are going to go sour for Yaniqui. She would have had a level of freedom and comfort if she had proved she was trustworthy. That door is closed to her now and they'll still use her as they like."

The sun was nearly at its crest. Sweat trickled down Ippa's neck like molasses. She had to keep reminding herself this wasn't a philosophical discussion. This was a real woman they were talking about. "You can't expect her to roll over and accept slavery."

"That's exactly what Akar expects."

"And not even try to fight for freedom?"

"It's better to be alive than dismantled for parts."

Ippa wrinkled her nose. She cleared her throat. "Anyway, she did it. She got free. And likely this independent planet won't take kindly to Akar's interventions."

"S'not the first time Akar has found humanoid resources here. The woman is in a city called Washington and that's not only a seat of power, but a wealth of human capital—did'ja studies teach you that? Those two things often go hand in hand."

They marched quietly for a few more minutes. Matts didn't seem to particularly mind Ippa's questions—they were a chatty one—but Ippa was thinking.

Matts was a bounty hunter. The idea was so abhorrent to Ippa that she hadn't yet analyzed it. All of what was happening was tender in her mind but Matts must have weaknesses. Ippa simply had to figure out what they were. Figure that out, exploit them until she freed herself, waltz out of the jungle, and do an epic research project on Earth that would win the good graces of Shou University once again.

"Hurry your sweet ass up," Matts called over their shoulder. "I don't want to spend another night in this shithole."

Her epiphany didn't come until late afternoon as they marched away from a stream they crossed, water still dripping from her hair. Before swimming it, Matts took a long drink. Ippa tried to convince Matts they should filter the water through one of their shirts, though jerry-rigging a way to boil it was best. Matts said there wasn't time. Ippa chose not to drink from the stream. She didn't want to die from the many forms of bacteria that could be living in fresh water.

That was when it dawned on Ippa. Matts's knowledge base had to be broad because of the territories they covered, the races they interacted with. They weren't ever able to specialize in one area. Their success came from mass generalizations. And what did Akar care? Either they were successful or someone else would be. So, it stood that Matts likely knew only enough about Earth to get by.

Ippa tested her theory as they followed a narrow game trail. "What do you think of the battle between Earth humanoids and the last of the Intelligent Earth animoids?"

Matts hesitated. "Oh," they started, "it will end soon. It always does."

"But what about the fact that the Earth leader is an animoid?"

"Sure, but that power structure wasn't going to last long either way."

Ippa nearly grinned as she pushed a fern aside. Not only did Matts have no basic understanding of Earth or the differences among Earth ecosystems, they were a bullshitter. They'd never let it be known they didn't know something, much less ask for help. The only reason Ippa hadn't realized it was because Matts was all confidence. That, and Ippa was 1,000 percent terrified. But, it turned out, not ill-equipped.

It was hard to give up the first opportunity, but Ippa wasn't certain it would work. A wasp nest of some kind hung on the side of a tree and Ippa considered telling Matts she could safely harvest food from there, but Ippa figured Matts would tell her to do it. And the frenzy of insects—it set anyone's teeth on edge. It was too obviously a ruse.

She scratched at a mosquito bite on her wrist and wished for some salve. "Matts"—it was the first time Ippa had used their name—"why don't you just leave me behind when we reach a human population center? You know I don't want to do any of this, but logically, I'm slowing you down. By keeping me with you, you're creating too many opportunities for things to go wrong."

Matts laughed. It was low and husky. Ippa didn't like it one bit.

"But you're an important part of my plan for getting to Yaniqui."

"Why?" Ippa was incredulous. "I have no idea who she is."

"I don't want to give away the fun." Their voice was rough velvet.

Ippa stopped in her tracks. "I'd never help you capture her."

"People never know what they will or won't do. Trust me, you'll do it."

Matts kept marching and Ippa reluctantly followed. She didn't want to be pinned down again with her arm twisted behind her back. And that's how it was. How much would Ippa do to avoid pain? To keep her family safe? Would she give up another person to do so?

No. Ippa was determined. She would never put herself in that position. She was fallible but smart.

And she had found her opportunity.

If she couldn't trick Matts into an unsafe environment, she would have to trick Matts into believing a perfectly safe environment was unsafe.

"Oh, it's a cannonball tree," she fought to build excitement in her voice. "We can eat this fruit."

Matts turned and evaluated the narrow columned tree. The brown fruit hung high in vined clusters. Ippa was terribly hungry. She knew Matts had to be too. "If you're able to get up there, you can knock the fruit down and they will crack when they hit the ground. We can even carry some with us."

It was clear Ippa would never make it up there. Her arms were ready only for the rigors of academia.

It took Matts less than a minute to shimmy up the tree. Their upper body strength was alarming. Matts hit down a cluster. They fell to the forest floor and broke. A slightly musky smell filled the already humid air.

Matts began carefully descending when Ippa backed away from the fruit.

"Crisps! It's a red-backed centipede."

Matts paused.

"It's right on the tree trunk, it's huge. I don't know how you didn't see it." Ippa let her body convulse slightly as if she were repulsed by the perfectly neutral collection of brown leaves she studied. "These are deadly poisonous." Ippa stood, as if she couldn't figure out what to do.

They huffed. "Get a tree branch and knock it away so I can get down."

Ippa jerked to attention. "Right." It was hard not to grab one of the fruits as she moved away in search of a stick, but if she did that, she may as well confess. She picked up a slender twig and cast it away. "Here's one." Ippa took a series of steps, picked up a thick stick, looked down at a placid little flower and screamed, "Snake!"

She tore off through the brush shouting, "Crisping papers!"

As she was running away, it occurred to Ippa that she actually would do anything to keep herself safe. Even be brave.

Chapter 10

D-68
Lake Michigan

"If you don't stick your head under the water, I'm going to steal a bucket and drench you in the middle of the night, and you won't like that."

D-68 regards Lozen suspiciously. He does not like the threat but even more, he does not like the idea of touching this poison water. Two days after the Many Legged One cast his venom on D-68, it still itches and burns at touch and movement, even between some of his strongest platelets. One eye and earhole are painfully inflamed and burn constantly. After saving Lozen from that little human, all he could do was lie on the rock floor of his cave, trying not to move. The only reason he left was because Lozen said she could heal him.

Now that he is here, he is frustrated at her lack of understanding. What does she know about battling? About his pain? He already tried to wash off the venom. It hurt walking to the lake. She's only going to get them caught. Only going to make things worse as she does.

"Is poison."

The human woman grabs her black braid and pulls it over her shoulder in frustration. "It's poison to drink but not touch. That's what the government says."

D-68 doesn't speak for he senses there's more.

The white moon doesn't glint on the choppy water surface but rests above. It is an alien sight, beautiful even. The birds are quiet and he and Lozen are many paces away from the Catchment. Patches of artificial light glow, but they are nothing compared to the haze of lights concentrated over what Lozen says is the capital city.

"Okay, so you already know about Monte and my life at the Catchment, but who I am—it's bigger than that. It's like there's me, Lozen, and then me, Lozen the Potawatomi slash colonizer descendent woman. A long, long time ago, I had ancestors who lived on the edge of this lake when it was pure. Like, for a very long time. This was the entire world. Well, we knew about other tribes, even a song all the way from a Florida tribe made its way here like some kind of viral phonk track—"

D-68 snorts and Lozen gets the message.

"But anyway, what eventually happened was other people. Earth humans came from another territory on this planet, another continent for fuck's sake, and took our land. Then they pumped a bunch of garbage and chemicals into the water. The people who were supposed to be in charge let this happen. They destroyed this lake. Or at least the southern part of it. I don't know, maybe if you go north enough." Lozen turns away from D-68 to face the dark waters.

This Catchment isn't her home. He thinks of it as her home, but she doesn't belong here, like him.

"There's a cleanup project, but they've made drastically more headway on the smaller waters. A lot of terrible stuff was dumped in Lake Michigan that those people never thought would come back to bite them. And it didn't. It's come back to bite their grandkids. I say all of that to say I don't trust the government one bit—can't—but they said the water is fine for bathing and washing in and everyone in the Catchment does. I've been doing it my whole life and I do think it's okay. Just keep your mouth shut."

These humans speak so fast, they say so many words, it is a nuisance. If only they were more restrained with their speech, they could say more. Still, he feels he got the center of what Lozen said. The Earth government has exploited her people and her land, the same as they are doing on his home planet. He's resistant to the thought that they're similar in any way. He looks to the distant, dim lights of the Catchment and pictures kits growing up in that disgusting pit. And not being able to do anything about it. A feeling he has grown too accustomed to.

Lozen stands in front of him waiting, apprehension on her face. D-68 knows this because the furs on her face burrow toward each other. It's only by a few degrees, but it is enough of a marked change to communicate her anxiety.

The tissues under his platelets still burn. "Fine," he ventures.

"Okay, so walk into the lake, like, um, submerge your body, but not too deep where you can't touch the bottom, and dunk your head. Try to stay underwater for a few seconds. We'll start with that and see how that goes."

D-68 takes a step into the water. It is cool and lively. If he had not tried to drink it when he first arrived, he would not know the water was bad. The surf washes back and forth across his feet on the sand, then limbs. There is buoyancy. When the water is midway up his leg, he halts. He feels foolish to be nervous, but he is not the same as the humans. He has seen their kits swim from a distance and they move like spiders, agile and lithe. These people were made for water. He was made for rock.

The great water slaps against him and sand pulls at his feet. The waters will swallow him and take him deep to where the poisons lie. He will die a watery death, far from the solid resting ground of rock.

Lozen is beside him, up to her chest in the water. He is shocked to see her shoulders bare in the moonlight. She pulled off parts of her clothes D-68 couldn't name. He already knew there were no platelets on these humans, but still he is unnerved how soft and vulnerable they are. Her bones are all in the wrong places, protecting nothing of her most vulnerable softness.

She watches him give her a once over and laughs when he says, "Fragile." He knows the last word because 'vo had said it again and again while they moved human cargo. 'vo was someone D-68 assumed he could trust simply because neither of them were humanoids. Instead, it is Lozen the Earthling who tries to help him.

She wades in deeper and he sees the tiny marks of a spinal column shine through her back.

"You only have to go a little deeper, then you can kneel on the sand for a moment."

D-68 cannot go deeper.

"I'll be with you the whole time. I taught Monte how to swim and while I don't think you're going to be doing any swimming, you will at least not drown."

It is laborious to go deeper into the water and find a position where he can allow the waves to wash over him. Lozen cups her hands and fills them with water and lets it trickle down the side of D-68's ruined face like rain. The water makes his platelets feel as if they'll float away and Lozen insists on using her dexterous fingers to run along inside the tiny spaces between his platelets. Her prying movements are uncomfortable. The water in those tight spaces is uncomfortable.

D-68 knows Lozen does not understand how her insistence is misguided, even rude. Yet he suspects it is helping. He tries to set aside what he knows of Lozen and imagine she is some kind of healer, which makes it easier. He has never imagined another being to be different than they are.

He hisses as she dislodges a wad of venom string and flings it into the surf.

"I guess it's organic. And it really can't make the lake worse at this point."

She takes extra time running her small fingers over his earhole and then they are done.

He is quiet as he comes onto land.

She notices this, at least. "You did good. How do you feel? Do you think all of Leggs's gunk got washed out?"

He is waterlogged and uncomfortable, but the burn has dissipated in several places. He nods his head stiffly. He stands, dripping, while she turns away and runs her hands over her own limbs, displacing water. The water slides off in rivulets and she slips on her clothes, getting stuck halfway into the little piece of cloth she wears around her chest.

"Brrrr. I didn't think it would be so chilly."

She gets her other arm through and straightens the fabric.

They talk as they walk back to the cave, Lozen mostly. She tells him more about how the Catchment runs. He is especially interested to hear how humanoids and animoids of all kinds interact. They have separate markets. In drinking establishments the groups haphazardly intermix and often fight. They seem not to understand each other on a biological level.

"—so, Jinn had his men tear down the hives and a few of them were stung and died and now no one knows where the hive settled, but it's definitely not in the Catchment."

He listens to the many words and chooses new ones to keep for himself.

Back at the hole, D-68 climbs in first, taking one last look at the stars through the treetops before he does so. Lozen goes to follow, but he tells her to wait. He can't see well in the dark, but he doesn't need to, not for such a small excavation project. He uses his broad talons and carves a few handholds for Lozen. Limestone dust sticks in the air, but she climbs down with ease.

She lowers herself a few footsteps down and then pulls at a pile of brush she had stacked earlier that day. She insists it is a new security measure because she is committed to lighting the fire indoors. The branches will block the majority of light from escaping the gap. The small gaps between twigs combined with the small hole D-68 burrowed out above will let most of the smoke out so they don't asphyxiate. At least so she assured him.

She sets about starting the fire with a piece of flint. She explains what she's doing and D-68 watches her movements but doesn't really listen.

Finally, with a small fire between them, Lozen speaks on something worthwhile. "Okay, so Leggs is out. The GIA is out. That leaves Charla."

Lozen tells him of the secret group of women humanoids in the Catchment. They call themselves the Karmas and Lozen had hoped to join their family. There is an element of resolution to their work. D-68 thinks Lozen would have done well with them if she was a follower. And she is not a follower but a leader like him.

So, one leader to another, they devise a plan. They will go to the Karmas's cave tomorrow and steal from the collection of devices so they can collect evidence to bring to the GIA—the holograph flashes in his mind—evidence that irrefutably shows that D-68 is innocent of the most bitter of the charges. And Lozen will get her new life away from her family.

Chapter 11

Ippa
An Earth Rain Forest

Ippa dotted clay along her arm. It went on thick but cool over the nest of bug bites that had gathered on every bare swatch of skin. She couldn't see the bites on her forehead but tiny throbs told her they were up there. She smeared the clay across her face and a bit more on her neck. There was no one to see how ridiculous she looked digging wet clay from the ground and practically bathing in it. She was alone. In the jungle. On Earth. Completely alone.

She stood from her crouch on the riverbank, grateful again it seemed she had left the swampy lowlands behind. She had wandered into them shortly after ditching Matts, but she couldn't be picky about the direction she fled to.

She had to put distance between her and that demented bounty hunter.

If only Bel could see the studious, only-one-from-her-home-planet-to-ever-attend-The-Shou Ippa. Bel might be concerned, but everyone else from Shou University would say they weren't surprised. Some might even take glee in the sight of her, clay and bites across her skin, flats full of swamp water, tunic dirty and brown.

How she looked didn't worry her as much as the reptiles. She knew in a jungle this vigorous there were predators.

She stood and moved purposefully away from the still water at the bank. She was still limping from the exertion she had put her hip under. A hairline fracture? A bruise? Either way, her relentless pace couldn't be good for it.

The afternoon sun would bake the clay on her skin soon, but she wanted to shiver. The mammals would likely emerge with darkness, but any oversize reptiles—crocodiles, snakes, anronos—could attack her at any minute.

Something cracked.

She spun.

Nothing was there.

Images of Matts, poised to strike, an anrono, blood dried in its claws, flitted through her head.

She had to move. Shake off the jitters.

A sudden step brought the creak back to her hip and Ippa pushed on through the humid jungle despite it. As she walked, she looked up at the sun overhead. It was hard to spot directly through the canopy, but she could make out its general location and kept it to her left, heading north as she knew Matts would. She wished she knew how much longer she'd have daylight. There were a lot of things she wished and she was going without each of them.

She pushed lacy ferns aside and checked for snakes, scorpions, and anything that might want to bite or sting her. Every vine looked serpentlike, every pile of forest humus able to camouflage something deadly. The giant leaves and low spindly branches pushed at her shoulders, holding her back from progress, from escape.

She couldn't help it. Tears brimmed and slipped over, pooling gently at the dabs of clay on her face. Ippa. The magnificent whiz kid, lost in a jungle on Earth. *Earth* of all places.

Ippa marched forward bleary-eyed until she heard the sound of flowing water. She came out on another bank, possibly another part of the slow rolling river she mined clay from earlier. Dense canopy strained at the open air over the river, but it was large enough to prevent the branches from touching. She paced the riverbank in either direction before deciding there was no other way around. But she must cross.

Ippa was a good swimmer—her mother had always insisted on practical swim lessons alongside Ippa's own chosen cram school activities—but the water was murky.

Nausea rung at the hollow of her stomach. Ippa slowly scraped together a handful of stones and flung them in the water. The stones disappeared instantly in the brown depths. No scrawny heads full of razored teeth reared their heads. Nothing shifted that Ippa could see at least.

"You're going to swim and it will be fine. What's not fine is having a panic attack and allowing that bully to catch up." Ippa kept her voice hushed though if Matts was near enough to hear her talking to herself, she was already a lost cause.

If she was back at university, the most strenuous thing she'd face in a day was a professor's wrath. Now on the other side of the galaxy, her expulsion felt, if not personally insignificant, then small. Still, she missed the crowded biblioplaza, her rigorous coursework, and the intense feeling of purpose, the driver behind all that she did.

Her only purpose here was to move her body forward across the landscape, skirting disaster when she could. One could say survival, but she was barely achieving that. No better than the beings who originally crashed-landed on Earth and got stuck.

Gods, she was never going to leave this jungle!

She fought to calm her breath and tucked her hair behind her ears. It had grown since she left The Shou and she had nothing with which to hold it back. The blunt edge she usually kept was uneven. Without knowing it, Ippa may have had the last haircut of her life.

She shook her head. "Don't get sentimental about a crisping haircut. You're going to get out of here." Ippa was an explorer. An adventurer. A scientist and researcher. She was going to get through this.

Ippa squatted and felt the water. Tepid.

She stripped her damp shoes and socks, pants, shirt, underwear, and underwrap. A musty smell rose and Ippa had a feeling it was from her feet. At least she didn't have to deal with her menses at the moment.

Ippa tied all her clothes to each other and rolled them up. Even if it came unfurled and she lost part of her grip, nothing would float away. The shoes though, there was no help for them. She doubted they could make it to the next bank if she threw them. Ippa tried wrapping her clothing around her head, and balancing the cumbersome shoes on top, but they kept slipping. She finally decided on a kind of sling made of clothes she could hang across her chest and tucked the plain flat shoes inside. She'd spend the rest of the day wet, but it was the only way she was going to keep a handle on all her clothes.

Naked, bundle of clothes knotted across her chest, mud smeared across her arms and face, stringy hair falling in her face, Ippa waded in. Mud and silt squashed between her toes. It was unpleasant but Ippa shoved the thoughts down. It was all unpleasant. That's how it was going to be. No use thinking about it. If only she had listened to her advisor at the Thought Prioritization Examination.

The slowly churning river wasn't deep. It took Ippa longer for her footing to disappear than she expected. Her limbs billowed out from her body. Though it would have been faster, Ippa didn't want all the splashing a breaststroke brought. It might draw attention from fish or animals eager to seize a creature they thought was drowning. She settled on a mild frog-like stroke.

Her legs kicked out, nothing to get in their way. The clothes hung heavy from her chest. The water enveloped every inch of her body in cool liquid peppered with sediment. She had no idea how deep the river was, tried not to think of what might be below her and behind her.

A thought stopped her swim. Why did she take her clothes off? She was going to wrap them up on her head to keep them dry. When that didn't work, why didn't she put them back on? Everything in the sling was getting wet the same as if she had worn the clothes.

Ippa kicked forward. She wanted to cry. The only thing she had was her mind and exhaustion and terror were overtaking her critical thinking skills. The only thing she could do was keep going.

She was closer now. The entire opposite bank was overgrown with shrubs, widely splayed ground plants, and low branches. Ippa would have to find a spot to squeeze through and hope she wouldn't get too scratched up.

There was a disturbance on the surface. A fleck of movement rippled out toward her. Ippa's body went cold and the cool water turned to ice around her. Two black eyes nestled low on a scaled brow appeared. She could make out the tip of a snout perched above the water's surface, close to the eyes, very close. It was mottled, deep green, perfectly matched to its surroundings. Ippa could have just as easily missed it. It flicked and moved from side to side in long powerful strokes. The body of the snake was too heavy and thick-ringed to skim the top of the water. Only the barest hint of the snake's arrow-shaped head appeared at the surface. The rest lurked in the depths.

Ippa wasn't going to make it. She wasn't going to make the bank before the approaching soulless black eyes reached her. She broke motion to tread the water, limiting her movement as much as possible. She wished she wasn't breathing at all, but her breath came in loud shaky gasps. She couldn't look away from the beast.

This was no mammal, influenced by the social orders of life. There was no intimidating the reptilian brain, no way to communicate with the pure instinct of a hungry animal.

As quickly as it appeared, the elegant head continued past Ippa. A heavy curl of the muscular body brushed Ippa's leg and she fought back a scream. She turned and watched the snake recede and pull itself into the thicket at the bank she disembarked from. Only snippets of scaled skin were visible through the branches, but it was clearly thicker and meatier than any snake Ippa could have imagined. Spots of black and brown overlapped each other, providing instant camouflage.

Ippa turned back to the spot of brush she was targeting and rushed forward with her own ill-equipped stroke until sticks sharpened themselves on her legs as she clawed on to land. She broke into a run, stumbling naked over logs and branches until she was heading in the opposite direction as the snake. She didn't even think to check if she still had all her clothes, only ran through the rain forest, stumbling over an anthill, feeling the fiery bites make their way up her ankles.

"Crisping madness. This is crisping madness!" she shrieked into the woods.

It took time before she slowed her pace and beat the last of the ants off her body. She shivered despite the warm air. All her clothing was stretched out at odd angles. She wrung out her underwear and underwrap and hung them on branches. She took turns with each item, wringing it out, spinning it through the humid air. Nothing was dry when she put them on and she couldn't tell what was filthier—them or her.

What was she thinking, leaving Matts? Even if Matts was a bloody psychopath, at least there was safety in numbers.

Instead, Ippa had doomed herself to a horrible death in this horrible jungle.

She marched on through the rain forest, still in an approximation of north. Her thoughts strayed to what would happen to that woman if she failed. Yaniqui. She'd never see Matts coming.

And Akar. Akar would what? Sell that woman? Skin her until they found the biological secret behind her people's ability to heal themselves?

Ippa sighed.

This was the most intense assignment she had ever received. She couldn't fail this time.

Seventeen hours later, Ippa staggered down a worn dirt path. A small building made up of faded blue-painted planks came into view. A thatched roof graced the top. It was the most beautiful sight Ippa had ever laid eyes on.

She dropped to her knees.

A woman in a red shirt came out and looked at Ippa in surprise.

She did it. She escaped the jungle. The village was the first step to finding Yaniqui and warning her. Saving her.

As the local advanced, concerned look on her face, Ippa's optimism withered. She couldn't possibly know if she was ahead of Matts.

Chapter 12

Lozen
The Catchment

Charla's dark eyes narrowed on Lozen. The air of the cave was still as it awaited her verdict.

"So, you're saying you found the culprit. The one who bombed the food station. The effing guard tower."

"Yes."

"And…?" She spread her hands, awaiting explanation. Even in anger she was elegant. And ruthless. The torches of initiation were gone. An electric lantern cast Charla in dramatic shadow.

Lozen responded immediately and emphatically. "He got away. He's no longer at any of the places I tracked him to and the minkin, an animoid I trust, said he fled the area.

He went south while he had the chance to escape before winter comes around again. The minkin thinks possibly the southwest. Desert, like he's used to."

Lozen held her breath as she waited for the ax to fall. She was a big drinker around her friends but she never tried uppers before. But this had to be what it felt like. Lozen's body hummed with the knowledge one mistake could get her killed. She could see the slight mole below Charla's eye stand out on her dark skin. Monte glared at her with fire over Charla's shoulder, so much so she seemed to vibrate. The two others who led Lozen in from the cave door stood close behind. Her back tingled.

And with her hyperaware senses, she heard D-68. Did no one else hear that? That subtle shift of a box at the back of the cave. They were going to get caught. She had to cover up the noise.

"So, that's, uh, why I wanted to follow up and report out." Lozen's voice was slightly louder than usual, but she couldn't help it. "I felt it was my responsibility."

Charla made an indiscriminate noise and flared her nostrils. It was clear she was disgusted with Lozen, but she wouldn't let it fluster her. The Karmas had chosen their leader well. This woman had the unruffled stance of the minkin. They were the only beings Lozen had ever known that were so effortlessly confident, knowing they'd come out one step ahead no matter what.

"I find that hard to believe after our sister Monte told us you didn't want to turn the creature in. That you...*doubted* my integrity."

Lozen shot a look at Monte. She had expected Monte to tell them something but the truth? That seemed a bit much.

She felt her resolve harden. If they couldn't keep their business between themselves, that was it. It wasn't simply a fight. She and Monte were no longer friends.

Uh-oh. More noise from the back of the cave.

"Yeah, and we had a huge argument about it. I was so fucking pissed off." Spittle flew out with her words. Maybe she wasn't playing it up. Maybe she really was that angry. "My oldest friend in the world"—Monte had the grace to look at least 5 percent abashed—"didn't help me. None of you did."

"It's called an initiation. You're supposed to figure things out yourself to prove you have what it takes."

"To find a criminal? Do you have any idea how out of my league this all was?"

The women at Lozen's back shifted. She had to tone it down, or she'd end up at the bottom of some cavernous shaft. At least D-68 would be able to carry her out. If her legs weren't broken.

She took a breath. "So, after Monte called me 'unworthy,' I went back. I wanted to prove her wrong. I checked all his hiding places. I was going to confront him and figure out what was going on so I could make the right decision."

Charla raised a barely there eyebrow.

"But his stuff is gone. And the minkin told me he bugged out. So. That's it. Now you know."

Charla sighed. "Damn it." She stared into the darkness over Lozen's shoulder for a moment. She snapped her fingers and Monte stepped forward. *Like a dog,* Lozen thought, offended on Monte's behalf.

"Is she lying?"

"Huh?" Monte looked nervous.

"She was your best friend. Is she lying?"

Monte turned her gaze on Lozen. She looked like the time Uzzie had been caught with Mama Teresa's bent chopping knife.

"No." It seemed Charla was waiting for more so Monte added, "She failed and she's embarrassed, but she's telling the truth."

Sweat gathered under Lozen's arms. *Did* Monte know she was lying? And if she did and helped Lozen cover things up, did that mean they were friends again? Or was she trying to protect her own reputation?

Charla shuffled two steps away, arms crossed, one hand under her chin. Her braids were piled on top of her head to reveal the narrowly shaved patch each of the Karmas had. "So, what to do with you, Lozen? We're careful about the women we offer initiation to. Everyone must make it."

Lozen's brain begged her to ask the question: What about the others? Did they die trying?

"We couldn't have it any other way, letting random people in the Catchment know about our operations. And none of your *news*," Charla exaggerated the word to make it clear Lozen had brought them no information of value, "changes the fact that you were working with the GIA."

Lozen saw a large shadow dart across the walls. D-68 was done. It was definitely time for her to go. She took a step back and one of the women pushed her back in place.

"You have no family. You have no friends except your masters in the capital."

"Hey…" Lozen disputed halfheartedly.

"We have nothing to hold over you to assure you won't expose us. The very fact you felt confident to come back here is troubling. It would have been better if you had forgotten our location." The corners of Charla's mouth turned downward. "It's too bad. Our sister Monte had such a strong feeling you'd do well with the Karmas. But I can't let you go. We didn't stay a secret society by giving our secrets to traitors."

"So, you're going to kill me?" Her voice cracked. "That seems like an overreaction."

The women behind her seized her by the arms. She started to struggle but they were fucking Amazons. She was puny, could-hardly-read, never-had-enough-food Lozen.

"Let go! Let go!" Pain shot through her left shoulder.

Charla's voice barely cut through the panic. "We're not going to kill you, you silly girl. We're just going to shave your head."

A huge woosh of tepid cave air blew her hair.

The two women holding Lozen staggered back.

D-68 stood, bag over one arm, knees bent, ready to defend her. It was easy to see him from the Karmas's perspective. A huge russet-colored animoid, a full head and shoulder taller than the tallest humanoid in the Catchment. Hard platelets lined his torso, arms, and legs. His black eyes were the solid black of a snake. The sensitive nasal pads couldn't be anything but revolting to human eyes. He looked like the dreaded alien bug they all thought he was and he had come ready to suck the marrow from their bones.

139

Someone shrieked as he grabbed for Lozen, threw her up and into the crook of one of his arms, and they were flying out of the cave. No, he was lurching across the cave walls, the talons of two legs and his free arm digging deep scratches upon the rock. Her sore back teeth felt strangely light in their sockets. The sound of grinding gravel filled Lozen's ears. Lozen had a wild thought that the Karmas would not be happy with this lasting reminder of their failure.

She could hear them giving chase.

A gun went off, the echo racing through the caves.

A louder blast rang over top the dying echo of the last.

But they weren't faster than D-68.

Instead of exiting the rocky archway that led outside, D-68 followed a series of tunnels as if he had a map of the place etched on his arm platelet. There were no lanterns lining the walls here. The dark was pitch.

Lozen couldn't hear the Karmas anymore, but D-68 didn't slow. She struggled to right herself in D-68's thick arms. He understood what she was trying to do and tilted her up. Lozen flung an arm around his basically nonexistent neck and wrapped her legs around his torso.

Uh-huh, okay. This is weird.

Speckles of cave grit washed across her face with each lurch forward. She could see nothing of what was in front of him. Only hope he wouldn't run full force into a cavern wall.

He finally stopped and dropped her neatly to her feet. She managed to keep her balance but put her arms out, totally blind.

"D-68?" she whispered.

A crawl like centipede's legs tingled up her back as she stood in the darkness, no idea where she was, unable to see anything.

A soft rose-colored light bloomed. She heard D-68 exhale pointedly and the delicate light brightened.

"What?"

"Air on stone. Glows," he said in a voice that was soft for him.

"That's amazing."

"From my home."

"From your home...and you had it with you all this time? Why haven't you used it before? Why wasn't it taken from you?"

"In my pouch." He couldn't shrug but made some gesture akin to it. "Didn't need. Need now."

Lozen rolled her eyes, then softened. "Hey, thanks for getting me back there." She crouched down and wrapped her arms around her knees. She was light-headed as she came to the realization, "I think they really hate me."

"Yes."

"Did you manage to get the camera?"

D-68 set down the cloth bag.

Lozen dug her hands in but knew quickly that he failed to discern between the supplies the Karmas had. Her hand touched cold metal. He probably just took what he saw first. She should have described the equipment more clearly. "Could you bring that light a little closer?"

He did and Lozen saw her hand rested on a gun. She froze, shocked. Did he purposefully take it? There wasn't any ammunition in the bag and Lozen didn't know how to open the gun to check for bullets. She set it aside carefully.

"That one's a weapon. Don't point it at anyone you don't want to kill. This other stuff…" There was another gun, this one a smaller handgun, and a jumble of electronics. A tablet that wouldn't unlock for them. A single communicator that was out of battery. Some other random stuff they'd have to sort through in daylight.

She sighed. "It's just a bunch of shit."

Which was why Lozen found herself in Lin's house the next day. She had entered the Catchment through the animoid side, wandered the streets until she found her way to the nicer blocks, and waited outside Lin's house, heart pounding the entire time.

How many members of the Karmas were there? Maybe twenty? How likely was it she'd run into any members? Would all of them be able to recognize her? What would they do if they spotted her?

It was a relief when she was finally allowed to enter Lin's home, just to be out of public sight, though she knew D-68 wouldn't be able to save her this time. She was adamant that he had to stay in the cave. He brought up that she wasn't so good at taking care of herself—first of all, rude—and that she needed him—second of all, *she* was the one helping *him.* Besides, there was nowhere for him to hide in the nicest blocks of the settlement—the Earthling corridor for fuck's sake.

A burly man patted Lozen down for weapons and wires. She resented it, but he didn't seem to enjoy it. She was sure he did it fifty times a day and it got old. Still, she resented him.

Then she was brought into the same room they had sat

in the only other time she had met Lin. When she was first trying to find D-68 for the Karmas.

She'd grown up a lot since then. She'd been commandeered by the GIA, failed to join a secret society, been outed from her own home, and was now cohabitating with a near-silent, rock-climbing giant of an alien.

She settled onto a flat cushion at the low table.

"Oh, you're back." Lin pointed at his mouth, to mimic her cleft palate.

With all of her growing up, she'd nearly forgotten about that.

"Did you come for a husband—"

She furrowed her brow and cut across him. "That's really rude, you know. There are other ways to remember me, and if you can't, you don't have to point it out like that. It really bothers me."

Lin's eyes bugged slightly. He was expecting demure Lozen.

That wasn't who she was anymore.

"I'll have you thrown out," his voice was even but held a buzz of anger. "You come bearing no gifts, speak disrespectfully, a woman no less—"

Lozen heard the guard adjust his stance behind her. She had to act fast.

"I found that alien responsible for the three bombings. You know, the bombing of the handout station, the guard tower, and, oh yeah, one right nearby your house. The one you failed to catch. You're lucky I want to turn him into you. You can do what you like with him. I want to see justice."

Lin pulled back, sitting upright. She had his attention.

His wrinkled face smoothed in concentration, Lozen's rudeness was not forgotten but was secondary to his own plans and needs. Lozen could tell he was reassessing her, trying to figure out who this common woman in front of him was.

She shook her head. "If you can't take on the responsibility, I'll go to Pellor." The bosses were constantly scrabbling to one-up each other.

Lin made a motion with his hand indicating she should remain seated.

He scratched his neck. "How did you come across the alien? We've been looking for him—the GIA is as well. How is it you, a rat from the low side of the Catchment, found him?"

Lozen answered his series of questions, making up a story about spotting the alien animoid in the woods while foraging. She made it clear she wanted him dead for all the pain he caused in the Catchment. The animoid was no friend of humanoids.

"So bring us to him—we'll take care of it." Lin pointed to the man behind Lozen, ready to give an order.

"No."

Lin turned back, frustrated. "What do you mean 'no?'"

"I don't want to be anywhere near the place when you take him. The animoid is immense. And extremely aggressive." Lozen swallowed. "Give me a camera, and I'll show you exactly where he is. I'll bring it back and you'll follow the footage to him. You'll know I'm telling the truth when I bring it back. I won't leave until you watch it to the end. This way, I won't be anywhere near him when you take him."

Chapter 13

Hloban
Lake Michigan

He was going make everything right by convincing Yaniqui that she and Adam had to be together.

The beach house was light yellow with turquoise trim. Though the ocean was far away, the vacation houses on the shore of the Great Lake mimicked what the citizens of the capital wanted—their grandparents' classic vacation to the cape. The cape when times were simpler, the coast was intact, and everyone could put their screens down long enough to talk about the future, who was meant to be with whom, and whether an intergalactic slaver had gotten wind of their location yet.

Hloban pulled into the wide driveway and he and

Loera stepped out. It was breezier than their suburb. He could hear the lake surf. A gull called overhead.

"Did you *forget* about me?" Obani pulled at the straps of his car seat, trying to free himself.

Hloban backtracked to unbuckle Obani while Loera took their two weekend bags out of the trunk.

This was a good idea, Hloban thought. A long weekend at the beach would get everyone together to relax. Yaniqui and Adam would finally see that they were right for each other at which point Loera would finally forgive him for his transgressions in space. Then, that problem solved, he could move on to the next one—warn everyone that Onlo had decided to fuck them over, convince Yaniqui to adhere to Cortez's plan so Earth would become devoted to their safety, and plan how to get Nica back. He could do this.

Obani wrapped an arm around Hloban's neck until they were a few feet away from the car and wiggled down.

"Is this my new house?" Obani asked.

"For a little while," Loera responded. She fell back to walk with Hloban as Obani ran ahead. Hloban took one of the bags from her.

The front door was open, and Obani was already inside and talking to someone.

"Hello, Loera. Hloban, you picked a good place," Amanda said and stood from the couch to hug her friends. The living room had the same light color palette as the outside. The whole common area was bright from the many windows, making the wooden floors gleam.

"Where's Adam and Yaniqui?" Hloban asked.

"Not here yet. Adam wanted to drive up separately.

Get a few more hours of work in."

Good. That would give Adam and Yaniqui time alone in the car.

"I didn't realize Adam found a job," Loera said. "That's great."

Keyad and Amanda exchanged smiles as Obani disappeared up the stairs to explore.

"Not quite employed. It's more of a passion project at this stage," Keyad said. "It's a blog. At least he's not moping around the house anymore. And he's been putting a lot of research in. Hopefully next time we have to fly across the galaxy, he'll know a little something."

Amanda raised her spritzer to that, then turned to Loera. "I'm surprised you could take time off so unexpectedly."

Loera scratched her neck below her cornrows. "It's good to remind my staff how much they miss me. And Hloban seemed to think this was the perfect house and a good way soak up the summer."

It really was the perfect space. Their house was relatively modest for their—mostly Loera's—income, but they always spent lavishly when they traveled. The nearest neighbor was more than shouting distance away. With direct access to the beach and the quaint vacation town a short drive away, there was plenty to do, but it wasn't overwhelming. But Hloban mentally reminded himself again, he had to have a conversation with Obani about not going outside by himself and to definitely never go near the water without a grown-up. He instinctively looked up the wide staircase and confirmed he heard Obani moving around upstairs.

"I hate to put a damper on things from the start," a growl came from the stairs. "But I think I broke the bed in the master suite. It's the only one I'd fit on, so I thought I'd test it out. I'll take that room. Now that the mattress is on the floor, no problem."

Loera's smile froze in place.

Jeb came down the stairs on heavy steps. Hloban and Keyad could blend in wherever they went on Earth. As an animoid, Jeb would always stand out. But it was more than that. His entire personality was a standout.

"It broke so easily?" Amanda asked and raised her drink to her mouth.

"It may have been more of a trip and fall than a test, but either way, dibs on that room."

A car door slammed outside. "Yaniqui and Adam?" Hloban wondered aloud.

The door opened and Yaniqui stepped inside, followed by Waquas stretching his arms over his head after being cooped up in the car.

Hloban soured. There was room for one more in the vacation home, but he hadn't invited Waquas. They had been—were—good friends. With no family and most people in the capital adverse to his green skin, Hloban and Loera had always been happy to invite him to family functions. Level-headed Waquas was, in fact, the only person Hloban originally wanted to bring to rescue Yaniqui.

But this was too much.

A round of greetings rang through the room.

Yaniqui threw her backpack down. She wore tan shorts and a loose, billowy tank top. "Ugh, that drive," she said to everyone, then turned to Waquas. "On the way back, we'll listen to my music."

He smiled in response and continued stretching. No, Hloban didn't like this one bit.

Soon Keyad and Loera were tight in gossip about an artist they both knew. Jeb had gone out to the ample porch and was sunning himself on a stack of pillows he pulled off the frail lounge chair. Everyone was settling in, but Adam had yet to appear.

Hloban was prepping a charcuterie board in the kitchen but glanced up sharply when he heard Waquas laugh. He frowned. Waquas didn't laugh. They'd been friends for almost a decade and he knew Waquas only laughed about once every six months.

Hloban saw it in the way that Yani and his traitor friend looked at each other. It cut so deeply through him that he had to leave. He set the colander he was rinsing on the counter, grabbed the bags Loera set by the wall, and went upstairs. Hloban scouted out a few of the rooms, found one with two beds inside and set their bags there. He brushed off thoughts of Yaniqui and instead fixated on the room with its bright bedspreads. He put Obani's little cartoon character bag on the smaller of the two beds and tried to calm his thoughts.

Loera came up a few minutes later.

"Keyad took Obani to walk the beach. I was very clear that he shouldn't go in the water yet." Loera glanced around their room and then finally settled her gaze on her husband who sat despondent on one of the beds. "Hloban," she said, surprised. "Are you okay?"

"I think Waquas is in love with Yaniqui."

Loera approached him cautiously, as if she were willing to give him the benefit of the doubt but not one iota more. "And why does that bother you?"

Hloban ran both hands through his hair and scratched at the follicles. It helped jolt him from his thoughts. "I thought she'd end up with Adam and everything would make sense. There would have been a reason I found her after all this time. I wouldn't have risked everyone's lives for nothing. I wouldn't have…" He sighed. "I'm not jealous. I thought—"

"—you were in control?"

He nodded.

She came to sit next to him and pulled at her simple chain necklace. "You know, I've never understood Wea Saavian notions about fate, but maybe that's where it all stems from. A desire for control. A need for certainty." Her face softened. "You know how often I've wished for that."

Hloban shrugged. "It feels like I've been outside any realm of certainty for a long time. Loera, I am so grateful for you and Obani, especially now. Thank you for being so steady while I've been"—he gestured erratically—"a mess."

"Remember when my company first went public? It happened, like, six months before we met, but I was still riding a wind of chaos at that point. You looked beyond the seventy-hour work weeks and board crises and instead proofed my emails and helped me prioritize blocking out space on my calendar just to be. To rest or do things because I wanted to do them, not because they were productive for the company. We're a team."

"I know. But I hate disrupting everything like this. I thought I'd save Yani, bring her back, and somehow everything would work out. Instead," Hloban's voice shook, "Cortez can't understand why Yaniqui isn't gung ho to sign up as a healer for a community of people she doesn't know." Hloban shifted, pulling one knee on the bed to better face Loera. He licked his lips. "And what's more is Cortez learned Nica is still with Akar. She's owned by a Joint Council member, but Akar has her on one of their spacecrafts. Cortez doesn't want to involve Yaniqui until she gives some indication that she's committed to Earth. That she plans to stay on Earth and convince Nica to settle here too if she's rescued."

"Shit."

Loera looked out the window, thinking. Tree branches bordered their view of a crystal-blue sky. Mares' tails drifted high in the atmosphere. Finally, she pushed her glasses up before speaking. "You have to tell Yaniqui. Even if the secretary-general of the United Nations doesn't want you to. You didn't sign an N.D.A. or anything did you?"

Hloban shook his head.

"Then you have to tell Yaniqui. Whether she stays on Earth, if she leaves to go try to find her mother and never comes back, it's all her decision to make. I know Cortez wants Yaniqui's ability to benefit Earth but seeking to control her like that is as bad as Akar." Loera put her hand on Hloban's knee in emphasis. "You *have* to tell her."

Hloban put his hands together and touched the fingertips to his mouth. He tried to breathe out the stress. *One problem at a time.*

Chapter 14

Adam
Lake Michigan

Blog Post #17 "Where Did All The Bikes Go?"

But the most damning fact in the search for bicycles is that four years ago, a government document was leaked from the U.S. Department of Transportation. It was a memo, actually, sent from the office of the United Nations assistant secretary-general, not from the Conference on Trade and Development. This short note has been available online since then but hasn't gotten much interest.

What did this little memo say? That it was essential to build trade with Onlo, a technology-manufacturing planet, specifically that their solar energy cells for vehicles were vastly superior than ours. Good, right? Well, the memo writer, one Lynda Rosen, looked at the data. She suggested that our relatively small population size (Onlo has fifty billion beings) combined with a still-significant portion of our population unable to purchase the cells or a vehicle at all, would not warrant enough demand for the trade agreement the U.N. desired.

So, how to fix this problem? Create higher demand. And Lynda suggested that there was a not-insignificant population of cyclists that could be swayed away from their chosen mode of transportation to become new consumers of solar cars.

Thus began the underground campaign to give bicycles the ick and increase trade with Onlo.

I know, I know, not as sexy as the wayward government propaganda that has allowed basically our entire population to believe we evolved here on Earth to satisfy the religious community, but I promise I'll make it up to you next time.

I'll post tomorrow about the U.N.'s immigration policy for aliens and how they're using it to increase our standing within the Joint Council.

Adam read it back through twice more and clicked post. It was a bit like writing papers for school. Though he wasn't the most eloquent writer, he had something to say. And people were listening. He had a growing subscriber list of people who had found his blog in the past week and wanted to know what he had to say right away.

Adam closed his laptop and leaned back on the fluffy

pillows of the bed. He was lucky to be sharing the room with Waquas instead of Jeb. Waquas wasn't in the room much. He knew Yaniqui's conversation with Waquas had gone more than fine, but he was still surprised how instantly the two had taken to each other. As an introvert, Waquas didn't make friends well. Adam would have thought their relationship would be a slow transformation, but it seemed like they were both happy to move quickly. The only time they were apart on the trip so far was when Amanda and Yaniqui tested out the dusty tandem bike they found in the vacation house basement. Adam took a quick picture of them riding down the road, just before they crashed. He included it in his post.

Obani popped his head in. "This is your room?"

"Hey, Obani. Yep, it is. Look at this." Adam flashed a gesture in the air and his window fogged over.

The four-year-old sniffed, unimpressed

"Well, try this one." He did a slightly different gesture and the window replaced the fog with photos pulled from his phone.

"I brought my dinosaurs from home. They're, they're in my room if you want to play with them," Obani offered, stony faced at the lack of dinosaurs in Adam's room.

"We should play with them on the beach. Why don't you go get them?"

There was enough late afternoon sun to play in the sand. And the short conversation with Obani meant that enough time had passed to check his analytics without reminding him how desperate he was. He knew it was too early, but he refreshed anyway.

He sat up straight. Already eighty-nine views? He

smiled. That little two-digit number meant that it didn't matter that he wasn't getting paid to expound on the internet or the fact that he was currently on vacation with his parents or that he was unemployed.

Adam put his swimsuit on and played dinosaurs in the sand with Obani. He tried to convince Obani to build a sandcastle, but it quickly became a sand tunnel. Then, when Obani had the great idea to make his dinos swim, they spent twenty minutes looking for the allosaurus in the surf. The kid was melting down when Adam finally stepped on the hard plastic spikes and Loera called her son inside to wash off. Adam toweled off and took a shower. Once he was out of the shower, he couldn't help but flip his computer screen on.

A number appeared: 3,077. Seriously? He had 3,077 views?

He let out a whoop and flung the bath towel into the bathroom.

Once Adam's dad talked him out of sharing publicly about his Wea Saavian heritage, specifically Yaniqui, it had taken him a while to come up with a topic that was enticing enough to catch the attention of other Gen Epsilons. And it was apparent that he was doing just that.

Adam grabbed his device and sent a text to Yaniqui. She and Waquas had gone into the little town to get groceries.

Over three thousand views in two hrs.

The three dots wiggled as she typed.

I would guess as much. I read it in the car.

And?

Shocking how the galaxy works but not surprised

at all. Tell me what else you find between Earth and Onlo. And I'd like to get a bike for home.

Dinner wouldn't be for a while if the groceries weren't even in the house so Adam took his phone and books out to the deck. Jeb and Loera were going back and forth about politics and Adam slid effortlessly into his book, *A Place in the Universe*.

The phone rang and he jolted. The ID read Bayler Luna Corp.

"Hello? This is Adam," he added uncertainly.

"Hi, Adam Jayul? This is Nick Yang with Bayler Luna Corp. Hey, I just stumbled across your blog, *Earth Secrets*, and it is, frankly, amazing."

"Wow. Thank you. Honestly, it's the kind of stuff I wish I knew before going into space." Adam had never heard of Nick Yang, but he knew enough to shift into his work voice.

"Can I ask you a few questions?"

The voice of Nick Yang did indeed ask a few questions about how long Adam had been building the site, what he wanted to do most with his time, and where he graduated from. Adam smiled as he answered, watching the sun set over the lake. He was happy to say he had a lot of other ideas and stories to expose. In the background, he could hear dinner preparation underway, but his mother must have warned others away from the patio.

"That is just so interesting. Well, it's not a surprise that the blog has caught people's attention but don't you think you'd like to do something more?"

"Um, of course."

"So this is just a placeholder until something else

comes along?" Nick continued before Adam had an answer for him. "I have a job for you."

Adam swallowed. "I'm not looking for an office job. I'm really looking to get into space."

"That's great, because that's what we do." The smile was evident in Nick's voice. "We're the third largest colony on the moon. It's a research facility, very progressive. You'll be a great addition to the culture."

Adam stood from the beach chair, looking at the immense lake, but not really seeing it.

Everyone was seated at the long table outside on the deck. It was dark enough that the string of solar lights flickered above their heads. The nighttime summer temperature was perfect. The food Waquas made was delicious.

Adam's mom whooped when he shared the news. His mom actually whooped.

"And did you take it?" Keyad leaned forward, elbows on the table, his plate of lamb and roasted corn slathered in butter forgotten.

Adam nodded his head, and then nodded his head more vigorously. His mom reached across the table to squeeze his hand.

"I'm going to start out as a maintenance process engineer. Maybe they'll let me change the filter on the oxygenator." Adam pulled a face at his dad who smiled in response.

"Congratulations, Adam," Loera put in. "Luna's doing some interesting work on climate monitoring."

Everyone was smiling. He deserved this.

"On Monday, I'll fill out the paperwork and get some

tests done, but from what Nick said, they're expediting the process for me."

His mom paused, then said, "That's great, Adam, they must really want you. But isn't that fast? Do you have enough time to think it through?"

He shook his head. "Bayler Luna Corp. moves quickly. Third largest base on the moon. They probably have to in order to stay competitive. Fast-paced work environment and all that."

"What does this mean for *Earth Secrets*?" Yaniqui said down the table.

That was the question Adam had been asking himself all evening. He couldn't keep up with both—writing a post or two a day didn't sound like much, but he'd been putting a lot of research into it.

"I guess it will have to go on hiatus until things calm down."

"You're going to give up your momentum?" Yaniqui whined. "But what you're doing is really important."

"More important than my career? And going to live on the moon?" He smiled. "That's what I've been waiting for."

Chapter 15

Hloban
Lake Michigan

Dark clouds moved overhead. Obani ran in circles with two children from another family not too far from the blankets laid out on the ground. The performance was supposed to start at dusk, but there was no movement onstage yet.

Like Zarbon-period dramas, Hloban had a soft spot for Earth-period productions. Hloban loved hearing the old language, an anomalous accent that Earth had developed, then gave up on. He saw last year's Shakespeare in the Park production when things were calmer. Everyone was there then. Everyone except for Waquas and Yani, and they wouldn't see it this year either. They stayed back at the house that evening.

Hloban remembered how the sky had faded and the lights had brightened a year ago, before he learned that Yaniqui was still out there, when he could look Waquas in the eye, and when he didn't know how happy he was.

A droplet landed on his nose, a gift of water from the sky.

All around him, families wrenched their blankets off the ground and held them overhead. Loera was trying to do the same, but Hloban realized it a moment too late, unaware until the blanket was half ripped out from under him. Amanda and Adam laughed at something, probably him.

Keyad shouted, "Do you think we should go back?"

Just then, the actresses and actors came out in their costumes designed to look like clothing from six hundred years ago, protected from the rain by an overhang. Some of the crowd applauded while others tried to decide whether to clap or hold their makeshift coverings up.

The ornate group bowed grandly. One of the leads stepped to the front and said, "'*It rain. It rainith every day.*' Or at least today. Sorry, folks, lightning is coming and we have to cancel the performance. We'll continue with the rest of the weekend schedule, weather permitting."

One more bow and they exited the stage.

Everyone piled up the things they brought. Jeb washed back the rest of his bottle of beer.

"No!" Obani shrieked. "You said we were going to stay here all night. Don't take me away from my friends, Mama." With no promise of a party to distract him from his tiredness, Obani was ready for bed. Loera tried to reason with him, but Hloban simply swooped him up and carried him, kicking and screaming, back to the car. He was disappointed the show wouldn't run that night, but he was eager to get back to the rental and have everyone in one place again.

Already in a full-blown temper tantrum, it was a struggle to get Obani in his car seat. He was strong enough to pull his arms out of his straps and it took a long while of pleading to calm him down.

It took thrice as long to get out of the park as it did getting in. The cars went gridlock and only slowly untangled themselves. Keyad, Amanda, and Adam rode behind in their family car. Jeb had his own vehicle, but Hloban lost sight of everyone quickly.

It was the last night of the trip. The group had spent the weekend swimming and grilling out on the rental's patio and playing on the beach. Jeb wouldn't go anywhere near the sand. He said it was impossible to get out of his hair, so he sat on the patio and gave Yaniqui suggestions of what to put on top of Waquas's head when she buried him in the sand. Up until the show, the weather was near perfect and Hloban's attitude, though slightly dour, was steady.

Now that it was the last night, everything was about to come crashing down on him.

Adam was going to blast off and live on a new celestial body so there went the idea for getting Yani and Adam together. Besides, she and Waquas were obviously committed to each other. He'd broached the topic of Cortez's proposal for Yaniqui that morning and she had been strangely evasive. He had wanted to try one more time to get her to commit before telling her about Nica. If she wouldn't accept the proposal that would put her to work healing members of Earth's population, he still had to tell her what he learned. It was the right thing to do. Cortez would be upset though.

And Onlo's threat.

In the days leading up to the trip, he'd made up his mind that he'd tell Loera about Onlo at the beach house. It was an unnerving thought that Onlo was going to—or already had—sold their location to Akar. He was going to have to tell Loera and he was going to have to tell Cortez. The trip had provided a much-needed break from reality, but once it was over, he'd have to soon fess up.

They drove away from the immense city park and toward the shore; commercial district replaced slowly by candy-colored houses.

"I wanted to stop for ice cream, but now it's too cold," Loera lightly complained. "Hloban, did you want to try for tomorrow's performance and drive home late? I know you were looking forward to it."

Hloban didn't answer. He was so upset the performance was canceled. How could they cancel it? People came to watch with their whole family. Something in his mind whispered that he was projecting his feelings onto the wrong thing, but he couldn't stop and take stock now.

Everything was going wrong and he just wanted to get back home.

At the vacation house, they parked the cars and Hloban ran up the steps, threw the door open, and there was Waquas and Yaniqui locked in an embrace. Kissing. Up against a wall. Her shirt lay on the floor, a meek, passive swatch of linen next to Waquas's own shirt.

"What do you think you're doing?" Hloban boomed.

Yaniqui looked up, alarmed. She let go of Waquas.

The rest of the group caught up at the entrance to the beach house and pushed past Hloban to get out of the rain. There was a split second of chaos as everyone fit through the door and then it fell quiet.

Adam laughed and Hloban had an immediate impulse to punch him.

"Uh, hey, guys. What's going on?" Waquas asked. He looked neither embarrassed nor in a hurry to put his shirt back on.

Jeb pushed past them all and gave a thumbs-up on his way to the kitchen.

Keyad adverted his eyes and started to explain, "It started raining. The perf—"

Hloban had been jostled to the back, but now he lurched forward. *"What's going on?* I don't know. Just that you both are embarrassing everyone."

The tension in the room turned from merely awkward to uneasy. Loera dropped her gaze from the couple.

Yaniqui stared at Hloban, her dark eyes hard to read.

"We didn't expect you all back so soon," Waquas said simply.

"But I won't say sorry for something I didn't intend," Yaniqui interjected. She reached down and grabbed her shirt.

"Look outside, Yaniqui. Water is falling from the sky. Soon electricity is going to come barreling down to the population level accompanied by enormous crashes of thunder. What did you think was going to happen? Of course, we were going to come back."

Keyad said, "I'm sure they didn't notice the *rain*," as if Hloban had forgotten the common word after living on Earth for the better part of a decade.

Yaniqui had her shirt on now and was smoothing out her static-infused hair.

"This is ridiculous. You are not allowed to do this," said Hloban. "You can't be together. This isn't right. Safe. It isn't safe."

Yaniqui's eyes went tight. "None of that is for you to decide. Hloban…what's going on?"

Hloban became aware that everyone's eyes were on him.

"He's jealous," Loera whispered, her voice more forceful than Hloban's yell. She turned to her husband. "Aren't you? You haven't given up on her."

Hloban stepped back at the venom in her voice. "Loera, that's completely untrue. It's that Yani's only been on Earth for, like, a month." Hloban turned and pointed, as he continued, "Waquas, you're taking advantage of the situation."

Everyone was quiet, except for Loera. "Hloban, Yaniqui can make her own decisions."

"You don't care because you don't like Yaniqui."

"That's not true at all and I will not let you accuse me of that in front of everyone." Loera stooped to pick up Obani who was standing in a sleepy daze. She crossed the room in a few strides and ascended the stairs.

"Hloban, things were good between me and Loera," Yaniqui said. "There really was no way to more effectively tear apart everything except for what you just did." She looked disgusted.

A door slammed on the third floor.

"Yaniqui. Just…just shut up. Waquas, I can't believe you're doing this. This is completely inappropriate."

"Hloban, you don't get to decide things about my life," Yaniqui said.

"I am your freaking sponsor! I brought you to this planet so that you could be safe. Instead of supporting the people who brought you here, telling Cortez you'll do your part, you spend your time chasing boys. You tried it with Adam. You tried it with me. And now you're trying it with him."

Too late, Hloban realized he implicated himself in all this.

"Yani—"

"No, Hloban. Leave me alone."

There was no moon that night, but the storm passed without more than a few droplets until it let go and lit up over the lake. Now, the sky was clear and the stars were out.

Hloban walked out on the beach, his feet sinking in the small brittle pieces of shell, fish bone, coral, and Earth. Although it was 1:00 a.m., there was a figure out on the gusty beach. Hloban walked closer, sure it was Yaniqui. She had a hood up and a blanket from a chest in the beach house wrapped around her.

She heard him but didn't turn. "You should go. I'm too angry to talk."

"I didn't come out here to talk to you, though maybe I should have. I didn't even know you were out here."

Hloban stood a few paces away from Yaniqui.

"I came to see our home."

He could practically feel Yaniqui roll her eyes in the darkness.

"What does that even mean?"

Hloban gestured to all the stars. "You know how the light from a star travels years and years across the galaxy to be witnessed by people on other planets? The sky is a like a map of the past and in that picture, Wea Saa is still there."

Yaniqui jumped up. She let the blanket fall to the ground. "Which star is it?"

Hloban pointed and directed. He moved a little closer to Yaniqui to shift her hand. She pulled it away sharply.

He could tell when Yaniqui locked on the star. It was as if all the other stars in the sky disappeared.

"That's why I came out here," Hloban explained. "The light we see began its journey when Wea Saa was still habitable. We will always be able to see it in our lifetimes. Our children will and their children. It will probably be visible in some manner until all memory of Wea Saa is forgotten."

Yaniqui spoke, more to herself than to Hloban, "How can a whole system, an entire race, just be gone from the universe?"

Hloban often wondered how the gods of his planet could let their own star blink out the entire existence of a population.

From time to time he wondered what they were doing now that they had no home planet to watch over. Did they die when it did? Or were they floating around in space, waiting to attach themselves to another piece of rock and water?

Or did they follow the last of the Wea Saavians? Forced to wander where Hloban would, resigned to take interest in the few beings they were supposed to care for. All parties ending their existence with a last strangled gasp for air.

"Yani…" Hloban let her name trail into the darkness. "There hasn't been a right time to talk about this, but Cortez told me they located your maemi."

Yaniqui straightened. "What? Maemi? Where is she?"

"She's in Akar's possession. But is, um, owned by a member of the Joint Council."

Yaniqui cut across him. "Do you know where Akar has her?"

"She's on one of their transversers. I don't know if I can find out, but I can try."

"Find out for me and I'll forgive you for tonight. Help me get her back and I'll forgive you for keeping this news from me."

They stood silent for a moment. The waves rhythmically crashed on the beach.

"Is it really only us?"

"There could be more," Hloban said.

"There could have been more," Yaniqui replied and walked away.

Chapter 16

Yaniqui
Lake Michigan

Unable to sleep, Yaniqui snuck into Adam and Waquas's room. The gentle roar of the great lake came through the window. She crept on soft feet past Adam's lanky frame sprawled across his bed. The rest of the house was quiet and still. An errant snore came from Jeb's master bedroom.

A streetlight glowed outside the window blind. A thrill went through her when she saw Waquas's bare chest, blanket thrown back from the mild heat. Her heart sped. She hoped he'd be okay with this. She placed her hand over his heart.

He was awake immediately. He didn't even seem surprised. He sat up, pulled on a shirt, and led her outside.

Her eyes traveled up ahead on the beach. She felt him watching her.

"Do you want to see something other than ice cream shops and Shakespeare plays?" he asked.

Yaniqui wondered if they hadn't been together, shirts off, when the cars arrived, or if Yaniqui had acted more embarrassed, things wouldn't have gone so wrongly. Heat came back to her cheeks, not from mortification but from anger.

No, Yaniqui decided, Hloban was in a mood to fight and destroy, whatever those around him did.

"No one saw the play. That seems to be the problem. You know, we're lucky the storm passed over. Otherwise, we'd be in the house right now and that is too small to house everyone's emotions tonight."

Waquas smiled. "A few miles up the beach is the boundary for the Catchment."

"Catchment," she repeated. "What does that mean?"

"Did you notice anything about this community? There are twelve waterparks. It's always clean. There are no poor people. More guards than I can count. Everyone looks the same."

Yaniqui wondered what Waquas meant that people looked the same. "I saw more aliens the past two days since I landed on Earth. Isn't this just a wealthy tourist area?"

"It's more than an area for visitors. It's a display. All the aliens you saw were rich and relatively Earth-like," Waquas said. "This area is international welcome land. It is a display for visitors to see what Earth has to offer and helps attract wealthy aliens.

"You don't see as many aliens around Hloban and Loera's neighborhood because they live in an upper-class but working suburb near the heart of the capital. Aliens typically don't live there because they are rarely allowed those types of jobs."

"So how can these newcomers afford this lifestyle?"

"They came here already rich. They were the haves. They don't need to work, but they did need a clean planet for their children, far away from war."

They started walking and Waquas took her hand. It was warm and it made her own feel small.

Waquas continued, "You may not realize this, but on the flight back to Earth, Hloban filled out forms and attained references for you to live with him and Loera. You did not have the resources to settle in the capital, but he couldn't bear to send you to a labor camp or the Catchment settlement up ahead. That's where the poorest refugees go. Just because you're an alien, even an endangered one, you weren't assured a place in the nicer communities."

"The Catchment is where you went when you arrived on Earth," Yaniqui said, slowly, coming to understand.

"And where I would still be, if not for Hloban."

Yaniqui pulled her hand away. "Waquas, you sound like you're trying to convince me to forgive Hloban for all the drama," she said.

There was no moon, but any lingering cloud cover from the storm had moved on. She could see Waquas smile gently. "I'm simply trying to give you the facts."

As they walked, the houses shrank in size. Gone were the elaborate estates. These were still cheery colors but crowded together, some sharing walls as multifamily units. One had beach toys strewn across a cement patio. Another had a light on in its upstairs window.

Yaniqui broke the silence. "You make this Catchment

sound bad. Why are we going?"

"It's not all bad. Kids grow up there. People fall in love there. Some of the food is decent. It's like any place where people live. I guess I have so little to show you about my history, about my life, this is one thing I can."

They walked a couple more miles, as Yaniqui shared the startling news about Maemi. They spent a long time on the subject talking about what the pieces could mean before they moved on to Adam's windfall job and then walking in silence as the lights around them disappeared one by one. With the vacation homes altogether faded away, the last mile was an empty stretch of sand and sea grasses of all shades. Thick shrubs and sparse pine trees grew at the edge of the dunes, blocking their way with shadows.

When the sandy beach turned into a rocky shore, Waquas steered inland. They climbed the sand dune, grains of sand littering the insides of Yaniqui's shoes, then another hill of sea grass and bushes.

At the top, the Catchment was laid out below Yaniqui. Faint starlight illuminated gray boxes. They weren't high enough to see beyond the fenced borders of the Catchment, but Yaniqui spotted one neighborhood that had sparkles of electric light. In the other pockets of darkness, the orange glow of fire or random single bulbs stood out. Unlike the towering spires of downtown New Washington, WI, there were only a few multistory buildings. It was hard to see in the dark but most of the structures looked less standard than they should.

Yaniqui took a shaky breath. "Wow...the size of it. These are all aliens?"

"About half Earthling refugees, half alien. Animoids

and humanoids."

"I thought Earth didn't take on a lot of animoids. Except for that restaurant, Jeb is really the only one I've seen."

Waquas spoke slowly, "Well, actually I'm classified as an animoid. I do not share DNA with this galaxy's humanoids though my people evolved humanlike."

Yaniqui took his hand and kissed him.

"Are you kissing me to prove a point?"

"I'm kissing you because I like kissing you."

They broke and walked down the hill.

"Oh," Yaniqui blurted out. "Is that why Hloban was upset to find us? Is he upset you're an animoid?"

"I think Hloban would have responded similarly to the thought of you with anyone except him or Adam, however, yes, I think he overreacted because we're from different galaxies. That doesn't happen very often."

Yaniqui took a shallow breath, afraid to ask, afraid she was intruding, but it was killing her not knowing. "Why are you here?"

"There was a war," Waquas said simply. "What I remember of my parents is that they wanted me to be safe. The only way they thought they could do that was to send me with a cousin who had a way out. I still don't know what happened. If I was separated from him or sold, or if our craft was overtaken by pirates—I was in stasis. When I woke, I was in this galaxy and I never saw any of my family again."

"I'm so sorry."

"I am too. But even with all the hard stuff, I like to think that my parents' dream was fulfilled. I'm here. Alive and safe. I can spend my time doing the things I like. They paid a very high price for that to happen."

"How did they afford it?"

Waquas smiled again. "I mean the price of never seeing their son again so that he might be safe."

"Of course," Yaniqui murmured, feeling entirely stupid. "That's a completely different way of thinking than a Wea Saavian parent."

"Why's that?" Waquas asked, interested.

"There's a cultural emphasis on fate and destiny. To Maemi"—Yaniqui swallowed abruptly—"it was inconceivable to take a great leap like that. Change was expected to come to *us*. Taking your child and sending them out into the universe, that takes a certain kind of bravery I don't think my people had."

The sand dune slanted down and then they skirted a fence until it took them to a copse of trees. There was a worn path, easier to walk on than the sand. The gusts of wind off the lake were gone.

Eventually they came to a gap in the fence. A short man leaned against one side of the fence, smoking, the concentrated red glow floating in the dark. He said nothing as Yaniqui and Waquas entered, Waquas bending slightly to make sure he cleared his head.

Inside, immediately on Yaniqui's right was a rubbish pile and then it was house after house after house. She could see ahead that the alley split in two. Everywhere there were more shacks and tents and other makeshift houses. She could practically feel the heat of sleeping children, feel the oppressive miasma of breath and woodsmoke that settled over the trapped community. She didn't want to admit it to herself—it felt uncharitable—but the stench grew. Agriculture Planet No. 4,278 had been ordered and streamlined for efficiency. This was chaos.

She followed Waquas closely, nervous to be separated. They took the left path, then the right.

"You know this area so well," Yaniqui whispered.

"I have no idea where I'm going."

Yaniqui let out a soft hiss of laughter. "I'll lead, then." She took his hand and they wandered through the alleys.

They passed a house with wood board walls. The sound of gossiping women wafted out of the fire-lit doorway. A group of young teens clustered around one girl with a video game device in her hand, the artificial light spilling across their faces as they battled for headspace to watch. Shouts of an argument came from Yaniqui's right and they kept walking.

Finally, Yaniqui noticed a low hum had turned into a proper buzz. Waquas said it was from a generator and pointed down another alley. They followed the sound and came to an open clearing among the shacks, a few lightbulbs strung across. A radio played. "It's called a jumpoko," Waquas said. "They spring up at night wherever someone has a working generator."

Once Yaniqui stepped through into the clearing, she realized how loud the buzz of the gasoline-run generator, the technology of past generations, really was. Men and women leaned against the walls of concrete houses and talked and laughed.

In one corner stood a street cart. Waquas asked Yaniqui if she would like something to eat and then purchased two soy-based flatbreads piled with chopped cabbage, veggies she didn't recognize, and sauce. Waquas rolled them up tightly. Yaniqui took a bite. Though she had had dinner earlier, she was hungry from the long walk. It was salty and nutty. He finished his roll in a few large bites and brushed his hands.

They people-watched while Yaniqui finished her food. The time finally occurred to her and they had a long walk back. "Maybe we should head out?"

They returned to the shadowed alley and Yaniqui worried that Waquas thought she was disappointed that they'd come because of how quickly they were leaving. Yaniqui stopped. Waquas bumped into her and put his hands on her waist to keep them both from falling. She settled herself against a wall and turned back to watch the scene.

Waquas squeezed between her and the wall and Yaniqui leaned into him. He bent down to her neck. She sighed when she felt his lips part. She pressed into him more.

They both were breathing heavily when they heard two whispers.

The voices grew closer, one strangled with emotion.

"Jerramy, *please*, I wouldn't ask if it wasn't important."

"What's all this about? You and Monte are fighting. She won't say a word about it. You leave your *house*? Where are you even staying?" A sharp pause hung in the air. "Uzzie is devastated."

"I get it, okay. I need your help to fix it all."

Yaniqui held her breath.

"Fine," the man said. "We'll do it in the morning, and

then you're going to tell me what the fuck is going on."

The man and woman continued through to the lights of the jumpoko but instead bumped into Yaniqui and Waquas.

The man made a surprised noise, but the woman grabbed Yaniqui by the shoulders and pushed her hard into the light. "You listening to things you shouldn't?" she hissed.

Yaniqui was shocked and looked into the face of a small woman with dark brown eyes. It didn't matter that she was shorter than Yaniqui, she clearly had venom on her side.

Yaniqui shook her head. "N-no."

Waquas stepped forward. "Trust me, we were back here for a reason. We didn't hear anything."

The woman gave one more hard stare and brushed by, her black braid swinging behind her. Yaniqui couldn't help but wonder what her life was like, living in chaos.

Chapter 17

D-68
The Forest

He crouches in the tree above the two humanoids. His, Lozen, watches the other type on a device. It clacks with each keystroke. The man does not know D-68 is there—D-68 is proud he can tell their males and females apart now. The human didn't even look up in the trees when he followed Lozen to the meeting spot. A thing called a squirrel mammal chitters two trees over. Their voices drift up to him even though they are trying to be quiet.

"You'll have to tell me at some point why you two are fighting," the man says, still typing, not looking at Lozen.

D-68 thinks his tone is disrespectful to Lozen. He doesn't like it.

"Can't you accept that it's personal?" Lozen replies. "I

know you can hear me complain through the walls about that weird hair growing on my chin, but you don't have to know everything about me just because we're neighbors." Lozen paused. Her voice went weak. "She's mad at me. Probably always will be."

The typing fingers go quiet. "But why would that mean you can't stay in your fucking house? We haven't seen you for days and then suddenly you hustle me out of the jumpoko to ask a favor. Lozen, my mom is really worried. Everyone is really worried about you."

Lozen sighs. "It's complicated. Even if I told you, you wouldn't be able to help me any more than you can by sending this video file."

The man shakes his head irritably but continues typing. D-68 has no need to adjust his bent knees or grip on the branch hanging near his head, but he would like this to be done. Once this is over, everything will be different. Everything will be better.

For the past three nights, he and Lozen filmed Leggs's operation as well as they could in the dark. They got clear recordings of the crates the first two nights and shaky ones of the unconscious humans being transported, five of them. Lozen's breath came fast that night. He had to pull her back as they watched members of the Catchment being taken away. It would do no good if the two of them got themselves killed. They were too small. They were already doing what they could.

With this Jerramy.

D-68 watches as carefully as he can in the dim but growing morning light. Fortunately, the screen lights the strange male's face. He watches the fuzzy fibers above his eyes and the nose closely. He is agitated at the thought this stranger may want to hurt Lozen. D-68 will not let that happen.

"Okay, it's set up. Where are we sending it?"

"Just give it here." The two Earthlings hiss at each other some. It seems difficult for Lozen to communicate with others not aggressively. Lozen wrestles the small computer away and peers carefully at a scrap of paper. The man typed quickly, but Lozen's fingers clack painstakingly at the device as she types each letter of what D-68 knows is Agent Tril's second name. Lozen described the hidden second name as a way for select people to get in touch with an individual. D-68 asked if Lozen had a hidden name and she called emails stupid and tripped over a tree root.

Jerramy has temporarily lost interest, marked by a yawn.

"Okay, but if you do make up with Monte, you tell her I did exactly what she told me to do, which was to forget you existed."

"Whatever. I'm done."

Jerramy takes back the computer and looks at the screen. He cocks his head. D-68 narrows his own eyes on the man.

"Lozen?" His voice is unsteady. "Why is this a GIA email address?"

D-68 hopes he does not have to smash Lozen's only friend.

Lozen licks her lips. She tries to smile, but it dies on her face. "Now you understand why Monte is upset with me."

Jerramy makes a noise of disgust. "Don't you dare tell

anyone I helped you." The man walks away through the trees, looking back once at Lozen, his face tight. His elongated form is soon out of sight.

Lozen pulls all the supplies into a bag and turns to go farther into the forest. D-68 lurches from one strong trunk to another. Thin branches crackle and break around him. It is nothing like climbing in a cave or cliffside, but it is manageable and preferable to the flat ground. They have to be careful. Angry Lozen never returned with the equipment or proof to Lin's people. They could be looking for Lozen and D-68, even now.

Soon he drops down to Lozen's side.

"See," she whispered. "Jerramy did fine. And he was quicker than an animoid would have been."

"Don't trust."

"I realize that you don't trust, like, any human, but I do." She tugs the bag higher on her shoulder. "I have to."

"It happens tomorrow?"

"What?"

"Go home."

Lozen goes quiet.

He turns his torso her direction to try to read her. "What problem?"

"Well…" Lozen sputters, "not a problem, it just doesn't happen that quickly. Agent Tril won't see the footage until later today and even if she believes it, it will take her some time to process it and gather her own evidence. We can't get into the encrypted inbox without Jerramy. He's upset with me, but I think he'll come around. Still, we'll have to wait until it's safe to meet up again. I'll try to talk to him in a few days."

More days. More Earth days. He expected to finally be safe. To go home. Instead, more Earth days.

He makes an indiscriminate sound in his throat. Nothing that any of his kind would understand, but something he picked up from Lozen. He has been around her too much. Been around all of them. The more he stays on Earth, the less he feels like himself, like his own kind. The more his brain feels disrupted, like a pebble is stuck under the edge of a platelet. Nothing he does will fix it.

Lozen sees he's upset. "It's really not that bad. These things take time. As long as we don't get caught in the forest, we hide out in the hole for a few days, and hopefully when we meet Jerramy, we have a calm message from Tril that she understands all of this got out of hand and she wants to talk and we go from there. Dealing with the government is hard. There's all these systems promising certain people certain things if they can figure out the right email to send or the right form to fill out. For people like us, it can take a whole life to finally get to where we were trying to go all along." She rushes on. "But it's not going to be like that. It's only a little more time."

D-68 is trying to go back to his planet, but for Lozen, the place she's been trying to get to all along is New Washington. She told him of her goal of living in a city bigger and cleaner than the Catchment. More food. For her. All of this will work for her. His planet is so far back, he can hardly remember the feel of the dry air. Returning is an impossible goal. Has he realized that all along? Has he been helping Lozen reach her own goals, neither of them with a clear mind on how any of this plan is better for him than running away?

He slows and stops.

A few paces ahead, Lozen turns and looks at him. Her brow wrinkles.

"You. Earthing help you go. To capital. Me?" He pauses. It is unusual for him to stay so much of his deep insides aloud. "Never go home."

"That's not true." She takes a few steps toward him, raises an arm as if to touch him, then thinks better of it. "They'll have to see." Lozen takes a breath and expels the air in a way that makes noise and a small gust. "You didn't do anything wrong. They forced *you* into defending yourself. They took *you* from your home. How can they expect you to follow their rules when you don't even know our language? Where everyone looks at you and calls you 'other.' I know how it is. You have to trust me. This is only the beginning of fixing it all. Things take time."

D-68 moves his head back and forth, back and forth in the way of her people. She doesn't see. She doesn't know. She's not an animoid. She's not an alien. She has a home. She can communicate. He has no one to help him.

He bares his teeth. "Go."

"What?"

"Leave me. Don't come again."

"D-68, you don't mean that."

"Not my name."

He's growing frustrated, feels the urge to throw himself, move between rocks, not walk on the thick, unruly grasses of her home.

"You can't do this. It's just going to take a couple of days." She takes a step closer, exasperated. "I'm *trying* to help you."

He turns his back on her.

"You're really going to just…just leave me behind?"

He takes another step.

"I have nowhere else to go."

D-68 can hear the shock and the surprise and the sadness in her voice, in a way he has never heard a human's emotions, their very thoughts carried on sound waves. It cuts him in his thoughts. But it must be this way. Everyone has put themselves before D-68. If he is going to have any chance at survival, he cannot trust these humanoids any longer. Even Lozen.

He scales a tree and she runs to the bottom like a squirrel, chattering like squirrel. He can swing from branch to branch quicker than she can run and she follows from tree to tree, but soon she is gone and he is alone in the morning light of a strange planet once more.

Chapter 18

Nica (*Nee-ka*)
The Akar Provenance

Every third step, the back of the high heel slipped off Nica's left foot. Her hands still warm from healing, the feeling of someone else's vargolo sickness still crawling through her guts, Nica couldn't take one more ill-fitting physical sensation.

She paused in the hallway and slipped off the shoes. Left them where they lay. She wouldn't have worn them in the first place, but there were no flat or non-ceremonial shoe options in her room. Even when she lived on Wea Saa, she had always been against any kind of dress that would restrict her movements. She was currently in a loose-fitting jumpsuit—a fashionable peach, not a spacefaring outfit—with a white shirt underneath.

"Ma'am, your shoes."

Nica rounded on the doe-faced attendant. "I can't walk in any of the shoes in my apartment. You will go and fetch me more practical options. Underwear too."

"But, ma'am, your clothing allowance is set at Constellation Vas. It's one of the premier allowances. I couldn't bring you needlessly ugly pieces." The attendant looked pointedly at the heels. "If it's a matter of fit, I will bring you a different size. Or we will use an insert to make the shoe fit better. Sometimes they're uncomfortable, but there's no better way—"

Nica drew a sharp breath. "I have been more than patient with you. I understand you are just as trapped as I am, but when you babble like this, it makes me want to rip out your hair. And not even I can fix a bald head," she finished dryly.

The attendant took a sharp step back and put a hand on her chest.

"There's no need for all that." The deep voice cut across both of them. Then more softly, "Polly, go and restock our guest's closet. She can't heal if she's uncomfortable."

The attendant gave Nica a dramatic side eye as she left.

"Walk with me, Nica," Savini said.

They left the shoes on the walkway.

"I know how cramped these suites can feel after a while. You haven't been to the upper salon yet, have you?"

"It must have been left off my social calendar." The carpet underneath Nica's feet was plush. Much more comfortable than the hideous heels.

They walked in silence. An Akar attendant clad in

cream passed. A man with a satchel noted Nica's bare feet and nodded to Savini with a carefully neutral face.

"This way." Savini guided her into a much wider hallway, this one with a cold marble floor Nica didn't care for it at all. Dozens of people stood between them and what must be the door they were heading for. The gilded gold framing shined above the open doors, giving view to patterned chairs and couches. The fabric was black with threads of brilliant green and sparkling, creamy gold running through it.

Guards clad in green so dark it was nearly black stood at either side of the doorway. Gods, Nica was getting sick of green and white.

Beyond the perfectly styled seating area was an enormous floor-to-ceiling window. Nica paused midstep. The dark ink of space was blurred by streaks of white stars left in the wake of traveling at Lightspeed+. She couldn't make out a single constellation or landmark. She couldn't guess where they were. Everything was tiny and far away from the Akarian craft.

"Give us the room." Savini's voice carried effortlessly.

Attendants and their charges filtered out slowly. More than one woman looked at Nica curiously. Nica could only imagine what they thought. What they faced since being abducted by Akar.

"Here, Nica." Savini gestured to a chair.

Nica pulled her attention away from the view of space but didn't sit.

When it was clear she wasn't going to, he sat, but not comfortably. His back was always ramrod straight. There was no risk of him sinking into the couch back.

"I have an update for you."

She sighed and decided to perch opposite Savini. She was tired. "Are we being recorded?"

She suspected so. Despite past words, there was an inconspicuous absence of desire radiating off him. He didn't take her hand under the guise of helping her get seated. He didn't move to sit next to her as he often did, knee brushing against hers. Savini was controlled.

Savini smiled, not unkindly. "Always. The information we've gathered in this room alone has made Akar a fortune."

Nica wondered at Savini's confidence. Was he not worried she'd give him away? Did she even have anything to give away? Did Akar care if he manipulated her holding to the benefit of himself?

"I have a meeting soon, so I'll get right to it. A rep from Onlo recently sold us some information on your daughter. She is indeed on the small planet we suspected— Earth it is called."

Nica's breath caught in her throat. She had been dreading each morning, agonizing over the fact that that day could be the one they stole Yaniqui. But Yani was still free, at least for now.

"Moreover, there's another Wea Saavian on-planet."

Nica froze her face and looked at Savini's eyes. Her instincts were right, he was watching every nuance of her face to see if she knew.

She shook her head. "I didn't know there was a Wea Saavian on Earth. I'd never even heard of the planet before you told me."

Savini turned his gaze toward the immense windows.

"We haven't heard from our bounty hunter. And we expected to by now. And if Matts can't do it—"

"Really? Them? They're some kind of psychopath."

"Nica, stop fucking around."

Nica looked up sharply. She'd never heard Savini speak with any kind of stress. His speech was as controlled as the rest of him, if not more. Her insides shrank at the thought of what could have scared him.

"Just before I came to you, I gave the command to turn our course toward Earth. I cannot afford for any more mistakes to be made."

"No, you can't." Nica folded her arms tightly, an elbow under each hand. "Which means I'm in a good position to refuse to perform any more healing."

"After a few days, I doubt that." Savini smiled at her dark look. "Did you know I was once like you? A rebel like you? The difference was, I was only a kid. My prefrontal cortex wasn't even fully developed yet. You...you have no reason not to work for your own best interests. Your daughter's."

She didn't want to listen to whatever sob story he had prepared. "Why go to Earth yourself?"

He put a thick hand to the breast of his suit coat in admonishment. "I thought you would have gotten there on your own. Where there's two Wea Saavians, there may be more. I can't have radio silence from Matts, but moreover, this could be the Wea Saavian holdout Akar has been searching for. You really didn't know any were on Earth?"

Nica hardly allowed herself to swallow. Savini was watching her with that calculated look of his. She didn't have anything to give away, but she also didn't want to appear she was trying to hide something and make them more eager to go.

It was almost too painful to consider. Yaniqui, among her own kind? Thinking she found safety at last, unaware Akar was slithering her way?

Whether there could be other Wea Saavians on the little planet was a thought that haunted Nica.

She shook her head.

Savini nodded. "We're retrieving stolen property. This doesn't have to be messy." An attendant and guard came through the salon door. "Guide Nica back to her room."

Nica and Savini stood at the same time. He brushed close to her as he made for the door. His hand was warm on her elbow as he steered her aside. Nica turned belatedly toward him and felt the catch of the guard's hand on her other elbow.

Chapter 19

Adam
Bayler Luna Corp. Base

The Earth glowed brightly above his head. The dark recess of space stood ready and waiting on either side. And there, in between, the size of a coin, was everyone he knew.

Adam had been at the Bayler Luna Corp. base for only one Earth week, but he wondered if any Earthling could ever get used to seeing their planet floating above, swirling with white clouds. It looked much larger than the moon looked from Earth. The sphere was enormous by comparison, even with the southern hemisphere in shadow.

Adam pulled himself away from the thick-glassed window and set off toward the dining hall. The food served that night was American dinner fare: instant potatoes, gravied meat, corn, and a dinner roll. Bayler Luna Corp.

was an international company so mealtimes rotated staple foods from countries around the globe. The one thing that was consistent—regardless of cuisine—was the school cafeteria quality.

Though the meal was marked as dinner, it would be breakfast for a third of the workers in the colony like Adam. For those who objected to strangely timed food, there was always chopped vegetables, hummus, fruit, and good ol' cereal, as long as you didn't mind pouring water over it instead of milk.

Adam took the offered dinner food and scanned the few tables. There were approximately four hundred workers at the moon colony at any given time and less than half of them were scheduled for this meal. Adam recognized two people and walked their way.

"Beth and Kabir, right?" he asked them.

Kabir gave Adam a big smile and said, "Yeah, take a seat."

Adam sat down across from Beth, next to Kabir. Beth angled her body grudgingly to accommodate Adam in the conversation.

"New this week," Beth said. Her long black hair was pulled back in a tight ponytail.

It was unclear to Adam if it was a question or a statement, so he said, "Yep."

"It takes a while to get used to, doesn't it? Don't worry, most people are still vomiting every hour at this stage from space adaption syndrome or extreme paranoia. You know, regarding the fact that this place could implode on itself any minute." Beth sniffed in Adam's direction. "You seem to be fine for now. I'm not going to stick around after you eat though."

Kabir ate another bite of instant potatoes and shot Adam a sympathetic smile. From that angle, Adam could see light acne scars along his chin.

Adam took a few enthusiastic bites of his own food, not because it tasted good but to show he didn't have any problems with a weak stomach. He shrugged. "I've heard of that happening but I've been fortunate to never get gravity sickness. As long as I keep up my muscle tone in the low G, I do okay."

Beth frowned. "And you've been in space for what, a three-day college field trip?"

"Actually, I've been on an extended mission before."

"Really?" Kabir flashed his contagious smile at Adam again.

"You've never been to the Bayler moon base before," Beth said and pulled at the end of her ponytail.

"No, I haven't." Adam left it there and focused on eating his food.

"Jupiter Station, then?" Beth finally asked, more curious than before.

"No, I stopped by there though on my way back in."

"Oh wow," Kabir said. "You've gone beyond the J Station, then? Where? What were you doing?"

Adam used one finger to help scoop the last of his corn onto his fork. "I can't really say. The voyage was a confidential, private venture. Nongovernmental."

Beth threw her fork on her plate. "Come off it. Don't act all mysterious. It was probably mining on Linkos."

"Beth," Kabir said in reprimand.

"No," Adam said. "But I read about how we're

embarrassing ourselves out there."

"If it wasn't mining, then what? Diplomatic? No, you said it wasn't a government operation. Trade? But why the big secret, then?"

Adam laughed. "I'll tell you later, if I can. Nice meeting you both."

"Bye, Adam," Kabir said.

Adam put his plate and utensils on a conveyor belt and left the cafeteria to start his workday. He felt like he had to shake off the interaction with Beth. Kabir was nice enough. Though clearly introverted, he seemed happy for the company. But Beth. There had been several Beths in Adam's short time on the base. After a lifetime of academic competition and cutthroat job hopping, it seemed some people couldn't drop the habit of sussing out the pecking order.

And Adam was still low on the company pecking order. He was still in training but finally in Phase Three.

The very first day, Adam was monitored closely for any physical issues. He attended several orientation sessions with four other new workers—all of them older than he—and was taken around the moon base, practically by hand, to be shown the very basic functions of moving about the confined space. He would have appreciated it if Hloban or Eeriva had thought to show him the essentials on the *Canielle* those first days, but after spending months crossing the galaxy, it felt a little childlike to take turns in a group practicing with the in-house communication system.

The three days after that, Adam shadowed in every department. It was essential for anyone working at the base to understand how their role fit within the larger mission of the facility. It was still slightly like babysitting but with more purpose as sometimes people asked him to run to a tool closet or get more coffee.

Now Adam still had to work closely with his mentor, his schedule was tightly controlled, and he didn't have more than a basic clearance level yet, but he was on his way. His mentor at least, another maintenance process engineer named Pearl, was all business and taught Adam more in an hour than the entirety of his time in corporate training.

Most of the work on the base was research. Adam wasn't a scientist but the projects required a lot of technical support in addition to keeping the base safe and functional. Pearl had already trained him on the software for ordering necessary parts from Earth and walked him through several stations. She had a quick way about her, giving workflow reminders to people who didn't stand up to her scrutiny and stopped spontaneously to troubleshoot with a security officer.

Adam couldn't help but filter his experience through the lens of his blog. He found himself composing new articles despite the immediacy of his work, and had to continually remind himself that he didn't need to do that anymore. He had gotten what he wanted.

Pearl sent Adam to help unload and organize a new shipment of material so he was, as Pearl barked, "Outta my damn hair while I write these reports." At least Adam thought there was a hint of a smile when she said that.

Adam's wrist communicator vibrated. It was time for him to go to lunch. He rolled the last spool of copper wire—tall enough on its side to reach his hips—into place and double-checked that everything was secured. The entire complex was fastidious about making sure supplies, tolls, and personal belongings were secured in their exact storage locations. He'd do the rest of the unloading and organizing after lunch.

Adam walked down the harshly lit narrow hallways, then backtracked. He peered into a room he just passed and, yes, there was Kabir. Low static buzzed through the room. Kabir typed rapidly, his expression blank.

"Hey, Kabir. I thought I saw you. Are you going to lunch?"

Kabir smiled but kept typing. Adam was about to leave when he looked up.

"Sorry, I'm on radio duty, but I'm writing a report. Have you had to do this yet?"

Adam walked a few more steps into the room. "No, I haven't."

"Everyone Level Eight and below has to take a turn at it. You can work on anything while you're in here, but you have to listen. That static, that's the emergency channel. It's rarely used but can help. A few months back, there was an astronaut who got caught during her spacewalk. The monitoring system said she was in the decompression room, but really the door was clamped around her foot and her communicator broke when she slammed against the floor. She was able to radio in on this frequency."

"Why don't they just—"

"—use this frequency all the time? The hardware for this is built into the helmets and of course all the ships can access it. But communication is moving visual more and more. It's usually more helpful to use a screen and camera than just verbal. Many times, astronauts on spacewalks have to record what's going on outside the facility so the necessary team members can see and evaluate it."

"Are there many accidents like the woman getting her foot caught?"

Kabir wrinkled his nose. "Not really, but enough to keep you on your toes. So, how have you been settling in? The culture can be—"

"Competitive?" Adam folded his arms across his chest.

"I was going to say hard to crack. My mentor is a psychologist. The things you should hear her say. It'd make your skin crawl."

"I bet. But why do you hang out with Beth?"

Kabir grinned. "She's not so bad. She worked really hard to get here. Besides, I only see her when I'm up here at the base. We live on different continents. She's here on this tour for another two months. I bet you're friends with her by the end."

The conversation paused for a moment. Kabir picked it up again. "You're from the States, then?"

Adam nodded.

"If this is your first time on the moon, if you didn't go to the Jupiter Station for your mission, bet I can figure out where you went."

Adam was taken aback from the sudden shift in topic. "Nah, that's a whole 'nother story."

"I know. That's why I want to know."

Adam watched Kabir type his full name into the search bar. The first result was Adam's blog. Kabir clicked through a few aspects of it quickly, his eyes bulging.

"You run...a radical left-wing website?"

"What? No?" Adam cleared his throat. "The blog's all about things that were kept from us, uh, things we didn't know growing up—" Adam could hear how crazy he sounded. He wasn't doing himself any favors. "It was a side project thing—"

Kabir was barely listening. "Look at all these comments. Five thousand pingbacks? You had a lot of readers."

"It was something to do while I was job hunting. And it worked. That's why I was called. And I wanted to work somewhere progressive."

"That's not the word I'd use to describe Bayler Luna Corp. I bet someone out there is fine with your blog going dark."

Before Adam could respond, Kabir asked, "You don't think humans evolved on Earth?"

Adam almost snickered. "Come on. Do you really think we'd look so similar to beings from other planets if we did?"

Kabir shrugged. "That's not what I was taught."

Adam bent down and whispered, "By who?"

Kabir edged back. Okay, maybe the theatrics weren't very helpful.

"It's in the interest of the government to make us think we're somehow different, better, than beings from other planets. Think about religion, man. What would happen to the church if people started questioning things? If there really was a supreme savior, what are the odds it would be an Earthling?"

Kabir wiped his face blank. "I don't know. I'm not religious. I guess I'll have to read your blog."

Adam made finger guns, nodded, and left with what he thought was an air of sophistication.

Chapter 20

Ippa
Paramaribo, Suriname

It had been a hellish seven days. It took five days to get out of the village, guided by a lovely couple who said they needed to go to a bureau in their country's capital, Paramaribo. *Paramaribo*, *Paramaribo*, Ippa repeated the word to herself. It was a lovely word made all the more valuable by providing her with the only shred of information she had about her whereabouts.

Ippa was quite sure Benito and Chimène moved up the date of their trip to rid themselves of a certain freckly blue-haired freak who emerged from the jungle. The trio started by canoe. A few miles down the river at a bigger village they hitched a ride in a back of a truck.

Paramaribo was a delight after days of slogging

through hills and swamps. Ippa first spied hastily built shacks and homes that peppered the landscape until they were in the midst of throngs of motobikes, vendors, and children walking to school in their uniforms. Ippa kind of wanted to go with them.

Finally, the truck slowed in the center of town—rows of orderly tree-lined streets and buildings with expansive latticed porches. Ippa was surprised how much she liked the ornate architecture on the government buildings, but it was in huge contrast to the chaotic feel of the rest of the city she saw from the truck bed.

Ippa was preparing to say goodbye when Chimène gave her a water bottle and Benito paid for her mototaxi to the airport.

"Thank you so much. You're the first Earthlings I've met, but you have been among the kindest people I've ever encountered in the galaxy."

Chimène's smile froze and Ippa thought she'd better just get on the mototaxi.

Her blue hair brought the occasional stare as they twisted through the city—mostly everyone else's was dark except for a few young people she saw with shockingly long blond hairstyles—but Ippa was terrified she'd see Matts around every corner.

It was a relief to finally be inside the airport where she used the last dredges of her bank account to purchase a flight with three layovers to New Washington, WI. It wasn't until Ippa was in the air that she noticed ocean-covered ruins on the edge of the city. Dark shadows outlined buildings turned coastal reefs. Partly crumbled rooftops stuck out at odd angles. A concrete wall cut through across the ocean and city like a fault line. It held back the last few feet of water waiting to trickle into the lives of the citizens.

Ippa knew Earth was facing a global warming crisis, had even given up a lot of prime real estate to the rising seas, but she was surprised such chaos could exist next to relatively peaceful and prosperous neighborhoods.

Comfort was haphazard on the airplane. The seats were entirely too small and everyone but her was plugged into the in-flight movies. At least she was fed. She ate her ham and cheese sandwich so quickly she nearly choked.

Could she really be making better time than Matts? Was she really on Earth, and not hallucinating all of this in a hospital somewhere, her mother stroking her head, the result of the extreme pressure of The Shou finally getting to her?

She did not have good dreams on the flight.

But when she woke on the fourth leg of her journey, the hardest part was over. She was landing in the capital city of one of Earth's more populated countries, one that housed the global network called the United Nations. Where Yaniqui Daful lived. Ippa could contact her, become a hero, and surely the woman would offer to pay Ippa's ticket off Earth.

The woman next to Ippa stowed her tablet, headphones, phone, passport, and a loose paper of some kind in her bright pink bag. Ippa had nothing to pack up except a thin plastic shopping bag she had captured blowing along the streets of Paramaribo that now housed her collection of papers. At every stop along the way, she explained her appearance on Earth. It seemed most officials were happier to give her a collection of papers that documented her delinquency rather than deal with her themselves.

She queued up and exited the plane, following her seatmate closely. She caught a breath of fresh air passing between the craft and the jet bridge. South America was humid and warm, nearly so hot at midday that she could be persuaded to take her clothes off. This felt more like the neutral air of The Shou. Not too hot, not too cold. She rode a sudden flashback to the biblioplaza all the way down the jet bridge.

It disappeared when someone clamped down on her upper arm.

Ippa looked up, shocked. It was a man in a uniform. Another man took her plastic bag from her hands.

"Hey, what are you doing? Let go!"

"You don't have the necessary documentation to be here," the man said.

The seatmate turned and Ippa saw disgust crawl across her face to say clearly, who was that criminal she had been sitting next to for past several hours?

Shortly thereafter, Ippa was fingerprinted. She tried telling them about the Wea Saavian, about Matts, but none of the words she said made any mark. Ippa wasn't used to not being heard. But ever since The Shou dumped her on her ass, Ippa had slid farther and farther out of the system and into something entirely different—a place of disgrace that invalidated anything one had to say.

After two days in a cell, she was herded into a swelteringly hot vehicle with three other women. They drove for over an hour and then the back door opened, sudden light pouring through.

"Not the fucking Catchment again," one woman murmured.

Ippa disembarked behind the other women. She turned to one of the security officers that drove them. "Uh, I think there's been some mistake? I'm not supposed to be here."

The man ignored her and got back in the vehicle. The other women were already gone. Ippa took one look at the dirt road under her feet and the pile of men standing on the sides of what looked like a tiny town square, if shanty towns had town squares. Ippa could discern from the tire tracks that whatever government powers were at work insisted the citizens keep this space clear so they could drive the truck in, push the people out, and run.

Ippa turned and ran.

The gate was shut. "No!" She pounded on the metal. "This is a mistake. I'm not supposed to be here."

She spun, heart racing. *Oh, crisping gods. How the heck did this happen?* What was she going to do!?

Ippa straightened her back and pushed her flat, sweaty hair slowly behind her ears. She clenched her plastic bag of rubbish that the agents were kind enough to return to her. She didn't look left or right. Couldn't. Just put one foot in front of the other as confidently as possible, pretending she belonged in a world where people were not moved around without their consent.

But this is where the agents said she belonged. The Catchment. Where the homeless went. Where illegal aliens were placed until a planetary sponsor could be persuaded to pay for their removal. Kidnapping, you could escape. A deadly jungle, you could escape. But systemic degradement? No one came back from that.

Her first priority had to be securing her safety. She needed…what the crisps could possibly help? An ally? Some food wouldn't hurt.

Fighting back tears, Ippa rounded a corner, then another. Rubbish littered the path. Kids, oblivious to the way her life was falling apart—to the way their lives were already ripped apart—darted down the path.

She felt mildly better when she was out of sight of the gate. If she walked confidently, the people around her wouldn't know she had just arrived, that she had no protection—

Rough hands pushed Ippa and snatched her bag. She fell in the dirt and sputtered her way back up to give chase for a bag she didn't particularly want. But no one was there, the culprit already gone. An old woman with few teeth stared hard from her place on a sack. She mouthed something, suspicious Ippa would try to take from her.

Ippa flung herself forward and around a corner.

It was a dark alley, no end in sight as it wormed its way through plywood homes, cardboard shacks, and bundles of garbage. Daylight dimmed around her and a breeze blew through the makeshift alley. It smelled of garbage and rot and humans.

Then she noticed it. There, in the center, watching her with intelligent eyes was a little four-footed mammal with a shaggy, faded blue coat. Ippa looked around frantically to see what the animoid was watching, but there was no one else. Ippa looked again. A minkin.

"Hello?"

It gracefully stood to its feet. "You'll want to follow

me," it said over its shoulder. "You're late. There's not much time."

"What? Wait, what are you talking about?"

"Let's get moving." The minkin's voice was already distant, the catlike creature faster on four petite feet than it had any right to be. Ippa forced herself to jolt to life.

"Could you stop? Hello?"

"There's no time, I'm afraid. You'll have to do that funny thing called trust if we're going to make it in time."

The long blue tail disappeared around a corner and Ippa sped up. She was running now and the minkin leaped into a full sprint, slender legs kicking out behind the creature. They passed houses and shops and the types of shady-looking places her mom always warned her about, but she barely saw them, eyes fixated on tracking the animoid. She banged her shin and someone shouted her, but she didn't stop. She didn't stop until her lungs were ready to give out, they were, they really were, her lungs had had it with Ippa's terrible planning and they were done.

The minkin skittered to a halt in front of a dark set of windows. *The Shiranhole* was carved crudely into the masthead of the building. A being with a canine face opened the door, exiting, and the minkin darted between her legs. Ippa followed a second later but wasn't quick enough and lost sight of the small minkin.

Inside was a bar. Animoids of all kinds sat in small clusters at tables playing cards or talking. A few stray lightbulbs hung from the ceiling. A large figure in a robe with black-and-white fur grunted as it laid down a hand of cards, its companions groaning good-naturedly in return. The minkin was nowhere to be found. Ippa had plenty of reason to drink, but no local money and no idea why the minkin would lead her there.

She found the quietest corner she could and tucked her hands around her filthy tunic. She startled when someone touched her shoulder. She had been touched many times that day, all without her consent, but this was the first done with care.

She looked into the dark eyes of a woman with a hood pulled over her hair. "Are you okay?" The woman spoke carefully, as if Ippa were a testy toddler ready to lose it.

Tears welled up. "Not, um, not really."

"You look it," the humanoid woman insisted, rudely, and handed Ippa a mostly clean cloth. Ippa dried her eyes.

The woman had a cleft palate. Even despite her circumstances, Ippa couldn't help but be surprised at the lack of basic medical care it seemed many Earthlings were denied access to.

"My name's Ippa. I just got here. To, um, the Catchment. I've only been on Earth like a week."

The woman nodded. "It happens."

"What do you mean?" Ippa asked.

"I mean," the woman said with emphasis, "the U.N. keeps putting more of you off-planet types here and we're full enough already." She seemed to think better of her words and pulled a long black braid from her hood to fret with. "I'm sorry. I can't imagine. My name's Lozen."

"I was following a minkin…"

"Yeah, that blue furball? He's always babbling on about something." The woman dropped her braid as if personally offended by the minkin. "He always acts like he's helping, but he's never very clear. He ran through the door just before you did, announcing to the room that sometimes in our own time of need, the way we can help ourselves is through helping others." Lozen rolled her eyes.

Ippa brightened. "Can you help me get out of here? I'm trying to get to New Washington."

Lozen snorted. "If I could get you out, do you think I'd be here?"

Ippa closed her eyes. She was losing her patience with this Earth woman. She opened her eyes and fixed the woman with a stare. There was at least one urgent thing that needed taking care of. "Could you please at least tell me where I could pee?" Her bladder had been bursting since before the ride in the vehicle. She was surprised it hadn't let loose on her chaotic run.

Lozen finally gave a small smile. She covered it up with one hand. "There's an alley right behind here. Make sure there are no men there. It's not pleasant to walk through, but there's a kind of ditch. When you're done, come back here. I'll try to help you, if I can."

Ippa let out a heavy breath. She thanked the woman profusely and made her way back outside and to the alley. It was dark now. Ippa was already losing her sensitivity to the foul smells in the Catchment, but the stench emanating from the pit was something else.

A hand covered her mouth.

"Ippa, what a surprise," Matts' gravelly voice ground into her ear.

Her bladder gave up the ghost.

Chapter 21

Yaniqui felt a surge of anticipation when she saw a craft descend through the light blue sky. It was a large craft but, even so, it was dwarfed by the immense buildings and hangars of the Winslow Space-Earth Station. While she told Loera that she didn't want to meet a stranger—and she still didn't—it was better to give in than go toe-to-toe with Loera, especially with how awkward the house had been since they got back from vacation.

Though everything was weird, Yaniqui figured the reason Loera didn't seem to harbor feelings of rage toward Yaniqui was because the moment Hloban got publicly jealous, Yaniqui was locked in the embrace of someone else. Yaniqui had done her part in moving on. Hloban was the one botching everything up.

Still, Yaniqui was the only one without a job, so she was the one picking up the student Loera was helping. It was odd, being connected to life off-planet once again. On Earth she was so far, far away from all the big things that happened in the galaxy.

Based on the size of the craft, Yaniqui was certain they were from outside the solar system. She knew that they would have been vetted at Jupiter and would undergo the final installment of paperwork at the Winslow Earth-Space Station. She stood, forearm pressed against the floor-to-ceiling windows, foot up on a railing, thinking about the huge number of things happening across the galaxy, all at once. And Maemi. She was out there.

For another two hours, Yaniqui sat watching Earth news on a wall screen. She got up once to go to the bathroom and once to buy a grilled sandwich with delicious melted cheese and sadly charred crust.

Announcements were made over the loudspeaker, spacecrafts came and went, but Yaniqui didn't know which one carried her guest.

Visitors wearing plastic wristbands came out in small groups clutching clearance papers. A family with two children—relocating for sure. A professional set of three that could either be diplomats or high-level tech workers. No animoids the whole time she watched.

A slight woman with close-cropped dark blue hair came through. Her blue hair was so dark, it was nearly brown. She looked around briefly, and then walked over.

"I won't pretend. I know it's you because I looked up your photo." She gave a friendly smile. "I'm Ippa, with

Shou University."

Ippa carried a bag across the tops of her shoulders. She struck Yaniqui as kind and dorky.

"My name's Yaniqui. Your university really sent you all the way out here for an interview?"

"It's called a site visit," Ippa said and looked around at the terminal. "I'm supposed to take soil samples, collect things, and do as many interviews as time will allow. When I get back to the university, I'll compile the most up-to-date anthology on Earth there is in the universe."

"Wow. Well, uh, we can go through this way."

Yaniqui led Ippa through the building. Ippa put on a pair of glasses and recorded video as they walked. She paused to slowly pan over a series of chip bags and candy bars outside a small shop.

"How many planets have you been on?" Yaniqui asked.

"Um. Now it's three." She sounded so embarrassed, and Yaniqui thought the woman reddened.

They walked quietly. One of Yaniqui's shoes squeaked against the floor. "You know, I wasn't going to meet you. I haven't been on Earth for very long."

"You have an outsider's perspective, then," Ippa said kindly.

"I've been thinking about leaving. There's a...friend I want to travel with me, but I haven't brought it up yet. Still, there's not much keeping me here. I'm not sure you're going to hear anything helpful from me. I've never even been to the ocean."

"The ocean looked close from the fly-in," Ippa said.

"It's pretty far away. It's hard to get perspective from

space."

Ippa shrugged. "My project has a general focus. Information from you will make up a portion of what I hope to cover." She turned back to smile. "There's really only one place I have to visit. My professor made me commit to visiting there for certain. He even said to send for more funds if I need to."

Yaniqui waved Ippa into an elevator that would take them to the parking lot. "Loera said you're to stay with us for the length of your trip. We can be sure to look it up."

"It may be much closer to the station than your house."

Yaniqui shook her head. "I doubt it. There's not much out here because of the security barriers." Yaniqui wondered if it was a geographical feature, or maybe a cultural site.

At the car, Yaniqui resisted the urge to tell Ippa she had just got her driver license. She didn't want to sound like a kid next to someone so accomplished that their university would send them across the galaxy to conduct research.

Inside Hloban's shiny black car, Ippa tucked her glasses away. "It doesn't record too well at high speeds. I should take it all in anyway," she said. "Oh, and I have the coordinates. Could we look them up at least? It's my top priority."

Yaniqui pulled up the coordinates on her dash screen.

Ippa leaned toward the map. "How far is that? Will it be too much trouble to get there, do you think? I really hope not."

"No, it's quite close." Yaniqui raised her eyebrows. "But I don't know of anything out there. It looks like it's a forest."

Ippa sighed dramatically. "You're kidding. There's supposed to be an underground cave system with the only traces of pati ervinus on the planet. There's a clear signal reading from space." Ippa saw Yaniqui's confusion. "It's a rare fungi from the Lentelle solar system. My professor wanted me to gather samples so we can decipher how it got there. Earth was closed off for so long, he wants to try to figure out if the sample is from before or since Contact...sorry, I can see I'm boring you." Ippa laughed. "Some of these academic projects are so specific you can hardly imagine how they'd be useful to anyone, but he did make me promise."

"I guess if it's a cave system, no one would know it was there until it was found," Yaniqui said slowly.

"Do you mind terribly if we go now? If nothing's there, I can take a photo and a ground sample and relax for the rest of the trip. If something is, I can determine what supplies I'll need to assess it," Ippa said.

"Okay...yes." Suddenly Yaniqui was excited. A short jaunt with a non-Earthling was wholly unexpected but exactly the distraction she needed from the stress of living with Hloban and Loera. Waquas had been working hard the past few days to make up for the weekend vacation in the middle of the growth season. She'd been lonely, and more than that, felt totally awkward and unwanted in the only home she had on Earth.

As they drove, Ippa excused herself and said she had to type initial perspectives and observations. She reached into her bag for her computer.

"Ouch."

Yaniqui peeked over while trying to keep an eye on the road. Ippa had a red gash across her finger.

"I guess this bottle broke at some point during the trip. Oh, that really stings." Ippa waved her uninjured hand around as if she didn't know what to do next.

Attention mostly on the road, Yaniqui held her hand out. "Here, let me see."

Ippa rotated her hand but that wasn't what Yaniqui had in mind. She clasped her hand firmly on her new friend's hand and felt the smallest pinch on her own pointer finger.

Yaniqui let go. Even through the drying blood, it was apparent the cut had been healed.

"Wow," said Ippa, "I knew from the information Loera had sent that you were, well, a Wea Saavian." There was awe in her voice. "But I didn't know—I guess you don't really believe it until you see it. You assume it's simply a heightened level of healing that has been overblown by gossip and wishes, but this…this was extraordinary."

Yaniqui smiled. It felt good to help someone, especially making a good first impression with someone who might turn out to be a very good friend.

There was no road out to the location, so with a look over their shoulder and a giggle, they parked the car on the side and walked out into the forest toward the location. Yaniqui used her phone to guide them through the trees.

"Do you want to stop and take samples?" she asked Ippa.

"No, that's all right. I'm more eager to get to the site to do that. I'm glad to be here during the summer. The weather sure is nice."

"Did you have to learn a lot about Earth before coming?"

"Yes, it was very difficult. Geography, culture."

They arrived in a wide clearing. Shrubs and ferns spilled out into the sunlight from the shadowed gloom of the forest.

"I wonder why this meadow is so open. It looks like it was once a farm field…" Yaniqui trailed off because Ippa wasn't listening. She was recording on her tablet.

There was the unmistakable hum of an incoming craft.

"I didn't think we were that close to the port." Yaniqui looked up and saw a gray craft with some kind of black logo she couldn't make out sprayed on the side.

"Ippa, I think they're trying to land here. Let's move away."

A crack rang through the air some distance away. Yaniqui spun, searching wildly for the source.

Over the light hum of the ship, another crack came. Yaniqui finally realized they were gunshots. She ducked and went to pull Ippa down with her, but Ippa's happy-go-lucky student expression went slack and Yaniqui saw metal and greed appear in her eyes.

Yaniqui jerked away. She turned and felt something hard dig into her back and sting her until she blacked out.

Chapter 22

Lozen
The Catchment

Lozen was hunched over, digging as quietly as she could. She didn't want Uzzie to hear her and come investigating. She clawed the dirt out of the way but the walls of the hole kept falling in on itself. She knew there was a canister buried there but she forgot what she put in there. If it was acorns, it might help her get D-68 back on her side.

Someone screamed.

Lozen froze, then flipped over so her back wasn't to the door. *Shit*. Lin found where she lived. Or Leggs.

The screaming continued. It was a woman's scream. A long-drawn wail of misery so sharp it pained.

Lozen crawled to the door. She was getting her knees dirty, but she didn't care. Despite the screaming, it was a relief to nose her face out the side of the blanket to peek. Her house was hot and stuffy.

The screamer was Marcie, standing in the middle of the alley, fists clenched on either side of her face. One of Jerramy's friends stood opposite her. Lozen thought his name was Rayco. A collection of bruises stood out along the right side of his face. Uzzie's little voice tried to calm his mother's.

Neighbors appeared in the doorways, asking what was happening. When no answer was forthcoming, they drew inward around Marcie on the path.

She collapsed against her siding with a huge sob. An older woman reached for her, but she would not listen, would not be consoled.

"I'm so sorry. I was the only one who got away."

Everyone turned to the husky voice.

A neighbor with a full black beard asked, "What are you talking about, Rayco?"

Rayco pushed back the flyaways that had escaped his bun of red hair. He looked daunted by the prospect of explaining things for a second time.

"I was at a jumpoko last night," he started. "Jerramy and some others went to, uh, smoke. They went with an animoid. I don't hang with those beasts. But when they never came back, I went to catch up with my crew."

He stared at the ground and Lozen's heart sped, willing him to get it over with and say what happened to her friend.

He took a deep breath. "They were all laid out under the trees. One of the animoids, one of those with the scaly tails, nearly caught me. At that point, the sun was already rising. I grabbed the nearest people I could find to help, but when we got back to the tree line, they were gone. I'm sorry Mama Marcie." Tears dripped down Rayco's cheeks. "I'm so fucking sorry."

"What do you mean *laid out*?" someone asked.

"Like tied up and shit. Sleeping."

Lozen's hand went to her mouth, not to cover her marred lip from others as she usually did but in shock.

If she hadn't been here to hear this news…this was the first time she had been back to her home. She'd been sleeping under the trees, tentatively exploring the animoid blocks, then bopped into the Shiranhole, trying to listen to find anyone who had a beef with Leggs, anyone who could potentially back her up.

She was so caught up in trying to solve her own problems, she forgot everyone in the Catchment was at risk, not just her.

And now Jerramy was missing.

Jerramy who helped her haul washing water from the lake the summer her aunt died. Jerramy who taught his little brothers to play football with a ball made of plastic bags. Jerramy who Monte had an epic crush on for years.

But it was Uzzie that did it. The sight of him standing next to his broken mother, little sister's hand in his, no big bro in sight, was too much.

Lozen set her face sternly before emerging completely. She didn't think anyone realized she'd been back. She tried to make her little hole look as abandoned as possible. Once she stepped out there, that would be gone. The place would be useless to her if people thought she was there sometimes. It would only be a matter of time until someone came for her when she was there.

The morning air was cooler than inside her house. Her flannel was tied around her waist and her shoulders were chilly from the stark temperature difference. How many times had she come outside her house to talk to Jerramy? He was a constant in her life. He was the only one who had agreed to help her.

Lozen felt her face collapse when she reached for Uzzie. She held him against her for a moment. "Uzzie, you need to get the little ones inside. Give them some water and calm them down." She pulled some dried food from her pouch and handed it to him. "We need to talk to your mother with them out of the way."

"But, I-I can help. I want to help," Uzzie said.

Lozen saw it in the little boy's face. The force of the world that makes a boy become a man. But that would not be today. Not if Lozen could help it.

"You are. You are helping by doing this. Your brothers and sisters need someone who loves them. Go inside."

Uzzie lured the group of children in with food. Conversations sprang up in the crowd that gathered.

Lozen pushed forward. "Marcie, I saw Jerramy last night. I didn't talk to him, but he was fine." Lozen had watched the jumpoko from the shadows. She had wanted to ask him to check the email, but couldn't find a moment to snag him.

"He was with that girl. Your friend. The slight one."

"Who. Monte?"

Marcie nodded. "They've been seeing each other."

Lozen turned to Rayco and grabbed his arm tightly. "Is Monte missing?"

He jerked back from her vicious clutch, but he nodded.

Shaky energy shot through Lozen. She was either going to vomit or keel over. "Where in the forest were they?"

"I went out through the fence break next to Big Tomma, the guy who sells gas."

A wizened voice broke over the crowd. "They're coming to eat us! The animoids are coming to eat us!"

Lozen's head snapped up. Mama Teresa ran down the pathway toward the group.

Rayco stepped back and a woman to his side instinctively crouched and put a bracing arm up. Mama Teresa's ridiculous outburst caused the group to shuffle against each other in the alley, nervous she was going to start thrashing about with a brick in her hand.

Lozen went back to her house and slipped the GIA handheld into the waistband of her pants. There wasn't time anymore. If Tril wanted to try to arrest her again, fine. But Lozen was getting help for Monte. She put the flannel on and did up two of her buttons to keep the device concealed.

When she came out, her neighbors had transformed. This time of day, they were usually gossiping and cooking whatever they had on hand for breakfast. Today, the voices came fast and harsh. Lozen spotted a machete tucked into someone's belt. A few women had gathered around Marcie, patting her back, looking at each other in shock. Mama Teresa stationed herself at a stretch of brick wall and was jittering on her own, her back facing the others.

A one-armed man came walking down the path, shouting, "We're collecting a group to search the animoid blocks. We'll find the kids if we tear the place down."

There were murmurs and nods of assent.

"You gotta be kidding me."

Lozen noticed too late that she spoke aloud, faces turning her way.

She blinked hard and then set her face. "Monte and the others aren't there. You heard Rayco. They were out in the forest." She cleared her throat to speak more loudly. "They were taken on a cruiser. I don't know where they go after that. You can't go destroy the homes of people."

The crowd went silent at Lozen's speech. Rayco turned to her, his face a brilliant shade of angry red. "What are you talking about?"

"You knew about this?" Marcie asked, disbelief in her eyes.

Lozen looked at the crowd. The way her neighbors were looking back at her...her knees went weak with fright.

"Listen to me," Lozen insisted. "It's not all of the animoids. It's just Leggs."

"You know about Leggs?" a voice wheezed.

Mama Teresa, in the same stained sweatshirt she always wore regardless of the heat, was inches from Lozen's face.

Lozen took an involuntary step back.

But Mama Teresa snagged Lozen's own long sleeve and pulled her close. She smelled like alcohol and bad breath.

"I'm going to go," Lozen stammered.

Mama Teresa cocked her head, her slightly hunched back making the movement difficult. "He got me once. He got me."

Lozen tried to catch Rayco's eye, or someone, anyone to help her, but they all just watched.

"Leggs is the one stealing people," Lozen said. "Always humans. I've been trying to get someone, anyone to take him out of here…"

Mama Teresa had let go, but she was lifting her sweatshirt. Bubbled, scarred skin lined her abdomen. Someone gasped. Lozen understood in an instant.

"Leggs did that," she whispered.

"I met him—" she stopped.

Lozen thought she wasn't going to add more.

"—two decades ago. When he first came to Earth. He spoke and I spoke for him."

"You were his translator? Why?"

The older woman glanced at Lozen as if surprised she was still there. "He was already on Earth for a year when I met him. I worked for him." She ran a hand halfheartedly along the web of scar tissue, then pulled the sweatshirt down. "Messanat began to trade in things that weren't pills and drink. He traded in meats. I didn't ask. I didn't want to see. I needed him to give me yellow powder."

Lozen folded her arms and cupped a hand around each elbow. How long had these terrible things been going on?

"I finally saw." Mama Teresa's voice had grown dry. "I told him I was going to tell. I didn't even know who I could tell. Then he did this to me and told me he'd be back if I ever told."

Lozen felt bad for making fun of the drunk woman her whole life. Sad. And angry that Leggs wasn't taken care of way back then.

"You should have told." Lozen's voice came strong.

"None of this would be happening if you had done the right thing then."

Tears appeared in Mama Teresa's eyes as she looked directly at Lozen for the first time. "It still hurts."

Lozen's head felt shaky. If only she could go lie down and not have to deal with any of this.

"He will take and kill until the last of us is gone."

Goose bumps rose on Lozen's arms.

"I am old and broke." Mama Teresa looked at Lozen with a desperate clarity. "But you can fix this."

"I don't know how. It's too much. I'm not smart enough."

"…that's what I told myself too."

She was really going to throw up. She wasn't anything like Mama Teresa. Lozen backed away. Away from Mama Teresa, away from her neighbors. No one stopped her. Most of them looked confused, trying to piece things together enough to understand who the eff Leggs was and what he had to do with all of this.

A thickset man returned, gun in hand. "Are we doing this or what?" he challenged the rest of the group.

Lozen didn't hear their response. She ran. She didn't bother to pull a hood up or shade her face. She flat out ran, jumping over a heap of rubbish and slipping in gods knew what. She ran, despite the excited chatter around her. The energy in the Catchment was palpable. If she was going to have a chance at doing anything to help, she had to get a call out to Tril. No one could know she was working with the GIA. In addition to being an animoid lover, she'd be a traitor, and she was the only one who knew who was behind it.

Guilt racked its fingers along Lozen's back. If she had acted earlier. If she had done better. Bile rose in her throat. She had to fix this.

At the hole in the fence, she heard a shout. She couldn't help herself; she looked back. No one was on the path that she could see. There was the single, splintered voice of a mob in the distance.

In the forest, she took out the communicator and powered it up.

"Yeah, Lozen? You're in hot water with Tril." It was Velazquez, sounding bored.

Lozen froze. She couldn't talk to Velazquez, she needed Tril.

"Where's Agent Tril?"

"Tril's on leave." He paused. "Do you have an update on D-68?"

Fuck fuck fuck.

"You need to put me through to someone else. The GIA needs to send a team of agents. Things are going crazy here." She had to act like she didn't know he was working with Leggs. She had to get someone else from the GIA involved so Velazquez couldn't manipulate the situation. "A lot of people disappeared last night."

"What do you mean people are gone?"

Lozen threw her hand up in the air in frustration. It was so stupid to be wasting her time pretending and explaining when Velazquez knew exactly what she meant. "I mean people disappeared in the middle of the night. They were drugged and kidnapped." Lozen shook as she ran through a controlled version of everything that had happened. She didn't mention Leggs at all. If Tril was out, did that mean no one saw the video Jerramy unknowingly helped her send in? "All my neighbors are going to attack the animoid blocks. I'm sure others are going to join along the way. They'll tear it down, but the missing people aren't there. I think we need help."

He wasn't going to do anything. Why would he? Lozen threw caution in the rubbish heap.

"You remember I mentioned Leggs to you and Tril? And you guys didn't want to believe me?"

Velazquez sighed over the phone. "That's a dead end, Lozen. Leggs heard of D-68 and wanted to wrangle a life in the capital out of the deal. That's it. Call us when you have real information—"

"I do." Lozen forced her voice to be strong. "I have proof. I'm going to the guard tower. I'm going to tell them what I know about Leggs."

"No, don't do that. This is above them." He muttered a curse to himself. "Okay, okay. I'll make a call. The squads will be slow coming though. No one's going to want to get in the middle of this. The jurisdiction issue alone." He cleared his throat. "You and I are going to meet though. Where we first met, quickly."

"I need to look for my friend."

"This will be the fastest way to find her. I'll help you. Meet me there but don't tell anyone. I'll send the police to calm things down, but you and I need to deal with the larger problem."

He hung up.

Lozen could hardly feel her body. What if Monte was gone for good? Gone from Lozen's life forever after that stupid fight. And what was she going to do when she met with Velazquez, gun at his side?

She needed a weapon too. And if she did it right, she could get two.

The forest moved all too slowly as she ran to the cliff outcrop. She didn't know how D-68 would take her reappearance, but it was time.

She was breathing hard by the time she got there. A stitch pulled at her side. She jogged the last few strides to the outcrop and then jumped back with surprise, terrified to almost have bumped into him.

Lozen put her hands up. "I'm sorry I haven't fixed all this for you. I promise I'm trying my best. But my friend is missing. Monte. You need to come with me. Everyone in the Catchment is going to be at war soon."

D-68 looked back at Lozen with dull eyes.

"No," Lozen said angrily. "You don't get to not care. You started all of this." Before Lozen knew what she was doing, she reached out and took D-68's arm and tried to pull him to standing.

For the first time D-68 looked fully alert. Lozen thought he might be shocked. Or…amused?

Lozen kept pulling and finally D-68 relented and stood. He towered over Lozen and she got a whiff of something briny.

"I never go home," he stated it plainly. With no emotion.

Lozen didn't know what to say. Hearing it stated so simply, yes, returning to his planet sounded impossible. "I'm so sorry. But we can keep trying. I'm not giving up. Please help me?"

An intensity came into his eyes and he spoke carefully,

"I am not there. Here with you. I will help you."

Tears blurred Lozen's eyes and she flung her arms around him as much as she could. A sob struck her and she could only hope that he realized she was crying and not purposefully getting tears on him in some weird human attack.

One of his arms came to rest on Lozen's shoulders.

It was slow-going, guiding D-68 through the forest. When they got close to the clearing, Lozen told him to wait behind a thicket, tucked the phone into a pile of leaves, and walked around to the other side. She didn't want Velazquez to spot her location right away.

The cruiser glinted in the middle of the clearing. It was the same model Tril had taken her to get ice cream in all those months ago. Lozen dipped lower into the green brush as Velazquez immediately began walking toward the tree line where Lozen placed the GIA communicator.

She didn't have long. Lozen crept half-bent until she got to the side of the ship. The open hatch was on the other side, in full view of Velazquez. She ducked and scrabbled under the craft and lay flat on her belly. Velazquez picked up the discarded communicator, took two steps into the trees, and listened carefully.

Lozen slithered out and prayed for Monte's sake her footsteps on the metal ramp would be silent. Inside, she heard a torrent of radio. She recognized one of the streams. It was Tril. Lozen turned that up and the others down.

"Velazquez, come in. This is not how I wanted to spend my anniversary, so you better get your butt in here. There's activity in the Catchment. I need your ass here now."

Lozen heard a tiny noise and looked up. There was Velazquez, with her communicator in his hands. His face was strained.

They both acted at once. Velazquez reached for his side holster, but Lozen already had a gun in her hand, the one D-68 stole from the Karmas.

Surprisingly, Velazquez smiled. "You need to stay calm, Lozen. You wouldn't want to misfire an illegal gun on a federal agent. You need to place it on the ground—carefully. It's not a toy."

"You are not to speak unless to answer my questions. I know you helped Leggs capture those people." Spittle flew from her mouth. "Do you have Monte and Jerramy?"

"Lozen, it's not what you think."

Lozen held the gun steady. She was getting her friend back.

Velazquez shuffled a foot forward and she pulled the trigger.

The bullet went past his head and a tree branch cracked. He rolled to the side and Lozen stepped forward to fix him with her aim. He paused.

"Where are they being kept?"

Velazquez shook his head. His perfect composure was broken. "It's too late. The other groups were held in a warehouse until they had enough to fill a ship to take off-planet. But this time, a slave ship came here."

Lozen fought the urge to look up at the sky, even though Velazquez pointed, hoping she'd take her eyes off him.

"How do I get to that ship?

"Fuck that, Lozen, you're smarter than that. They're

gone. Those people were a drain on our planet," Velazquez shouted. "Our government couldn't do the hard thing and get rid of them, so I did. You all were put into that camp to die. *That's* what their lives were worth." He dove at Lozen and she discharged, more afraid of hitting him than missing.

Velazquez slumped over on the ground, holding his leg, groaning and panting.

Oh fuck. This was happening.

She walked over and knelt by him. "Where are they?"

He didn't answer. Blood trickled out of his leg wound in heavy bursts. She took the gun he had on him.

Lozen found a rope in the transporter, threw it to him, and told him to knot it above his wound. When he did so, she put the Karmas' gun in his gut and made her face mean.

"You're going to take us to them. If you don't, I'll put another bullet in you and let you bleed to death."

Lozen looped more rope around his hands and went to get D-68 from among the trees. Something caught Lozen's eye. Did Velazquez have backup? Lozen threw herself on the ground and lay on her stomach. Images of a hulking GIA squad ran through her head. She shimmied forward through the grass.

She lay quiet, trying to peer through the brush to see what caught her eye without it seeing her.

A spaceship was faraway in another clearing. A woman with muddy blue hair lifted another woman from the ground. Lozen stood and jogged forward to crouch behind a tree and watch.

Wait, Lozen recognized the unconscious woman as they disappeared inside. Those were black curls. That was the woman she bumped into that night. The one who heard her fighting with Jerramy.

Had she been watching what had happened to Monte? A life forever changed in seconds. She wasn't going to let it happen.

She fired at the ship, but her blast went wide. Lozen put on an extra burst of speed, but she was too late. They took off.

The ship faded into the blue of the sky. Lozen swept the ground with her gaze. There was an expensive red device. Definitely not from the Catchment, then. She flipped open the phone. She looked at the call log. There was one number contacted much more than others, a very strange name. She clicked on it.

"Yani?" a deep male voice asked. Sexy as hell.

Lozen gasped.

The voice responded differently, alert. "Who is this?"

"I'll tell you if you can first describe the owner of this phone."

"She's humanoid. Has dark hair, shoulder-length. She's young, in her midtwenties. Who is this?"

"This girl, that's who I saw." Lozen's voice caught in her throat. "She was just taken by a woman with short blue hair. Up. They took her up into space."

"Yes, this is a rescue operation," Velazquez said. "I know it's not my jurisdiction, Dave, but you know, I guess sometimes you have a feeling about things. Tell Tril for me and don't shoot us down."

Lozen jerked the gun at D-68. "Uh, I have two others with me. They're from the Catchment and they have inside information on the situation."

"Hang up," Lozen mouthed.

"I gotta go, no, no, I really have to go. I'll update you in fifteen."

Lozen heard several voices on the phone cut off when she ended the transmission, but Velazquez kept talking. "Listen, this is the worst idea I have ever heard. Lozen, we need to land."

"What's wrong, you don't want to meet your friends up there? You were eager enough to sell to them. Stop that," she snapped. "I can read the altitude control. Go up." Lozen didn't mention that that was only one of two controls she could read.

"So," Velazquez challenged, "we just go up there, demand your friend back, and then you help this beast escape? He needs to go to court and answer for, in case you've forgotten, murder of your own kind."

Lozen took a deep breath. She didn't really know what the plan was. She gently touched her cleft lip with a finger. "Those people you sold are up there. D-68 helped move them. I didn't act fast enough to stop this. So, we're all going to fix this. We're bringing the people from the Catchment back."

"You really don't understand. This isn't some rinky-dink operation. An *Akarian* ship came to Earth four hours ago. This is an aboveboard quintillion-dollar organization backed by galactic politicians. There's no way the three of us can go up against Akar. You are from a small life, Lozen. The things that happen on Earth are much bigger than you. The things that happen off Earth are even bigger."

As much as Lozen despised him, she knew he was right. She was gambling with people's lives here and she didn't know what was right thing to do.

D-68 finally spoke, "Leave I. Leave I."

"Yes, yes," Lozen muttered. "We're taking you off-planet."

D-68 nodded in response. "Not home."

Lozen looked surprised. "I thought that's all you wanted."

"Yes."

"Then you need to go. Maybe we can get you a ship up there."

Lozen couldn't read any of his features, but she felt the immense struggle in his hesitation. "No. Dangerous them."

Lozen didn't know if he meant it was dangerous for his family if he came home or that the beings were dangerous, but she supposed it didn't matter. "What are you going to do, then?"

D-68 pointed at dumb-butt Velazquez and made a big effort to shake his head, his shoulders holding back most of the motion.

Yes, Lozen agreed, it was better that he not know. There was nothing else to do but go up and away.

Chapter 23

Hloban
New Washington, WI

The voice over the phone seethed. "Mr. Milson, do you want to repeat that again for me and the sixteen other people listening in on this call?"

"When I rescued Yaniqui, I misled officials on Onlo to think I was going to trade them seawater. They finally realized that I don't have the rights to the water." He paused. Forced himself to keep going. "And I believe they sold our location to Akar to get even."

The call was quiet for a moment. He thought they must be muted because there was no way there wasn't an intense vocal reaction to that admission.

The secretary-general's voice finally came back. It was steel. "You really fucked this up, Hloban. I've been putting things in place to burn Council Member Kilberg to the ground for his ownership of Nica. Last week we forwarded our information to a special Joint Council task force on corruption. Nica is a clear case. She did not sign herself over to Akar. She was kidnapped. I was"—Cortez took a shaky breath—"*this* close to getting Kilberg removed from the Joint Council. But now, for the past two hours we've been trying to make contact with a spacecraft docked right outside our borders. We never even saw them get past our outer perimeter. The Jupiter Station picked up nothing. With no idea what they wanted, we thought they might have been here to attack. Possibly sent by Kilberg. You don't want to know how close we were to launching missiles. And now we know they just want you."

Hloban's heart lurched. "I'll go. Please don't let them get my son."

He could nearly hear Emmett's eye roll as the secretary-general spoke. "We're not giving them *anything*. Don't be a fool. But you will come here and give us every detail of information you can. Stop all communications, no one's making contact with that craft until we have the full story and can strategize." Hloban could tell Cortez was directing her voice to everyone she was with, not just him.

"You understand, Mr. Milson?" The voice was unidentified.

"Yes, sir. I'll come right away."

The call went dead and Hloban set his phone down. So, Akar was already here. He looked about his office, dazed. He had to get moving. Get to the U.N. Help them negotiate. Keep his son safe.

"Hloban, did you hear me?" Loera stared at his face

and touched his arm. He jolted. He didn't even hear her come in.

He looked closer. Anxiety was written across her face. "What?"

"Keyad called. Waquas said Yaniqui is missing." Loera tried to tug him up to standing but stopped and looked at him fearfully when he didn't move.

Hloban's mind reeled. They knew to come and take her. Akar knew exactly where they were because of him and now they already had Yaniqui.

Loera tried again. "It was her! Ippa, the woman I've been communicating with. She said—oh God. It was me. She said she wanted to write a book about Earth." Loera started fanatically laughing. "I thought she wanted to know more about our salt oceans." She was crying now. "But she wanted to take Yani. I sent Yani to pick her up from Winslow. I thought it would be good for her."

Hloban's voice was stuck deep in his belly. His communicator buzzed. He answered it. It was Waquas. Hloban struggled to understand the words. Waquas wanted to leave on Hloban's spacecraft.

"Waquas—"

"I'm coming to pick you up. It's not full of fuel, but we have to go."

"I don't—"

"A girl from the Catchment, Lozen, she said a woman took Yani."

"Stop. Stop, Waquas. I don't know if we should go." The words lay there, limp and ugly. Loera was in the midst of pulling their passports and paperwork out of the wall safe, but she turned with her mouth hanging open. Hloban continued, "It's not just a bounty hunter. There's an Akarian craft."

"What are you talking about?" Waquas's voice was cold and hard.

"I talked with the U.N. And-and we can't protect her. Not anymore. They could be searching for me and Obani already. It was a mistake to bring Yaniqui to Earth."

Waquas's voice thundered with anger. "How can you say it was a mistake? We risked everything to bring her here. You know what they're going to do to her. You fucking know."

Hloban hung up the phone. Pain and stars blinded his left eye and suddenly Hloban was on the ground.

"I *cannot* believe you." Loera prodded his shin with her foot—half a kick, half a prod to get up. "I made excuses for you. And because things didn't go the way you planned—"

Hloban rolled as her foot came his way again and it glanced off him. He crouched and got on his feet. Loera came at him like a wraith. He struggled to contain her arms and legs. It seemed like once he got a hold of something, something else got free to hit him. Loera's glasses fell off and clattered on the hardwood floor.

"Damn it, Loera. Stop it."

A sob came from the doorway. Hloban turned and saw Obani, standing with big eyes and an open, crying mouth. Obani had never seen a person hit another person, much less his parents physically grappling. He ran.

Hloban took advantage of the pause to rapidly expel his guilt. "I promised Onlo rights to salt water I don't own. They traded our whereabouts to Akar. That's why they're here. It's my fault."

"What do you mean, Hloban?" Loera looked nervous. Hloban hadn't ever seen her look so afraid. He made her look that way. He was the one.

Hloban felt like he wasn't getting enough air. He breathed deeply and felt the room sway around him. "When we went to save Yaniqui, we needed access to Akar Evion." He paused. "I-I took out a cloaking device…on loan. I promised Onlo access to salt water for exportation."

Loera inhaled sharply. "How could you do that, Hloban? How could you ever think that would come out okay at the end? Resource companies like that are ruthless about getting what's owed to them."

"I know," Hloban said. He saw the anger on Loera's face, but it was the fear there that scared him. "At the time, it seemed like I needed to get to where Yaniqui was, no matter the cost. It was impossible for me not to go save her."

"But she wasn't your responsibility. You were a galaxy apart. There were other people who could have helped her. And did. She helped herself."

She doesn't get it, Hloban thought. How to make her finally see? "Betrothal is *nothing* like marriage. Her life was worth more than mine. We are linked on an essential, cosmic level."

"And that's why you want to throw our marriage out the window. You love her?"

"No, I don't love Yaniqui. I hardly know her. It was something that should have happened, but maybe our link died when our people did. We both should have gone on with our lives, but she was in danger and I thought she needed my help. I never could have left her." Hloban shook his head. He would feel foolish about that for the rest of his life.

Tears crept into Loera's eyes.

"But I love you, Loera. I got to choose you. You took a chance with me. I'm so sorry for all of this."

"Just stop. We don't have time. And you told Waquas to let Yaniqui go," Loera snapped.

"I know. I know that's terrible. But they could be after Obani next."

All he wanted to do was crawl into bed and lay blessedly unconscious. Hloban's hip was sore from when Loera knocked him to the ground. He was sure he'd find bruises on his shin.

"Jesus fucking Christ." Loera put her hands over her eyes and shook.

Hloban reached out to Loera and she slapped his hand away when she felt it rest on her shoulder.

"You put our entire planet at risk because you didn't think of the consequences. You've fucked us all on a previously unimaginable level."

"Loera, everything was complicated."

"Then you could have talked to me, you ass. I may not be your *betrothed*," she said with dramatic emphasis, "but I'm your fucking wife and the mother of your child and the one who took you in when you had no home."

"I'm sorry." Hloban dropped his hands to his sides limply.

"No, *I'm* sorry. *You're* going to fix this. You're going find a way. If they want to take you and your blood instead of Yaniqui, you're going to agree. It makes more sense anyway. You can reproduce with a thousand women if they want to build some freaking army. Why do they always want to mess with the women?" Loera's tears were gone, replaced with pure rage. "I am taking Obani."

Hloban tried to interject but Loera only talked over him.

"Where? You will not know. You're calling Waquas back and getting on that Akarian ship. If you can't fix this, you will never see me or Obani again. Obani will live his life knowing nothing about you or the Wea Saavians."

Loera called Waquas. "Come and get him. Hloban has important information concerning what they want and how to make them leave." Loera listened. "Okay, he'll be on the way."

She hung up. "They all left already. You're going to have to find another damn ship to take up there. I suggest you visit the bathroom—I don't think there will be time in space."

Loera left the room, her perfume lingering in the dusky air.

Chapter 24

Adam
Bayler Luna Corp. Base

"We are at a level yellow security threat, level yellow security threat," someone announced on the loudspeaker.

Adam stood up from the computer station he was working at. "What does that mean?" he asked the person next to him.

They looked at him, surprised. "It means there's a security warning, but we're not on lockdown yet."

"But what's going on?"

"I don't know."

Adam decided he would find out. He left the lab and found a knot of people in the corridor.

"It's apparently a huge commercial ship from another system, but no one knows why it's here."

Rebecca M. Zornow

An older man with soft white hair down to his shoulders waved a hand. "I've seen my share of unexpected arrivals. It's always refugees. They're going to fill up the whole planet."

"Stop that, Robbie," a woman fired back. "We invite them here. And this isn't no rickety vessel." She picked up her handheld to show a photo.

Adam leaned in. His blood went cold. The spacecraft was immense. Polished black, it was hard to make out all the features against a dark drop of space, but it was clear no expense had been spared.

But was it Akar?

Adam turned right and followed the narrow corridor. The bright lights were making everything surreal. It was a relief when he saw Kabir, still on his shift covering the emergency frequency.

"Did you hear?"

"Yeah," Adam said. "I have a bad feeling."

Kabir looked unconcerned. "It's nothing. A trader or something."

"Who's head of security here?"

The static picked up, interrupting Kabir midsentence. He and Adam both turned expectantly to the receiver.

A voice jumped out from space, "My name is Ippa." The person breathed laboriously. "I was taken from the Jupiter Station and crash-landed on Earth." Her voice cracked. "I was captured along with a Wea Saavian named Yaniqui from Earth. I require immediate emergency assist—"

It was the most stunted fifteen minutes of Adam's life.

240

Kabir called a superior into the office and played back the recording that cut out so abruptly. No attempts to contact the woman named Ippa were met. The superior called their own boss in. Soon the cramped space was full of officers with patches on their jumpsuits indicating rank and achievement. Them and Adam. Worried for his friend.

The group moved to one of the larger meeting rooms. Adam felt like he was wading through water. He tried to will them not to see him, trying not to make eye contact and sitting in a chair along the wall with the people who mattered at the table. He caught a curious look of one of the older women, clearly wondering why Adam was in the room, but she left it.

The way Adam figured, one of two things could be going on.

One: Earth was under attack. Someone flew from some galaxy far, far away to siphon up the salt oceans or steal what was left of the rhino DNA or eat the president. Someone from some planet decided to ignore treaty twelve thousand-whatever and take what they wanted. Yaniqui was a side note. There were no intergalactic forces out here. They only thing that could stop them was Earth's defense. And Adam had zero faith in that.

Two: it was Akar or someone acting on their behalf. They were here solely for Yaniqui. And maybe him and the others. Adam had no idea who Ippa was, but that seemed unimportant in the moment.

Adam wasn't sure which was more terrifying: that Earth, his home, would fight and lose or let them take someone he loved.

Someone from Earth buzzed in on the wall screen. The

conversation moved rapidly. It was clear the person had already gotten some kind of update. Another person chimed in. There wasn't just one unaccounted-for ship but two smaller security vessels flanking it. And what looked like many smaller ships coming to dock in trade. Some were unregulated Earthling ships, others seemed to be pirates who must have known to meet the larger ship at Earth.

"The U.N. has put out official communications. Do not try to contact the ship."

"Which one? The central one? You don't mean the one that sent the distress call?"

"Either of them. Any of them."

A clearer image of the mystery ship came up on the screen, the Akarian logo stamped on the side.

It was about Yaniqui, then. It was about keeping Yaniqui safe. And deciding what Adam would do to make that happen when someone already had her.

Adam stood and walked calmly but quickly out of the room. Everyone had left their work tasks and were standing in the halls speculating. He walked confidently to the bay. He spotted Beth working on the bumper ship, called so because it was only good for bumping into things in space. Its ability to dock had been down for more than a month. Even with new parts, it was useless.

Adam walked seriously over. Beth looked at him expectantly, frown already forming on her face. Another mechanic appeared from the starboard side as Beth closed a panel. The mechanic looked between Beth and Adam, probably used to inordinate amounts of tension between Beth and others, and steeled himself against whatever bickering was coming.

Adam opened his mouth to say something important. "You're not going to believe this. There's birthday cake in the break room."

"No way!" Beth squealed and ditched her electric soldering iron in the work box. Her partner quickly followed suit and ran after her.

They'd be there in three minutes, maybe wait around for another minute or two before asking about the cake, and then hurry back to see what was up. Fortunately, Adam was suited up in forty seconds.

He hopped in one of the functioning ships, questioning his sanity. He was risking his job and life to zoom off into a dangerous situation he knew nothing about. And this ship was much different than Hloban's ship. He took a deep breath and nodded. There were fewer buttons.

Adam powered up the ship. It rolled forward through the open sealant lock. The massive door shut behind him and the one in front opened. His breath came fast and his radio exploded with commands. He ignored it.

There was nothing he could say that would excuse this. Even if he stopped, he'd be fired. Never get another job in space. There was nothing to do but move forward.

Adam piloted the ship forward into the vacuum of space.

Please don't let Bayler shoot me down.

Chapter 25

Ippa
In Transit

Even though Ippa was a captive herself, watching the poor woman groan and snap to as she felt the braces around her hands made Ippa feel strangely like Matts's accomplice. A strangled cry started in the woman's throat, but nothing came out. Like Ippa, the woman with the curly dark hair had a silencer around her throat. She could open her mouth, but Ippa already knew no noise would come out, nothing beyond a small grunt. Her eyes looked around a bare gray cell. Her hands started to shake.

Ippa tapped the manacles around her hands gently on the floor and the woman looked up.

It had to be Yaniqui. Now that Matts had their bounty in hand, they were sure to be leaving Earth. Ippa had no view as to what was happening outside of the storage room, but she knew they had taken flight.

Yaniqui seethed as she looked Ippa over. No one had ever looked at Ippa in that way. She was an academic! She didn't normally get mixed up with bounty hunters.

She didn't blame the Wea Saavian. Ippa had always thought she would do the right thing in any situation, but a few minutes with Matts and an electric charger showed otherwise. She gave up information about Loera and their communications far quicker than she ever would have believed. And Matts had a sly way about them. They wouldn't do well at The Shou, no, but they had some intuition about how people operated. It took only a few forced sentences from Ippa to come up with the entire plan. Matts hired someone to dye their hair blue to pretend to be her.

Yaniqui went mad with rage, jerking her hands and glaring at the woman. Then, there was a shift in her eyes. Ippa willed her to see that her blue hair was brighter. That freckles dotted her skin and the imposter had none.

They were trapped in silence, to wait until someone came for them. The silencers were good ones. With Matts's own spacecraft dead on a jungle floor, Ippa had been surprised when Matts whipped them out, that Matts had secured a backup craft at all. Ippa only wondered for one moment how Matts had managed to find such brutal technology on Earth before the silencer was forced around her head and across her vocal cords. She supposed that with Akar's funding, one could get whatever supplies they needed anywhere. Ippa could eat and drink but could only make the smallest, wordless tone with her mouth open and no noise with her mouth closed.

Ippa tried mouthing a sentence to Yaniqui. Yaniqui caught on and did the same, but it was clear neither of them could read lips.

She tapped her hands on the ground. Ippa winced. Her shoulder had been bothering her ever since Matts hiked her arm up in the putrid Catchment alley. She pushed through and signed out the Trans-galactic Emergency Code.

From Yaniqui's blank face, it was clear she failed to register the code as such.

Ippa gave a slight grunt in frustration. That code was the only nonverbal communication tool they had in common—they were two strangers from other star systems speeding away from a little planet called Earth.

That was it. Ippa tapped in a pattern.

Yaniqui shook her head.

Ippa hummed. *Come on. You were with a four-year-old.*

Deep in the recesses of the Shou University biblioplaza was an audio file from Earth. Ippa could visualize the label without effort. Copyrighted first in 1835 by a music publisher from Boston, nearly every child learned the song hundreds of years later—the impact of simple catchy composition.

A B C D E F G... Yaniqui had to know it.

Yes. The Wea Saavian turned Earthling nodded. A spark came to her eyes as she recognized the tune.

Ippa hummed the first note and tapped once. Then the second note with two taps and then the third note with three taps. It was a juvenile pattern, one that couldn't be missed.

Yaniqui nodded and hope eked into Ippa.

There was only once chance for them to get free. Once Matts had them outside of Earth's airspace, they might as well be in Akar's cages. But until then, Ippa thought there was opportunity.

What had stumped Ippa for the longest time was why Matts was on the Jupiter Station to begin with. If Matts had never gone there, Ippa would be on Earth. A laborer but safe. Ippa couldn't get the thought out of her mind.

So why did it all happen? Matts had no compelling reason to pose as an ambassador and travel through the Station. It only provided opportunity for them to slip up.

Ippa came up with two hypotheses.

The first was that Matts was an opportunist and opportunity never came if you sequestered yourself away. After all, their decision to travel via the Jupiter Station was what put Ippa in their path. And—Ippa thought this grudgingly—she turned out to be more than useful to Matts.

The second hypothesis was that Matts operated within lawful bounds even when they didn't necessarily need to but doing so lowered risk in their career. Ippa thought maybe Matts would kill her doppelgänger—Why leave a stray end behind?—but shortly after they brought in an unconscious Yaniqui, the craft landed briefly and Ippa heard the wretched woman leave, presumably paid well enough. It surprised Ippa, but it ultimately made sense. If Matts broke the law a hundred times a day, they'd be caught a lot quicker than if they broke it only once a day when they really needed to.

Ippa tapped in slow sets, breaking extensively in between letters so there could be no mistake. *I-M-M-I*

Yaniqui shook her head, frustration clear beneath the silencer.

Ippa looked at her with calm but pleading eyes. She shut her lids. They started again.

I-M-M-I-G-R-A-T-I-O-N

Ippa pointed over her head with her locked wrists. If Matts wanted to leave Earth's territory with the lowest level of suspicion, they'd have to pass through official channels. And with the two women nearly silent in an out-of-the-way storage room, Matts could be assured their live cargo wouldn't be found.

F-L-O-O-R. Ippa pointed up again. They were under the main floor.

Yaniqui tapped back. *N-O-I-S-E?*

Finally. A breakthrough. She got it.

Ippa was physically and mentally exhausted by the simple act of tapping numerical sequences—if only her classmates could see her now—but she couldn't stop until their plan was set. *O-F-F-I-C-E-R-S.*

Yaniqui nodded back in agreement and silently whipped her hands back and forth and mimicked banging her feet on the floor to demonstrate how they could make noise. She made a low hum in her throat. That was it. They would have one shot with the meager tools they had—quiet voices and bound hands.

Yaniqui pulled against the chains. She soon gave up. The women sat in silence for a long time.

The sound of an opening port came from above. And an Earth voice. Ippa nodded at Yaniqui and banged her chains against the floor. She hissed a quiet scream from the depths of her throat. She stomped her feet, but the muted bangs didn't carry above the hum of the air system.

It was futile. The footsteps faded.

Yaniqui slumped over, crying. Ippa tapped away, trying to get her attention, but Yaniqui wouldn't look up.

A noise came from above. Part of the ceiling lifted off and Matts looked down at them. Ippa growled in her throat. Matts smiled.

"I thought I heard the tiniest creak as the floor settled under the immigration staff." Matts jumped down. "It's so nice to see you again. *That's* Ippa." They pointed. "It was easy to find an Earthling willing to dye her hair and do a little zappy zappy in exchange for some money money." Matts smiled again. It was maddening how cavalier they were.

Matts kicked at the food wrappers around Ippa from earlier. "Glad you enjoyed the food, Ippo."

Matts spoke directly to Yaniqui. "You'll have to wait to eat with Akar. One of their transversers came to pick you up, but I beat them to you. I wonder how much they'll pay for you this time." They turned to the ladder. "I know it's crappy. You didn't listen to the advice I gave you. *Co-op-er-ate*. Both of you." Matts looked serious now. "You're going to Akar, there's no denying that. Make it easy on yourselves." Matts raised their eyebrows as if waiting for one of the women to respond. When no response came, they climbed up and replaced the cover.

Part of Ippa's mind raged. She wanted to release a soundless sob. Dwell on the terrible things to come. Think how she'd never write that book, never see her mother again.

But the other half of her mind was entranced by a shiny

object.

Ippa had been eager to eat her meal earlier. It was a variation in an otherwise dull gray room. Inside the durable wrapper were two water packets. She saved one for later; still had it. There were also grain cubes, dried fruit, and a protein packet, all individually wrapped.

She ate the fruit. She didn't know when Matts would next bring her food. On the way from the Jupiter Station, food had always been regular, but Ippa didn't know about their current stock of supplies. So, it took her a long time before she ate the grain cubes and she decided to save the protein packet.

But when Matts kicked the wrappers, the protein packet shifted out of the meal wrapper. And the top part of the plastic was clear.

Now Ippa opened the shallow dish. She looked hungrily at what was inside. Small cubes of meat in neat rows on skewers. A light brown sauce covered them. Ippa picked one up slowly, so careful, her mind racing. The skewers weren't wood or plastic, they were a thin tin with a cork handle. Ippa supposed it was metal so the meat would heat thoroughly over a fire. Ippa slid one of the pieces of meat off with her teeth and made up her mind in an instant. She had a gut feeling she needed to explore.

With her finger, Ippa pushed the rest of the meat off the two skewers into the sauced dish. Yes.

They were cheaply made enough that there was some give. Ippa placed the tip of a skewer under one of her gray-stained shoes. She pulled the handle up delicately, using the bottom of her nearly disintegrated flat and her own force to manipulate the end, bending it to a ninety-degree angle.

Ippa looked over her work. She now had a tension wrench and a pick.

She couldn't navigate picking the locks on her wrists, but if she could do her ankles, she'd be free enough to move around. Ippa's hand shook as she slipped her makeshift tension wrench into the lower end of the lock on her ankle. She didn't want to think about what would happen if Matts came back.

Ippa rotated the tension wrench one way, then the other to subtly feel for which direction had more give and held the wrench there. She picked up the bent pick with one hand and slid it in, feeling for the bumps of the lockpins. She rocked it back and forth. Then, she pushed at the farthest pin with the pick, feeling for give. It went quickly. On the second farthest-back pin, Ippa felt a bead of sweat drip by her ear. She pushed at the pin but lost her grip on the tiny wrench. It was slick with sweat.

Ippa took a breath and listened to the surrounding transporter. She let the hum of machinery calm her. Deepened her breath. This was a test. Another test. And she was nothing if not excellent under pressure.

She repeated her steps and felt the first, second, and third pins slip into place. Then the fourth and it wasn't long before the fifth one snapped and Ippa's lock fell loose.

Her shoulder burned from the focused work, and she stretched gingerly as she stood. She crossed the tiny room to work on Yaniqui's fetters, hands and feet.

Soon they were standing. Ippa's locked hands in Yaniqui's free ones. Yaniqui tried to pick Ippa's last lock, but she didn't have the knack, didn't know what mechanics to feel for and Ippa couldn't coach her through it without a voice.

They each tried to pull at their silencers. The pick had no effect. Ippa could wiggle hers only the smallest amount. She stopped, overwhelmed by the claustrophobic feeling of metal wrapped around her face.

She looked at Yaniqui in panic. Yaniqui was pulling the back of the silencer up over the back of her skull. Like Ippa's, the ears caught it. Unlike Ippa, she kept pulling. Ippa's stomach churned at the sight of her ears twisting under the pressure.

Ippa tried to gesture to Yaniqui to get her to stop. Instead, hot blood ran down the side of Yaniqui's head as the silencer burst over her head.

Bile rose in Ippa's mouth. Yaniqui handed the soiled silencer to Ippa who set it quietly on the ground, unwilling to touch it for long. Yaniqui went pale as she felt the side of her head. She unrolled the fleshy mess her earlobe had become and flattened the skin, adjusting it down a little. A whine broke from her lips.

It was one thing to hear about Wea Saavians, another to see one of them reattach part of their skin. Ippa felt dizzy and disgusted at the thought, but it had given them a chance.

Yaniqui reached for Ippa with her bloody hand and slipped a few fingers under the collar of her shirt. They both tensed and then Ippa felt Yaniqui's hands warm. She felt a little giddy as her shoulder ache subsided. Crisps, the papers she could write on the physiological experience alone.

Yaniqui wrapped Ippa in a hug. Ippa couldn't hug her

back but leaned in. They might die together, but at least Ippa had a friend with her.

Yaniqui whispered, "Any ideas?" Their first verbal communication.

Ippa had had a long time to think what she'd do if she ever got free. She tilted her head toward a metal pipe that ran along the wall and stopped, broken, partly hanging down.

Yaniqui stretched toward the rod as much as she could. A few finger-widths shy. She tried again.

Struck with an idea, she peeled her shirt off. She knotted the fabric until it was a flexible but stiff object and used that to press slowly against the rod. She pushed up, let artificial gravity pull it back down. She repeated this and flakes of rust showered down on her. She shielded her eyes.

Ippa panicked as the rod careened toward the ground when it broke. Yaniqui caught it inches above the metal floor.

"Use it as a weapon?"

Ippa nodded. She jumped when the vessel creaked above them, but there were no footsteps.

Ippa gestured, pointing her locked hands toward a shallow vent in the corner of the room. Yaniqui reached inside as far as she could, grasping and fingering everything. She found a sharp, jagged bit of metal she was able to pry off.

That was it. They had a rod and a jagged edge and only one voice and one set of free hands between them. It was time to move.

Ippa shook with adrenaline as she struggled to climb the ladder behind Yaniqui.

Suddenly the entire ship jarred. It was an unmistakable pull. They were docking. They had arrived at the Akarian transverser.

Yaniqui pushed on the cover and softly set it aside. It didn't make a noise that would be overheard over the docking sequence and adjustments. They moved as silently as they could toward the front cockpit.

Matts conversed up front with someone on a radio.

"Initiating atmospheric climate conversions."

"Disarming security triggers."

A new voice came on. "Matricia, this is Jay. We need to make this switch quick. When we get Yaniqui, we'll transfer the resources."

"I brought you a bonus one too," Matts said.

Ippa's blood ran cold at the reference to herself as a bonus.

"We'll take a look."

Ippa wondered if Yaniqui was nauseous, because she definitely was. Sweat built on the back of her neck.

With a lunge, Yaniqui jabbed the shiv into Matts's throat. Ippa's stomach roiled with revulsion as Yaniqui pushed the sharp edge deeper into the meat. Blood bubbled out and their eyes bulged. They grasped the iron piece but sagged just as they touched it.

Yaniqui fumbled but got the keys off Matts's belt. She shook as she removed the wrist cuffs and silencer from Ippa who immediately went to the dash. But the docking sequence was complete. They were locked there.

"My name is Ippa." Her voice cracked after being quiet for so long. "I was taken from the Jupiter Station and crash-landed on Earth." She heard the craft doors automatically unlock and willed herself to speak faster. "I was captured along with a Wea Saavian named Yaniqui from Earth. I require immediate emergency assist—"

The doors opened and a finely dressed man stepped inside, a look of disappointment on his face.

Chapter 26

D-68
In Transit

An unfamiliar thrill burrows into D-68's stomachs. The ship has really left the ground. He is leaving Earth behind him. Lozen holds a gun to the man human's neck. D-68 does not fit in the chairs, so he towers above Lozen. If the man, Velazquez, tries anything, D-68 will kill him, but then they will be stuck in the spaceship. He cannot fly it. And Lozen, for all her showmanship in front of the agent, likely can do little more than call for help.

The thrill of excitement disappears. Hopefully Velazquez wants to keep his life.

"Fuck," Lozen whispers. The spaceship shudders as they leave behind Earth's atmosphere.

"This is ridiculous," the man mutters. The scent of

human blood still wafts through the air. The man is in pain. D-68 knows this as the man shifts, trying to find comfort in an awkward chair.

"Shut up, Velazquez. This is happening."

Lozen has the gun ready, but she drinks in the appearance of Earth on the screen—a wide expanse of blue and brown, growing farther away with each moment. The inky black of space appears on one side of the image.

Velazquez taps buttons. "It's been a long time since I flew in space." His omission is different. The bravado is gone. It is a confession.

Lozen turns one eye on D-68, the other still trained on their captive. "We're going to do this. We're going to get Monte back and then we're going to find a way to get you home."

He knows she is making a promise she cannot keep and he chooses not to respond. The fact that she said it makes him care for her even more.

Chapter 27

"How many beings are you selling?"

The speaker's neutral tone sent shivers down Lozen's spine. This was what they did day in and day out. Buy people. Take people. Use them.

Lozen pretended to slump over in a chair, unconscious. Velazquez was bound hand and foot in the back. It was both easier and far harder than Lozen expected. The story was believable. D-68 looked like someone who would hate the Earthlings. Someone who would profit off the sales of humanoids.

"Two now. Have many," D-68 responded.

No, Lozen didn't like this at all.

The console beeped with the passcode permissions to

dock. D-68 hovered over the panel of tiny screens and buttons. Lozen heard a thump from the back that must have been Velazquez. The video messenger continued to play. *Shit. He doesn't know what commands to type in.*

D-68 tentatively pressed a digit to the touch screen. Nothing happened. Lozen fought an inner groan as she realized his skin wasn't compatible with the touch screen. Her head and shoulders were in the frame so she tried to keep those steady as she reached out slowly to turn off the video feed.

Once that was done, she typed in the code, and instantly their craft lurched forward, docking initiated.

"We need to figure out what to do when we get in. All we have is one gun. We'll have to work fast. Or I could go along with things and maybe they'll put me with Monte and Jerramy," Lozen said.

"Captivity you," D-68 said.

Lozen nodded in response. It seemed like the best way to get to Monte without rousing any suspicion.

The ship groaned as they passed from space into a medium docking cavity. The wide door behind them began rolling shut on its own and Lozen peeked out a porthole to find their ship was already on the ground. Once the door behind them closed, the stolen government craft rolled forward of its own accord. Lozen could feel a distant hum of large machinery as the door in front rolled open and they were pulled forward.

The hangar before them was immense. Lozen couldn't see the end of it. Instead, there were rows and rows of doors like the one they were pulled out of. Ships and shuttles and cruisers of all kinds lined up in an orderly fashion. Little bodies like ants moved among them in the distance.

Lozen sucked in a breath.

"D-68, you're going to have to go first. I'll stand behind you looking disorientated. If I can, I'll sneak away, find where Monte and the others are being held. Otherwise, I guess we follow their process until we get to Monte and Jerramy, then fight our way out and back to these ships."

A hiss came from the side as their hatch powered open. Before they could exit, a woman with an inlaid tattoo of orange crystal entered. D-68 shunted Lozen aside roughly and she nearly fell on the ground. Lozen didn't have to hide her glare, in fact it probably helped.

"I'm an associate with Akar," the woman said smoothly. "We have a translator with Linkos on it for your convenience."

She held out the device and D-68 put it near his mouth.

He said a few words. Lozen didn't understand his language, but she knew his voice. Instead of the halting speech, his words were translated effortlessly and expanded into many sounds. "I have twenty and three of these beings secured on another ship. I want to get rid of them before I leave this solar system, but I want a good price. Immigration and detective technology on Earth was much more advanced than I expected. I had heard this planet was still in the formation stage and planned to fill my hold, but could gather only a few groups before detection."

Lozen wasn't prepared. Even with her hands loosely bound, even with a kidnapped GIA agent on the floor beside her, she never expected her version of D-68 to be challenged. He was good, but…he couldn't be this intelligent. She thought she knew who he was in his entirety and she was nothing but wrong.

The woman nodded respectfully as if she dealt with traffickers all the time, which Lozen had to remind herself, she did. She said, "We wouldn't have bothered with such a small planet, but we were picking up some other cargo. We'll give you a decent price, but there's not much market for Earthlings. In the future, if you want to do business with us, know we typically only do business in exotics this far out. We can breed the rest ourselves."

D-68 growled, "I want 58 yurr each body, nothing less."

The humanoid frowned, the crystals glinting off her temples. "This one's mouth is damaged. How do the rest compare to the sample here?"

Her friend's voice came again with ugly words but articulate sentences. "It's hard for me to age them, but I had an Earthling check that they were all in their prime. Several will be good workers, very tall and fine."

"We'll start processing these two. You can retrieve the rest, but you'll have to hurry. We'll be closed to new business soon. If your stock all checks out free from the poid virus and have all their body parts, we'll take them for two yurr each," the woman said. "But one yurr for this blemished one."

Lozen's face burned. She was terrified but also embarrassed by that asshole. Who was she to subscribe less value to Lozen? She reminded herself it didn't matter. Orange fancy pants could think what she wanted. She didn't matter.

All D-68 did was make an approximation of a shrug.

Chapter 28

Yaniqui
The Akar Provenance

Savini sighed deeply. Yaniqui's first thought was how much older he looked, even as a guard strong-armed her and Ippa across the floor of the hangar. His otherwise neat suit strained at his middle. Was that a white hair?

But in one deep breath, the anxiety lifted from his face—because he had his captive again. He had Yaniqui, last of the Wea Saavians.

"You can't do this, Savini. I have a temporary status on Earth. They won't let you take me." Yaniqui tried to instill confidence in what she was saying.

Savini closed the gap between them and motioned to the guard. The pressure on Yaniqui's arms released.

"Akar's holdings usually like to inform me of what I

can and cannot do." He smiled. "They rarely turn out right in the end."

Yaniqui wanted to shiver, but she wouldn't do that. Not in front of him.

"All of this over not wanting to heal others, Yaniqui?" His voice was measured. Calm. As if Yaniqui really was the ridiculous one. "I've never been to this part of the Orion Spiral Arm and definitely not to the Sol System. I'm glad I didn't have to set foot on that little planet." Another guard appeared. "What is it?"

She licked the corner of her mouth. "The bounty hunter was dead. *These two* took her out."

An assistant at Savini's elbow froze and looked up at him.

He turned his attention back to Yaniqui. "You killed Matts," he stated baldly.

Yaniqui didn't say anything. She didn't feel bad, but she was watching Savini's face intently. It looked like he was shocked but also sad.

"Matts was one of the best bounty hunters you could contract," he said, annoyed. To the guard he ordered, "Take their body to the morgue. Have somebody from Information Services try to contact their family."

The guard took a step away, then turned back. "And if they don't have family?"

Savini's response was instant. "Mine them for parts."

Yaniqui was done. She couldn't stay quiet. Just as she opened her mouth, Ippa broke out in a loud voice. "I am *not* here willingly! Neither is Yaniqui. We have been taken by *force* by a paid bounty hunter—"

Savini sighed again. He gestured around the room.

"No one is going to care."

"—and I have no wish to be here. I am being *trafficked* against my will—"

"Savini," Yaniqui said over Ippa, "Will you at least take me to my mother? She's still on this vessel, I know it."

Savini's lips pinched. His wavy hair was styled, but a lock had popped out of place and kept falling in his face. He pushed it back. "How could you know anything about who is or isn't on the *Provenance*?"

"—Shou University is expecting me, *a university student*, back for report on my research—"

"How could you keep the news secret of a Joint Council member keeping a Wea Saavian woman against her will? It's a political scandal."

Savini batted at the lock again. "No, I'm afraid I can't take you to see Nica."

Yaniqui looked at him sharply. There was something in his voice. Regret of some kind?

He gave a sad smile back. "I actually would have preferred to reunite you. It would have made something else a lot easier, but the board has other, more immediate, plans for you."

Yaniqui and Ippa were separated. Yaniqui kicked at the shins of two guards who were called to prod her along, but she was a good foot and a half shorter than both of them. She was finally shoved into a room and forced into a chair. Manacles clamped shut over her wrists. Yaniqui thrashed and could stand in an awkward crouch but the chair was fixed to the floor and eventually she sat, glowering.

"Leave us," Savini commanded the guards.

The room was simple. Yaniqui figured it couldn't be Savini's office. There was a standard desk and swivel lamp but no papers, computer, or writing supplies.

"As I told you the last time we met, Yaniqui, this could have been as easy." He swallowed. "But you've made it difficult for me and especially for you."

"Savini, you can't do this. This can't be my future. There has to be more than this." She fought back tears. She wasn't going to cry and she wasn't going to freak out.

He ignored her. "You're going to be expedited back. That means cryosleep and an independent launch straight to our maximum-security location. You'll likely be sold by the time you land so you may not wake until you're within custody of your new owners." His voice was purposefully neutral.

Yaniqui started shaking. No delicious fruits and soft dresses this time. She was going to be treated as a criminal for simply fighting for her freedom.

"That's not necessary. I'll cooperate." She had to stay conscious. That was the only way she'd escape.

"That's no longer an option." He sniffed. "But, as you already know Nica is on board, I will share word of her. She would want you to know she's well."

Yaniqui narrowed her eyes. "How would you know what she would want? Did you speak with her about me? Tell her that you captured me again to try to sell my insides?"

Savini looked taken aback. "Don't be so dramatic. If you're dissected, it will only be because you drove your new owners to it."

"How long will Maemi be here? Where will she be

taken?"

"Nica will be here for the foreseeable future and then taken somewhere safe."

"Please let me see her before I go. This could be the last time I'll ever have the chance."

"As much as she would like that, I'm afraid I can't allow it."

"Stop that," Yaniqui said impulsively. Then, "Why do you keep doing that? Why are you talking about Maemi like you know everything about her?"

"It's my responsibility to know and safeguard all of Akar's holdings."

Yaniqui's voice became steel. "But you don't blush when you call them by their first name, I'm sure."

Savini's face went ashy and some of the harried look came back. "I suggest you leave it alone. I'm doing you the courtesy of informing you of the process—"

"Gods, Savini, do you have a crush on my mother?"

Savini glanced at his wrist tech piece and Yaniqui wondered if they were being recorded.

"You've always been this way, Yaniqui, seeing ghosts where there are none. I suggest you focus on preparing yourself right now for a new future."

He stood and the guard stepped in. Before the door closed, Savini was already giving orders in the hallway.

Chapter 29

Adam
In Transit

Adam slowed the government-marked ship. This was the stupidest thing he had ever heard of, much less done. What was he going to do? Adam punched his thigh repeatedly, thinking. Could he sneak in? Perhaps don spacesuit gear and jump from the ship, propelling himself with an air canister, looking for an opening, and run rampant through the ship searching for Yani before getting the hell out of there, blowing up half the Akar craft in the process?

No. That did not seem likely.

An alert for an incoming message came on. It wasn't from Bayler Luna Corp. so Adam answered it, uncertain who was on the other end.

"Attention Earth craft, Amendment 12 to the

Fraternity Act guarantees a safe perimeter around corporate spacecrafts in time of peace. We are concluding business nearby and will depart within the visitation rights for corporate entities."

If Akar was open to business, that was one way to get in. "Hey, I don't have any problem with that. It's just me on here. I alighted from the government satellite station on the moon. I'm done with this place. I'll work for free for a ride to the next terminal."

There was long pause. Adam could have sworn he heard a murmur, but then all was silent again.

The voice from space returned. "Permission to dock granted. Be prepared to sign papers and submit the craft to Akar Enterprises."

They sent him a passcode to relinquish control of the Bayler Luna Corp. ship. The craft lurched slightly as they reeled him into the docking bay. Adam stood from the console, no longer needed. His heart raced despite sitting in a chair for the past hour. He stared at the sideview camera feeds as his stolen ship was absorbed by one mouth, then another. Inside the hangar were rows and rows of wildly colorful racing cruisers and fighter ships and massive transversers. It spoke to the far-reaching hand Akar had. They went everywhere, traded everywhere. The collection of ships was a by-product. Far from where his own was directed, he saw a sizable fleet marked with Akar's logo and colors.

Within minutes of off-loading, three small animoids in collars began powering it off and scrubbing it down, their tails flicking all the while.

A woman in a light-colored uniform approached him.

She was bipedal but that was where the similarities stopped. Fur even lighter than her bland cream uniform coated her body. Her face was pointed, nose thrust forward. The impulse to touch the fur tugged on Adam.

She ignored his quiet assessment and said in a bored voice, "You're agreeing to trade the spacecraft and work for Akar Enterprises as the corporation sees fit in exchange for transport to the Nervis Terminal." Her voice tipped up at the end of her sentence, almost as if she was asking a question. "The craft is ours as well as your clothing and any resources within or on the outside of your body." Despite the harrowing language of legal ownership of his body, Adam expected her to snap gum any moment. "All I need is a verbal agreement."

"Uh, sure. Yes."

The uniformed woman gestured to a worker passing by and directed him to take Adam. "This one's new, hopping a ride. Show him to imprinting."

Adam followed the quickly moving human who looked much like him. There was something unsettling about his face though. The eyes were farther apart than Adam was used to, or else the face was too wide. After two hundred thousand closed years of development of humans on Earth and the isolated Wea Saa, the man and Adam were the same but different.

"You must be crazy," the man said. He was in a uniform, but grease stains pitted his knees and forearms. "You realize you signed away your body for a trip?"

"It's just for a short ride," Adam said.

The other shook his head. "Once you're in, there's no way they'll let you go. They own you now. Legally. Even if you escaped, you could be brought back in."

"I still have basic existential rights," Adam said.

"You have nothing. If they want to work you, they can. If they want to kill you, they can. If they want to breed you, they can and will own your offspring. You have nothing," he said bitterly. "All for a ride to a terminal. As if you'll ever get there, stupid." The man snorted disdainfully.

Conversation halted and Adam wondered if what the humanoid said was true and what they would do if they found out they now had a half-Wea Saavian in their paws.

Adam shoved the thought away. He wouldn't be staying long enough to get tied up in the business of the corporation. No one would know unless they saw him heal.

"How long have you been working for Akar?" Adam asked.

His guide scratched his jaw and responded, "I was traded four years ago. Before that I ran an enterprise for a private owner."

It was time to probe. "And what is Akar doing so close to Earth? I've been waiting quite a while to jump ship, but nothing's come through."

"Jump ship. You rural folks come up with the weirdest sayings. We're reclaiming an asset that escaped to Earth. Ever hear of Yaniqui, last of the Wea Saavians, the quick healers?"

Adam tried to not to show any emotion at the sound of Yaniqui's name. Were his arms swinging too much? Too little?

"Who?"

"Her kind has self-healing properties. She's one of only a few left in the entire galaxy. They tried auctioning her off, but she escaped." The man was quiet, then said, "With a dragon, I hear." Adam heard the wistfulness in the man's voice.

"There's no such thing as dragons," Adam lied.

The man didn't quite smile, but something crossed his face. "You see a lot of amazing things, owned by Akar Enterprises. That's true at least." The conversation lapsed, then he said, "We're here. This is imprinting. Well," he hesitated, "good luck."

A woman came over to Adam. A soft squash of stomach rolled over her belt. "The name's Melenda. Take off your shirt. I'm going to take the blood sample first."

Adam paled. "Oh, I'm…uh…I'm very squeamish at the sight of blood. What is this for?"

Melenda smacked her tote of gauze, plastic tubes, and clear-wrapped needles down on the table. "It's a mandatory part of onboarding to the corporation so that you can be properly placed for work."

"I'm going to be working in shipping operations for a little while, that's what they said. I don't understand why you need my blood."

"Listen, boy, how old do you think I am?" She didn't wait for an answer. "You think I got this cush job on my first day? You're going to work exactly where you're placed. Take off the shirt," she enunciated each word of her last sentence.

Adam slowly took off his shirt, searching the room for any distraction.

"I suppose it takes a while to process the blood?"

"Not really," she responded. "It's almost instantaneous. They invested a lot in the system. The speed comes in handy in certain environments."

Adam put his shirt back on.

"What are you doing?"

"I really, really have to relieve myself. I'm a nervous pee-er and I told you I hate the sight of blood. Where, uh…"

Melenda rolled her eyes and pointed toward a door on the side of the room. "You're going to have to get your blood drawn eventually. Don't make things harder than they have to be."

She watched Adam walk to the door and shut it behind him. He slid the door open a tiny amount. Her back was turned. Quietly he walked out of the imprinting office, just like that.

He didn't have much time before Melenda knocked on the empty bathroom door. Adam had no idea how the ship was organized. Where would Yaniqui be? He guessed because of the value they subscribed to her and as well as her previous escape, she'd be secured tightly.

Adam wanted to stop and hit his head against the wall. And cry. What had he gotten himself into? When would there be an alert about his evasion?

Adam saw something he recognized, a maintenance closet, and he ducked into it. Inside on a shelf was a cast-off uniform jacket. It was cream colored and a little big on Adam. It smelled like sweat, but he would take it.

He was hoping for more. He waved his hand and a wall blinked to life. Yes. Water mains and air vents for the part of the spacecraft he was in. There was a vent inside the closet, but it was sealed tightly with strange-looking clasps. *Of course, they would want to make sure their slaves had no means of escape,* Adam thought. And water? Adam doubted any of the pipes were big enough for him. Besides, he'd drown.

Breathe, he thought. *Breathe and think, you stupid idiot.*

Adam pressed his ear to the door, but there were no clues as to whether Melenda noticed he was missing.

With a leap of faith, Adam walked confidently out of the closet. He passed two individuals but neither of them bothered to glance at him. They had a harassed, piqued look about them and Adam didn't want to stay long enough to find out when he would start looking like that too.

On impulse, Adam turned on his heel and walked back to the imprinting room. He stuck his head in, "Hey, Melenda! The guy who dropped me off gave me a jacket and told me to come right away. They're onboarding a new being, an expensive one, and they need extra security."

Melenda waved her hand dismissively and a communicator holo shut off. "I was about to call a notice on you. I thought you were a runner. You're going up to the private holds, then?" She hiked up her pants.

Adam nodded.

"Come back when you're done."

"I will. I want to make a good first impression…"

Adam trailed off because she wasn't listening and he took the chance to walk briskly and quietly away. That was taken care of, at least for a little while. Adam's only clue where to go was up. There must be levels to the ship and, like most people who lived in a hierarchy, they put what they thought was important at the top.

Adam walked on. He saw a room with a lot of activity

and slipped in. No, definitely the wrong place to be. It was a technology swipe. They had the hungry look about them. The rows of gray faces and red eyes were not decision makers but information locators. Adam wondered if one of the people in this room was the one that had tracked Yaniqui to Earth.

He found a transporter and rode it up, striving to look purposeful all the while. When he stepped off, he noticed the difference immediately. On the lower level, things were mechanical and practical. Here there was an air of wealth. He passed a wall with a depth hologram of a beautiful woman with violet hair. She showed off an intricate tattoo of circles along the back of her neck.

Adam saw a man repairing a sensor panel. He took a gamble. "Someone needs a panel fixed up in the private holds—can I take a fuser?" The man handed it wordlessly, studying Adam's face.

Adam tried to stop blinking. Why was the man looking at him that way? He just had to not flip out. "I was only told to deliver the fuser. I've never been in the private holds, could you direct me?"

"Lucky bastard, best place to be. I'd sell myself again to spend some real time in there. Follow the corridor and take entrance 60Q." Adam had noticed the numbering system at all the junctures in discreet script. The electrician turned back to the open panel of wires and Adam swiped a key card off the cart. With the spare tool in his hand and a key card, he walked confidently to 60Q.

A cluster of beings passed. A very short man with brilliant red hair said, "There's an Earthling man on the communicator that wants to make a purchase."

"No, we're leaving as soon as the girl's secured. Let him order online through the Interstellar Wave like everyone else and tell him shipping prices are up because of the Janvo strikes."

Adam kept his head down as two more workers passed him.

Ahead was a set of doors. Adam cruised full speed into them, expecting them to automatically open like all the others. They did not.

Fortunately, there was no one around. Rubbing his nose, he waved the scan card.

The hallway had thick carpeting and a mixture of promotional script, commercials, and holos along the walls. This was where clients came to view a potential purchase. Adam tried a few doors by chance. Two were locked. The third revealed a crimson room with a luxurious bed and light drapery that looked like it was made of feathers. One corner had a shallow platform. It read like a setting in a porno. Bingo. He heard voices outside.

"Put her in here. Once we leave Earth's boundaries, ready her sale profile."

Adam heard a voice murmur in response.

"No, after we leave. We need to be in intergalactic space territory. If her sale goes up while still in Earth's sphere of influence, it's bound by their laws."

Adam's heart leaped. Yani was on the other side of the wall from him. A door closed and voices faded away. He crept out of the room. This close, he prayed nothing would go wrong. With the key card, Adam set the door lock for maintenance work and slipped in.

There was an undeniably gorgeous woman, but it

wasn't Yaniqui. She had medium-length blue hair, but it wasn't a polished cut. It looked like it was a short haircut in the process of growing out. She was absolutely filthy.

The room she was placed in was nice but plain, like a hotel.

She sat perched on the bed as if she wanted to touch it as little as possible. Her arms were folded across her chest. "I'm a member of the Shou University on an expedition. Science exploration regulations prohibit molestation of scientists at work for the greater good." Her voice came fast with a slight lilt.

"I wasn't going to molest you."

She turned up her snub nose. It was sprinkled with freckles.

"I can help you escape, but I'm looking for a woman. Her name's Yaniqui and she has black hair."

Blue Hair's expression remained impassive. "I've heard of her. She's a big catch for Akar. What, you want to whisk her away and make her your slave? Have lots of genetically superior babies?"

Adam smiled. "Actually, I had the chance at two of the three, but it didn't work out. My name's Adam. Are you sure you didn't hear anything about her location?"

The woman hesitated. She knew something, Adam could tell.

"I'm from Earth. Well, I'm half-Earthling," Adam said.

"What else are you?" the woman asked.

"Wait," Adam said. Her voice was stronger in person than on the transmitted message, but he was sure it was her. "I know your voice now. You put out a call for help." He lowered his voice. "I'm half-Earthling and half-Wea Saavian." Adam shocked himself. He didn't know why he would utter those words to a stranger, especially while in Akar's nest. It could be very dangerous. But he needed her help.

He placed the tippy corner of his thumb in his mouth and bit hard. Blood pooled around the cut. Then, he showed her the skin healing. "I was with the team that brought Yani to Earth."

The woman's mouth opened and her demeanor changed entirely as she watched Adam's skin knitting together. When she realized she could trust him, her false confidence slipped like melting ice. What lay underneath was fear. "My name's Ippa. I know where Yaniqui is, but I don't know how to get her."

"She's not being kept in one of these rooms?"

Ippa swallowed. "They're going to cryogenically freeze and expedite her."

Chapter 30

Hloban
In Transit

"This is bullshit, Hloban."

Hloban didn't look up from the console of the commandeered government craft. "Then why are you helping me?"

Eeriva turned a smoldering glare on him. "It was obviously your only option, which means it was Yaniqui's only option. I'm just letting you know: this sucks."

Waquas, Keyad, and Amanda were already up in space with Hloban's own *Caneille*. He had no other options but to skirt the U.N. and call Eeriva. He hadn't talked to her since they had said an awkward goodbye at Winslow Space-Earth Station shortly after arriving on Earth with Yaniqui, but when he called, the first thing she said was,

"What'd you mess up?"

Though there was much bitching and casting of blame, the important thing was that she said yes. As an operations manager on Earthling missions, she had access to plenty of spacecrafts.

The scene laying out before Hloban—Yaniqui captured and in need of his help, him alone piloting a difficult mission, Loera vaguely out of the picture—was so close to what he had imagined long, long ago in the dark of the *Caneille*, it felt like a guilty dream. Except now, he didn't want any of it. All he wanted was to be home with his kid, on good terms with his wife, and not at all the reason for a slavecraft's appearance in the Sol System. That would be nice.

Eeriva sat in the faded copilot chair. It was an older craft, not much to look at and had been sitting in government storage for a long while. While Eeriva had showed the guard some paperwork and her coveted U.N. ID, it was mostly bullying that allowed them to taxi the craft out and take off. The musty smell hadn't faded when the oxygenator kicked on.

Hloban was aware of how dangerous approaching the Akar Enterprises craft was for him. He had the healing blood of Wea Saa and if anyone knew…well, he had to make sure no one found out. That would be the end of his life and his son's. And now Eeriva would be on his conscience too.

They turned off their radio warning them not to try to make contact. They weren't the only ones ignoring the government's cautioning. When Akar's craft appeared on their screen, they could see a whole host of other spacecrafts—smaller security vessels, traders from Earth, pirates from deep space. It was like when a whale carcass drifts to the deep-sea bottom. Everything emerges for a bite; in this case for business and trade opportunities on levels rarely seen in the Sol System and the surrounding recess of space.

Hloban switched on his communicator, radio waves reaching out tentatively to the corporation's ship. He planned to ask them to buy his craft, just another impromptu sale from an inhabitant of a remote planet looking to make a buck. It would grant him access to Akar's craft and he could search for Yaniqui.

No one answered his query. Instead, he got back an automated message that the *Akar Provenance* was now closed to new visitors and trade agreements.

"Are we too late?" Eeriva asked. "Are they already getting ready to leave?" She sounded worried but also relieved. Maybe she was having second thoughts about going up against a galactic trafficking corporation again.

Hloban cut the contact and turned on the invisibility cover of the black box, the one that had cost him so much, that had led to Onlo outing him to Akar. Since arriving back at Earth, he kept it near him at all times, terrified lest the object worth more than an entire block of homes in his neighborhood get stolen or broken. He felt bad that Keyad and the others didn't have the coverage, but then again, they shouldn't have taken off in the *Caneille* without him.

"If they are, then I have to get on that spacecraft before they do. Once they're gone, it will take months to track them down, time Yaniqui doesn't have."

Hloban repositioned the ancient craft as close to the

Provenance as he could, firing the breakers carefully to avoid colliding. A craft that large wouldn't notice his small jab, but it would be detrimental to them. His eyes went bleary looking for an opening on the immense craft.

He found it on the wide side, out of sight of the main docking station. It looked like a maintenance access.

"Can you hold us steady here?"

"This is an even worse idea, Hloban."

"It's the only one we have," he fired back at Eeriva. "Once I'm out, get back to Earth."

"No problem with that, but this is a good time to remind you I'm captain here."

Hloban looked up, surprised, but Eeriva was smiling. "Good luck."

Hloban was already in a jumpsuit thick enough to resistant the dire environment of space but the smell was atrocious. This definitely had not been properly cleaned before it was left to sit for half a decade. Hloban attached a helmet. He grabbed a utility belt and strapped it on.

Hloban's breath was shaky. He couldn't go out there like that. He made himself take a very long, deep breath and exhale through his nose, pretending he was just fine— as if he was on the beach, not floating next to a death trap. Hloban secured a tether with a practiced motion and did the same to a metal ring on his suit. He linked a canister to his suit with a metal clasp.

He stepped into the exit chamber. A door hissed behind him. Someone else couldn't have fit in there with him.

Then he opened the second door to bleak, dark, open space. Hloban placed his back to the interior of the craft and bolted forward over the few steps. On his last step of solid ground, Hloban pushed hard on his foot and bounced forward. He moved slowly and weightlessly through nothing.

He didn't risk a look back. He wouldn't see anything anyway.

The *Akar Provenance* was in perpetual motion passing before him. The spot he aimed for approached rapidly, but he was still too far away. He flashed the canister. It sputtered, caught, and boosted him forward, and then died in one breath.

Hloban cursed himself and the dated equipment. A sweat broke out on his back. He should have checked the level in the air canister.

Fruitlessly, he strained forward, but with nothing else to push off, his only choices were to wait, or rein himself in by the rope and try again, but he didn't know if he had another canister to boost himself with. And if he didn't, he wouldn't get closer than he was already.

Hloban threw the canister at his feet and pushed slightly off the momentum.

He wondered how far the cloaking camouflage extended. He should have asked the reps on Onlo more questions about it when he signed over the assets he didn't have to purchase it.

After what felt like a long time, Hloban braced for impact. He put his hands forward to claw against anything he could grasp. If he didn't catch something, he'd bounce off and have to return to the craft and come up with another plan.

One hand caught a gap between two plates and he

settled himself in. Hloban couldn't look up because of the limited range of his helmet, but he guessed that the spot he needed to get to was five meters ahead. He reached forward as much as he could and grasped a tiny bolt end and pushed himself forward. It was difficult to grasp something so small through the thick anti-radiation climatic gloves. He made progress by finding the tiniest inconsistencies on the smooth ship.

His tether was growing short. If he didn't want to be wrenched off, he had to let it go. Unclasping the metal hook, he watched it float off into space from the corner of his eye.

Hloban felt ill and fought to gain another handhold. There was nothing else he could do. He could not turn back.

It wasn't Yaniqui's life to save, it was his own. Sweat ran down Hloban's spine. He had a wild desire to let go of his measly handhold and scratch his back. Hloban zeroed in and focused. Ignore the itch. Ignore the rope. Ignore Yani and Loera. *This is your life*. Desperately, Hloban found another hold.

Now, he could see his destination in his peripheral vision. He had overshot to the left.

Hloban couldn't see anything else to grasp between himself and the repair door.

With everything to lose, he launched himself with all his strength, but he drifted sideways piteously slow.

Hloban got a good handhold on the vertical metal bar next to the door and steadied himself. He pressed the outer lock and the maintenance access door shuttered open. Hloban struggled to fit his bulky frame through the small door. He finally got himself inside. He spun around in nothing as he pressed the button to shut the outer door behind him. He used the handholds to propel himself forward and pressed the median regulator. He slowly sank to the ground as atmosphere returned. The helmet caused a struggle, he was shaking so bad. When he finally got it off, he closed his eyes and scratched the back of his neck, which was drenched in sweat. He stripped the rest of the suit and piled it on the floor.

Okay, the easiest part of this is done.

Chapter 31

D-68

The Akar Provenance

After what feels like a lifetime of hostility—the disgust of Earthlings when they look at him, the condescending nature of the Many Legged One—none of the workers on the *Akar Provenance* view D-68 with surprise, much less fear. They are used to beings of all shapes and sizes. The only metric they respond to is that of capitalism. Moreover, he is treated with respect for the first time. Besides Lozen, he admits to himself. Still, despite all the time they spend together, he sometimes catches her looking at his body in surprise, his size, his platelets with curiosity and mistrust.

They wind their way down the different levels of the ship. What he has seen so far of the bowels of the immense spacecraft rivals D-68's home hamlet. The tang of rust and metals sour his nasal pads but not in the way of the Earthling craft. There is something nuttier about the composition of these metals that wasn't so abrasive. D-68 thinks of the dim corridors as similar to Lozen's Catchment. It is forever winding. The scent of bodily fluids hover.

Lozen marches beside him, grumpy-faced but not panicked. He thinks she should do a better job at pretending. He never saw the humans awake during the trafficking, but he knows how much these beings chatter, chatter, chatter. She will give them away if she continues to resist speaking.

Her hands are bound behind her back by a measure of hard plastic. It is more economical than what 'vo used to bind and cover both hands. This is simply a loop of plastic to hold the thin frail arms together. It could never hold D-68, but it is enough for her.

"Will we arrive soon? I acknowledge the time you are taking to show me the holdings at my request so I can better source beings Akar is interested in purchasing, but I don't want to leave my extra product for too long as you ready for departure." The translator turns his few words into many, too many. He does not like how much longer conversations take, but he has to admit, the translation device is effective for the purposes of communicating with humanoids. They need many sounds to understand the nuance of speech.

"Almost there. The main cell group is down this hall. We put them together with others of their planet. It's a more humane way to transfer them. Survival rates increase when they are around others of their own kind." The woman with the orange crystals inlaid into her skin answers. She wears a pale green uniform and walks casually behind Lozen. If D-68 were inclined, he could tell her how fragile those crystals are. But she will likely find out firsthand someday. "If you are concerned about treatment, I can assure you Akar follows all Joint Council regulations concerning ownership and transfer of beings. Food, water, and toilet areas are all provided. Your cargo will be safe until they reach their destination."

At last, the associate waves a flat key to power up a wide door. It slides open to reveal a guard who steps aside.

The stench is immediate. If Earth was a humid ball of disgusting, wet humanoid smells, this is a nightmare. His nasal pads flare and he clenches his fists, fighting the urge to cover his face and back away from the scent. If he is supposed to be a practiced hunter, he cannot show surprise at the results of the capture.

"What the fuck?" Lozen cowers openly.

"You'll get used to it," the bedecked woman says and prods Lozen forward.

The noise comes next. The ever-sustaining murmur grows at their appearance. The beings swell to the bars and speak and yell and call. Hands slip through, reaching for him. He remembers being the one to reach through metal bars once.

There are slurs and threats and pleas and D-68's brain goes into overdrive trying to sort all the sounds. He cannot synthetize the moment. It comes all at once in fragments and pieces. His senses struggle to take in the tidal wave of voices and smells. They wash over him, threatening to pull him under. D-68 shivers and fights against covering his ears. A child is crying. A child in a cage. A child crying like the kits he has never seen.

The power of the moment nearly brings him to his knees. He can't let it inside him. Akar does not see him as a being forcibly taken from his home. If they did, he would be in a cage too. They see a hardened presence like theirs. That is what he must be.

He takes a step back. He loses sight of Lozen and the guard. There is only a wall of bodies behind the bars. No, three big holding cells, separated by corridors, and each with smaller sections inside.

His stomachs churn as he thinks of how many humanoids he helped the Many Legged One consign to a fate like this one. His solitary cell with the Earthlings on their craft was abhorrent. But this…this is an abomination. They cannot be kept like this, tight as legumes in a pouch.

He turns to Lozen to see if she has spotted her Monte and the others from the Catchment.

Instead, the dreadful woman is waiting next to the guard. "Akar says they purchase all species equally." She has to speak loudly. "But if you ask me, your best bet is to bring species that populate quickly. Brood stock fetches a higher price. If you're up for it, I can also put you on the bounty list for rare species. The notifications for special purchases are fulfilled quickly so you have to be fast."

She goes on, but D-68 can barely hear her, much less understand her despite the translator device. He is scanning rapidly, looking for Lozen.

There!

Lozen stands at the bars. His vision doubles in scope and he blinks. Lozen is standing inside the bars. Lozen was standing. She is inside the cage. She was in the cage.

Someone pulled at her sleeve trying to get her to look their way, but her eyes were fixed on D-68.

He shook his head. They were supposed to take the guard out before this happened. She and him.

D-68 looked around. The associate was at the door. Dizziness washed over him. He felt like he would fall.

Terror is etched. Was etched. On Lozen's face. Deep. He knew she was trying to communicate everything through her glance. That it wasn't the plan. That she couldn't say what she needed to without giving him away. That she protected him at risk to herself. That he had to fix this, come back for her.

Tears wet her face. She didn't say anything. Only clutched at the bars.

"Come on, I've got to get back," the associate called. The doors slid open and the guard returned to their position by the door.

D-68 turned and left with the wrong human, his mind forever altered.

Chapter 32

Ippa

The Akar Provenance

Ippa and Adam—the half-Earthling, half-Wea Saavian apparently—ran down the hall. She still wore the outfit she was kidnapped in, waded through a jungle in, was detained in, and was kidnapped again in. Her tunic is splotched with stains. Her shoes want someone to just bury them already. What Ippa would give to be clean and settled at a reading desk.

"Do you have a gun or something?" Ippa choked out in between gasps.

Adam turned to her. "Gods, no. It's not like I had time to prepare for this. A couple of hours ago I was on a station on our moon. I stole a ship—"

"The rest of the galaxy calls them spacecrafts."

"—and no one knows I'm here."

"What the crisp?" They were going to die. Things couldn't get any worse than being inside an actual Akar slaver and having no weapon and no way out and especially with this stupid boy. Her steps slowed. "You have to have *something* planned! Did you not run a Dempsey Situation Analysis at any stage along the way?"

"Shh!" he hissed. "Stop groaning. Someone's going to hear us."

At the corner, Adam yanked Ippa's arm, and she had no choice but to follow him into a closet. A clean soft floral scent hung in the air. Rows of white linens and pale green soaps lined the shelves like some kind of ordinary hotel supply closet, a hotel that was prepared to sell the people staying in its rooms at any moment.

"What are we doing in here?" Ippa demanded. "We need to keep moving."

"Shut up, let me think. Think, think, think."

"Seriously, Adam?" *He* was the one in need of a thought prioritization exam.

But he seemed to not hear her. He was pulling things off the shelves. A bin for dirty linens stood in one corner. He pulled out a light-colored jacket with a purple smear along one breast pocket. "Put this coat on. You clearly aren't going to blend in in whatever that is you're wearing."

"It's not exactly like I had a choice. You don't know the things I would do for a new pair of shoes."

Ippa snatched the jacket out of Adam's hand and wrinkled her nose. The coat smelled faintly of cleaner and someone's lunch. Despite that, Ippa pulled it on and tied a green sash around her middle. She'd already started to categorize the types of uniforms and their corresponding positions on board, but she didn't recognize this one. A dark green insignia stood out on the pocket opposite the stain.

She froze. Muffled voices and footsteps carried from the outside corridor. They were growing nearer and Ippa could tell it was a man and a woman, bantering rather than bickering, but Ippa couldn't hear enough specifics to know what about. The steps stopped outside the door and Ippa looked up in shock, terrified, when Adam lunged at her.

He pressed his lips to hers. He tasted like chips and smelled like sweat, but he was warm. Ippa's body went stiff and she almost pulled away, then realized what was happening. He tucked a hand into the small of her back and pulled her close and while it assumed way too much, it was also kind of nice?

When they broke for air, the two workers were watching them, door open.

"Oh. Sorry," the woman said, covering her smile with a pale pink fist.

The other gave Ippa a thumbs-up and they shut the door, somewhat reluctantly.

Ippa's head was spinning when she turned back to Adam. "Heh, uh, good thinking."

"I am *so* sorry," he whispered. "I couldn't think of anything else to do."

Ippa pushed her feelings down, the way she would push panic down during exams. "It made them leave us alone. But what are we going to do?"

"I have to find Yaniqui. I can't leave without her. If you need to go your own way, I understand. Once I do get her, all I know is we have to steal a ship and hightail it back to Earth."

"Right"—Ippa covertly wiped her mouth—"I don't think Akar will land on Earth without government permission. They break just the right amount of laws to keep going." She swallowed. "I'll come with you. But my hair's a risk. If they put it out among the staff that they're looking for a woman with bright blue hair, then we'll both get caught."

They spent a minute wrapping Ippa's hair in a contrived head wrap. Ippa flung her head back, right into Adam's nose.

"Ouch! Hold still. I'm *trying* to help you."

"I don't need your help!" Ippa tucked one end of the fabric.

Footsteps approached the door. They looked at each other with wild eyes as the door knob turned. Ippa lunged for Adam this time. She had to stand on her toes to pull his head down to hers—he really was taller than she was—and kissed him. She broke away abruptly and turned to the door. "Excuse me," she said as snottily as she could manage to the person standing in the bright doorway. "Can't you see we're in the middle of something?"

"Adam?"

Adam looked in horror at the man with dark hair. "Hloban? Wow, I'm glad to see you. Uh, this is Ippa. We're helping her escape too."

Hloban looked completely nonplussed.

"He's Wea Saavian too," Adam explained, then turned back to Hloban. "How did you know to open the closet?"

Hloban fought back a smile. "I passed a woman in the

hall talking to her friend. She mentioned wanting to, um, wreck, a guy she saw in a closet. Run her fingers through your black hair. Then I heard your shout."

Ippa pushed Hloban aside and decided it was better to not address what had just happened. "Three of us will seem more natural than each of us sneaking around on our own. Let's go," she said, resisting the impulse to look back at Adam. She set off down the plush hallway in her dirty shoes.

Chapter 33

Lozen
The Akar Provenance

That fucker.

Lozen watched D-68 disappear through the sliding metal door with the orange bejeweled jerk. Gone were her thoughts of worry that he was suffering from sensitivity to the metal, her wonder if he was enjoying the translation device, and the overall anxiety that she felt to take care of him. She was pissed he left her there.

Women jostled her on both sides and though she was getting used to the smell of bodies in a captive space, it still threatened to smother her.

The voices in the room roiled in a general rumble so that it took a moment to realize someone was directly addressing her. Someone shrilled into her left ear fighting to be heard. "Why did they bring you in by yourself?"

Lozen couldn't answer. She was fighting hard to hold her insides together. She didn't want to cry, *really* didn't want to cry, but she was absolutely going to.

She pushed away from the locked metal door and the Earthling women. The noise was atrocious, like some kind of colony of birds that all decided screech at the same time. Outside their cage was another captive space full of men. Some stood in small groups arguing, some crouched on the floor in despair.

She wondered how they went to the bathroom, how women dealt with their periods, what did they do when it was time to sleep? Lozen didn't want to be around to find out. She kept moving.

Outside the initial throng of people that had fought their way closest to the locked door, there was a little more space. Lozen slipped between two women, one in a bubblegum pink dress and the other in a denim jumpsuit.

"—I was only there for you!"

"—I didn't ask you to come!"

She let their fight go in one ear and out the other.

A row of open-door closets emitting a terrific stench answered one of Lozen's questions.

Oh gods, if only she would be rescued before it came to that.

"Lozen!" A wall slammed into her and she toppled over. Her hand splashed in something wet that she cringed away from.

"M-monte?" Lozen sat up and peered at her best friend. Her face crumpled. "I thought I'd never see you again."

"No, Lozen," Monte wailed over the top of her. "The only thing I was still hoping was that you wouldn't be taken."

A pair of hands yanked Lozen up, not unkindly.

"So, you're here too. Any idea what the fuck's going on?" After hours in the communal holdings, Charla looked only slightly more put together than Monte, but a thousand times more pissed off. As if she couldn't believe anyone would dare lay hands on her and it was only by her grace they hadn't been smote yet. She asked, "Who was that who brought you in?"

Lozen took a deep breath. Her worries seemed so small—no, not her worries, her efforts to keep herself and Monte friends. The lies she told to get by. The hope she had to go to the capital and get her surgery. She had put herself out there to help D-68 when no one else would and look where that had landed her.

She explained as well as she could what she hadn't been telling her best friend the past few months. Monte punched Lozen in the arm hard, but Charla only asked more questions. When they exhausted Charla's deep train of thought, it was Lozen's turn.

"But what happened to you two? Did Leggs get you?"

Charla shrugged. "I was in the forest and someone passed around a joint. I woke up in a warehouse with the others from that night, this plastic thing wrapped over my hands, everyone screaming."

A few other women around them shared similar stories. One woman said she was held captive on Earth for days, watching them bring new unconscious bodies in. It was only in the past twelve hours that they were loaded up into a craft and brought here.

"So, Leggs must have known Akar was coming here. He stored up Earthlings to sell."

Monte rubbed her nose, leaving behind a layer of dirt. "Why is this Leggs doing this?"

"He hates Earthlings. I think he hates all humanoids but especially Earthlings. I don't know what he's doing with the money, if he's keeping it, funneling it out of the Catchment, or what."

"That fuckin nonbeing," a woman muttered.

"I'm not making excuses for what he did, but he is—was—an endangered species. Earth was supposed to be his new home and instead he was stuck in the Catchment. It's bad enough being born there, but I can't imagine coming as a refugee looking for a new life and then being thrown in there." Lozen didn't have any sympathy for him, but she tried to think of what Mama Teresa said. How he had been on Earth for two decades. Trapped in the Catchment that whole time. Growing more and more angry.

Charla bristled. "No, it's fucked up. He could have worked like us to make it better."

"Yeah, it is fucked up," one of the Karmas said.

The conversation fizzled.

"So, what do we do?" Monte finally asked.

Lozen put her hands around her neck. They felt cold. She was thirsty but kinda had to pee. She couldn't think of any of that. "I think that all depends on my friend D-68."

Chapter 34

Yaniqui
The Akar Provenance

Yaniqui lay on her back. The raised cot was stiff like an impersonal medical bed, plastic and sterile, ready to be wiped down for the next product. Straps wrapped her shoulders, knees, ankles, and wrists. Another silencer covered her lower face. She wanted to scream and rage and burn the place down, but just as much, she was mourning the last chance she had at a good life.

She should have asked Waquas to leave Earth with her.

Even if she managed to escape, the threat of Akar and anyone else who wanted to use her would continue her entire life. Did that mean it was better to be sold and be done with it all? Perhaps. But what Yaniqui didn't know was if she was going to be sold as a slave to the health care industry or as brood wife or if she would be dissected until her body gave up its secrets of self-healing. She wondered if Maemi had decided it was worth her safety to negotiate with the terrible forces around her.

The door opened and Yaniqui flinched when she heard voices. There was nothing more claustrophobic than the approach of strangers when one is unable to move.

Then she opened her eyes wide. It was Hloban. She made a noise in her throat but couldn't speak. Her heart broke. How did Hloban get on the *Provanance*? Did they have Obani? Adam and his dad too?

"Yaniqui, I'm so sorry. You deserve so much more than this—"

Someone forced a silencer over his head and securely around his throat. They heaved him up on another ledge and strapped him to the surface. His hands were already bound and they made quick work of his legs and torso. Hloban thrashed and screamed in his throat, but there was nothing that he could do to stop his fate.

Tears leaked out of the corners of Yaniqui's eyes. They could keep her from moving and speaking, but they couldn't keep her from expressing her grief. She hated this moment of her life more than anything else she had been through so far. She would have thought her original capture and separation from Maemi would have been it. Or learning Hloban had replaced her. Or being captured by Ippa's look-alike.

Instead of expanding her capacity for endurance, it seemed like her capacity for hatred was the thing that grew. She wasn't free. She had no future. But she could hate more than ever before.

Officials and staff went in and out of the room. She felt someone prick her foot and take her blood. She assumed the same was being done to Hloban next to her.

Wouldn't they have brought in Adam, Keyad, and Obani if they captured them as well? Maybe Akar didn't know about them. Maybe the small bright spot in this was that some would survive. The Wea Saavian people, her history and culture, the fate of them all, would survive in someone.

A man leaned over her and checked her eyes with some sensor. The light made her blink hard. She vaguely wondered if her eyes were dilated, or what he was checking for. Could they control her eyes? Would they take that freedom from her too?

Yaniqui looked up and into the gaze of the man examining her and saw black eyes, so black they were almost endless. Yaniqui shuddered in her binds, but no one noticed.

It was Adam. He was the doctor. Yaniqui's brain dreamily wondered if it was delusional.

No. Adam was there.

Adam turned away, his face partly obscured by a medical wrap in Akarian green, but she was sure it was him. Yaniqui looked out of the corner of her eye to see if Hloban noticed, but she couldn't see his face.

Yaniqui let out a gasp no one heard when the room shook and then settled into an imperceptible hum. It was familiar. The feel of an immense craft readying itself to leave. Very soon.

Amid the casual busyness of their work, Adam slipped an immobilizer into someone's stomach and the person fell hard to the floor. Yaniqui thrashed, but she couldn't do anything to help but add to the confusion as Adam struck another member of Akar's staff.

Someone punched Adam in the gut and he doubled over and lunged at the person's legs. Then she couldn't see what was happening. Her friend disappeared from view.

Someone scrambled at Yaniqui's locked hands and she panicked until she saw it was Waquas. She had never felt so much relief in her life. Yaniqui was able to sit up again shakily, breathing heavy. Ippa was at Hloban's side, releasing him as well.

Waquas spoke rapidly, "We need to go. Keyad and Amanda rushed the control room to buy us time. Defenses will be high there and I don't know if they'll be successful. We have to get you off this craft."

Yaniqui was up and moving, but Waquas pulled her even more quickly out the door. She struggled to catch up, to understand how the group had come to be there together—and Amanda? Her relief was short-lived as she considered how many people had again put themselves at risk for her, and how to get everyone off the *Provenance*, free and alive.

Blood streamed from a cut on Adam's head, but it was healing already. He had a stolen blaster in his hands. Adam clasped Hloban's shoulder haphazardly as they ran. "Thanks for the distraction, man."

"No problem," Hloban said though his tone said otherwise. "Next time, you can get caught."

A whirling warning system crashed down around them, alerting everyone that Yaniqui, the last of the Wea Saavians, was escaping captivity. Two workers ran across the hall and Yaniqui struggled to keep from shrieking.

The craft shuddered again, jolting the entire group left and right. It wasn't the powerful pull of departure. It was something else. Something with chaos at its root. Yaniqui was certain she could smell smoke.

"Waquas, where are we going?"

"The docking bay—it's our only shot. The government cruiser Adam came in on is there. It should still recognize his bioprofile. We rammed the *Caneille*, so we can't take that anymore. They wouldn't give us entry. They were leaving. Keyad and I didn't have any other choice. But we need to get off before they really do leave."

Her breath came fast, but Yaniqui didn't dare stop—

No. She had to turn around.

Yaniqui ground her feet. Her head was finally clear. "We have to go this way."

Hloban crashed into her and Waquas pulled on her arm to right her.

"The main cells are down below."

"Yani, we don't have time to talk," Adam yelled, glancing behind him.

"You don't understand. There are people down there. Children. We can't leave them."

Everyone in the group looked at each other, fear on every face.

"We can't save them all," Waquas said.

"We have to try. This is what I should have done before. Instead, I went with the dŏsvengar and they kept cycling through people. Those people need help and they can help us take the craft." No one responded. "We're not going to be able to do it alone. It's the only way we're going to get Keyad and Amanda back—with everyone's help."

Chapter 35

Adam

The Akar Provenance

Adam stared at Yaniqui as she pulled out of Waquas's arms and ran down the hall, not checking to see if they followed despite the fact that she was the one without any weapons. Ippa and Waquas followed her right away, and Adam and Hloban exchanged a brief glance that said okay-this-is-what-we're-fucking-doing-now.

A slender guard stepped into the hallway, a furred tail flicking behind him, a painful look on his face despite the fact he was the one aiming the gun. Waquas sped up and slid into his feet. They grappled. Waquas got the gun from his hands and hit him over the head. That was two guns now. Adam tightened his grip and wondered if he was really the best one to hold it. He'd never even been in a fight until that day!

They ran through two corridors and jumped down a service stairway—they didn't dare take any transporters for fear of being locked in—then through a door where a guard in dark green appeared. She clicked her trigger and looked confused when nothing happened. Adam shot back on instinct. She slammed into the wall and dropped the blaster. Hloban picked it up and the group kept moving.

But Adam stayed, staring at the woman he shot. He couldn't help imagining his own mother, lying on the ground, dying somewhere on this ship. He bent and put his hand on her abdomen where her uniform was turning black with blood. His hands shook as they warmed. He tried to give enough to staunch the bleeding and then Ippa was there, grabbing his arm and pulling him ahead.

Through the door, things were immediately different. The pleasant veneer of sales was gone. Even the factory aesthetic of the lower hallways was absent. Here, the walls and floors were bare bones. Inside a gigantic cell were the live bodies of a hundred or more beings. Beyond that was another cell. And another cell. And another.

Looking closer, Adam realized one cell housed men and boys. A cell of animoids. Two cells of girls and women. Their fate was common sex trafficking, organ harvesting, and domestic slavery. They were the collateral that the company picked up along the way with larger purchases and sale deliveries.

They screamed.

Yaniqui reached for a dead guard's keys. Adam didn't have the strength to wonder who shot him.

Waquas caught her arm. "Yani, you don't understand.

You don't know who these people are. You want to save them, but some of them are criminals. Some of them would trade places with the guards and staff here in an instant if it meant food and water."

"We can't leave them here."

"Sometimes releasing someone isn't enough to save them. You need to be able to protect them and give them their life back. Yani, I'll help you, but please don't let them out yet."

Adam heard the roar of a man cursing and swearing at Waquas—the one who would keep them locked away.

Hloban tried. "Yani, this is it. We came to save you. And now we need to go."

A shadow passed over her face. Adam knew she was struggling with what was right and what was safe because he was too. "If I was worth saving, I'm worth following. This is what we're doing. This is what will get us out of here."

"Let us out," someone screamed.

Different tongues babbled and it blurred together in Adam's head.

Adam saw Ippa turn when a voice caught her attention.

"Hey, it's me! Lozen, from the Catchment. You know, the Shiranhole?"

Ippa closed the distance to the bars.

"Why didn't you ever come back?" the woman with the single black braid asked. Adam noted her top lip was misshapen and he looked back up to her eyes, uncertain if he should cover his response.

"Fuck that," a woman next to her snarled. "Get us out of here.

"Of course, I remember you," Ippa whispered. She turned to the rest. "They'll help us." She turned to Lozen and the others from the Catchment, and asked, "Won't you?"

Inside, they all looked to a tall, fierce woman. "That must be why we're here," she said.

Waquas looked at Yaniqui and then took the keys and opened the door. Lozen and a handful of Earthlings made their way through the clear path and stepped outside.

The door was still open. The women stood back, afraid of freedom.

Yaniqui walked to the door and gently pushed Waquas away. "Is there anyone else who will fight with us?"

One more came. Two. Four. The women took a great step forward, pushing children back with the older girls and the grandmothers. A mother hugged her young child and kissed her head goodbye. A woman pulled a simple necklace of twine off her neck and placed it on her daughter or niece or sister or beloved. They knew what this meant. That a chance at freedom meant an acceptance of death.

The intimidating women gave directions to those that remained with the children. Others lined up, gravely quiet next to one another, arms wrapped around friends, a burly woman to the side stretching her arms in preparation. Waquas unlocked another door and women flowed out. Adam wondered why the guards hadn't come yet, if they knew what was happening inside the chamber. With the women alone, they had a small army.

Adam followed Yaniqui to the metal bars separating a huge group of men. One of the men in front shouted to be heard over the din, "I'll fight too. I need to protect her." A woman came and grasped her partner through the bars. Adam noticed they each had a black circle with something inside it tattooed on the backs of their hands.

Charla came close. "Are you sure about this, healing girl? There are good men and good women and bad of both. But a few bad men could ruin our chances."

Yaniqui's voice dropped. "We need help."

The men pushed and shoved as they mirrored Yaniqui's movements.

"We don't have time for this," Adam shouted at them. "Form a line so no one gets crushed." He had no idea if anyone could hear him, but Waquas unlocked the door and the first four came cautiously to waiting family members before Charla pushed it shut.

"Give me the keys," she demanded.

"No!" A black-bearded man rushed the door and tried to slam it open. Adam saw the desperate fear on his face and that was all it took, as men pushed at each other to get out. A woman tore at Charla's back, trying to dislodge her from blocking the way.

Adam and Waquas pushed together, the door heavy under their hands, trying to assure there wasn't a stampede. Someone ground their fingers into Adam's forearms, their fingernails sharp.

"Move out of the way," Yaniqui commanded Charla. "We have work to do. Together. Adam, Waquas, move out of the way."

There was a squash as the crowd pushed for the door that was only as wide as three men, but slowly the panic settled to purposeful urgency. Before even most of the humanoid men were out, Yaniqui went to the other cage.

"The men, okay, but you cannot let these beasts out of their cage." Charla scowled at Yaniqui's ignorance.

Someone moved at Adam's elbow. He looked up and stepped back, stumbling over his own feet. The someone was an immense rust-colored creature. Adam's first terrifying thought was this was a guard sent in by Akar, but the woman called Lozen was at his side. Others shrank out of the being's path. Adam took a few more steps back himself, but the creature only flipped a switch. Buzzing that Adam hadn't even recognized until then shut off. It took him a moment to realize the last cage had been electrified.

The large animoid tore the iron door from its hinges. A black panther prowled out, assessing the mass of humans. It skirted to the side to watch. Two more animoids followed, assessing the group of humanoids, especially Charla. Others followed, most of them bipedal. No one wanted to be there, no one wanted to be working together, but it was all they had.

"We're going to the bridge," Hloban spoke loudly over the chatter, his voice resonating off the walls of the immense space. "Is anyone here a pilot?"

Two raised their hands, a man and a woman.

"Good. We're not going to fly the craft. Just hold it where it is until we have the Akar Enterprises workers secured and we can get support from Earth's government— the planet we're currently at."

"What are we going to do with Akar?" someone yelled out.

"In the cells. We'll put them in the cells."

There was a dark murmur Adam didn't like, a growl

of retribution.

Yaniqui said, "Safely. They're just like us. Some of us might have been turned into them by Akar."

Waquas spoke and the crowd quieted down to hear him as he gave directions to the control room. He also split up two mixed groups of beings to go the opposite ways and secure the two wings of the ship.

It was time to go. Adam fought hard to keep from shaking as he caught Yaniqui's eye.

"No dŏsvengar this time." Her voice cracked.

"And I thought that would be the worst thing we could ever come up against." Adam tried to smile but knew it was a grimace. He wanted to find his parents and take them far, far away from this entire mess. But he agreed with Yaniqui. If they didn't stop it, it would always be there, waiting to envelop them.

He saw Yaniqui startle as she realized everyone was looking at her. They were waiting for her to lead them out.

The guard's body stood in her way. She walked across it, stepping over it without looking at it. Charla took a spot immediately behind her on her left and scanned her gaze across the fighters. Yaniqui wrenched the door open.

Chapter 36

D-68

The Akar Provenance

D-68 heard a clamor coming from the massive room. When the ship fired its engines, D-68 flashed back to when the Earthlings' ship took him from his planet. He was shocked to be filled with memories of a time that had previously felt so distant. He had carried only the barest picture in mind of his partner and their hamlet.

Then he was on his knees, heaving.

The official who had been leading him bent over, uncertain if she should touch him. "Fra, are you okay? It's the engines warming up. If you want your payment, you'll have to go retrieve those other bodies now."

D-68's eyes narrowed and he threw himself into the woman. She cared not for the humanoids and animoids that her company bought and moved. He felt her bones snap beneath his fingers. He felt revulsion. A strangled noise came out of her, and then it was quiet. D-68 struggled to rise. He looked down at her mangled body, the crusts of orange crystal lay scattered upon her like dust. Self-hatred welled inside him. He had played a role in all of this. He told himself it was fine to steal the Earthlings because they were both lesser and crueler than he was.

A surprised shout came from behind him and he leaped forward.

"Calling security to X254—"

The voice faded behind him as he made his way back through the maze of tunnels, simple for one who could navigate vast cave systems in the dark. He would get back to Lozen and take her and her friends home. As he said he would. There was no hope for him to return home. He knew that now.

When he arrived, clusters of beings poured out of the giant cells. He saw easily above their heads but in the mess of flesh-toned, hairless faces, only the animoids stood out.

Then suddenly his one was in front of him.

"You're okay?" D-68 said. The translator was long dropped. He sounded like himself, but that didn't explain why he felt so different.

Lozen opened her mouth to reply but nothing came out. Instead, she flung her arms around him. She only came up to D-68's lowest chest platelets and her arms felt no stronger than a slender new shoot of a tree branch.

He worried he might break her even as he placed his own taloned-hands gently on her back. Lozen looked up at him and he shifted the position of his hands to allow her to tilt back.

"You came." Lozen gave a half laugh. "I thought you would but I—"

"You worried?" he said. "You doubted we are friends?"

She nodded sadly.

"I would not leave you here." He barred his teeth at the immense metal cell. He was overcome with the urge to dismantle it, tear it down and spread the pieces in the abyss of space.

His friend turned at the approach of another woman.

"D-68 this is Monte; Monte, this is my friend, D-68."

After spending so much time with Lozen, she looked odd. The fibers of her head only came down to her neck. In the enormity of the room, full of humanoid smells, hers was just one more, but D-68 still had to force himself not to draw back.

"Yeah," the friend of Lozen drawled, looking at his platelets and nasal pad warily. "I don't know if you guys are aware, but we're about to be forced to fight for our lives, so I'd, you know, get ready or something."

Chapter 37

Hloban
The Akar Provenance

The hallway was suspiciously deserted. The alarm still rang. It made it hard to think.

Yaniqui moved forward, a mass of eager people behind her. Hloban looked back after several strides and saw the two groups moving away in the opposite direction as Waquas had directed them. They moved quietly, but the pound of feet was evident. Hloban had offered his gun to one of the other groups. Now they only had one and he wondered what they were going to do. Numbers wouldn't do shit against a small army of trained guards.

A shot rang behind them. Another shot. The air smelled like ozone and Hloban felt his hair stand up. Screams came from the back of the crowd and in a moment, it turned from a rebel army to a horde of pinned animals. Those in back ran faster to escape the running, pushing, and tripping over each other. Hloban looked over his shoulder but could only see the fearful faces behind him. They had to do something fast, or they'd all be overtaken soon.

"They're going to trap us," he yelled at Yaniqui and Waquas. "We need to split up from the others."

"But—"

Hloban pulled on Yaniqui's arm so much it had to hurt. They crashed around a corner into another hall. Some people kept running in the chaos, others poured behind them into the hall, filling it. A shot fired close by.

"This way," a short man called. "I worked for Akar." He waved his hands in a panic, afraid they would draw the wrong conclusions. "I was stealing to support my family back home. I'd been—well, just come on. I know where an override control panel is. You want to get to the control bay, right? This way."

The group hustled around two more corners then up a flight of stairs, then down two more hallways. Workers in various green uniforms saw them coming and disappeared into locked rooms or down the opposite hall. Hloban wondered how many wounded they were leaving behind. And why weren't the guards heading them off? He could see the security cameras. Akar knew exactly where they were.

They scaled a massive twist of stairs up too many flights for Hloban to count. His heart pounded and his mouth was dry.

At a set of doors, the man removed the cover from a sensor panel and pulled wires apart. The hydraulic door went slack and Hloban helped pull it apart manually. Inside, the man flicked a hand in front of a screen and entered a code. The lights flickered and then went off. A gun fired in the distance, then faltered.

In the quiet, Hloban could hear the escapees breaking off handles and glass, anything that could be used as a weapon. He thought Yaniqui was still near him but had no idea where Adam was.

"Are you sure you want to go to the control room?" the man whispered.

Hloban could nearly hear the perspiration in his voice.

"It's the only way we'll take the craft," Yaniqui said.

The lights flicked on and then off, and the alarm cut out. Hloban's ears rang with the silence.

The ex-employee sighed. "If you really want to go, follow me. The dark will give us cover at least."

Hloban moved as quietly as he could with the others. A round of gunfire popped off in the near distance. Around them was stark silence. Hloban wondered where Loera and Obani had gone. And, assuming he survived, if she'd ever talk to him again.

"This is it," the man whispered. "Right ahead is a set of doors. I can spring them for you, but there's no way I'm going in there." He paused. "I'm sorry."

"I'll go in," Hloban murmured.

"No, we do this together," Yaniqui insisted.

"You're too important. You don't think I've continually risked my life to let you get captured again? Why do you think they haven't overridden the lights yet and put them back on? The control room can undo anything a maintenance area has access to. I think they want to let us do what we think we need to do. Once you and I and…well, once we're taken, they'll mow through the rest of the ship, killing indiscriminately. We can't let you get captured."

"Hloban, I said we go in together."

"You're already here," a clear high voice came and the lights turned on.

Chapter 38

Nica
The Akar Provenance

Nica ran along the carpeted halls, passing door after door after door. She would be caught in moments by a guard in a dark green uniform, collapse when they dug a charger into her gut, and dragged across the floor back to her locked room.

Instead, she kept running. The alarm had blessedly stopped, but she was certain the chaos hadn't. Savini had told her they were at Earth when he brought her a cup of some sweet light-colored liquor in a crystal tumbler an hour previous. He casually stated that they had recaptured her daughter.

"Can I see her?" Nica had asked.

Savini shook his head. "That won't be allowed."

Nica set the glass down without sipping it and willed her hands to hold steady. "Why not? And by whom? It seems to me you run most everything on this craft." She wasn't trying to flatter him. It was true.

"You know," Savini said conversationally, "the more I rise within the ranks of Akar, the more uncertain I am of who is in charge here. Certainly, I don't feel like I have any more control than previously. I wish I hadn't thought ambition would be the best way to preserve my life." He took a drink. "It would be nice to be a cook. Left alone in the kitchens. Perhaps we would have met. I could have rescued you."

Nica eyed him. "Gods, Savini, are you drunk?"

He frowned carefully. Dissatisfaction set upon his face like smiles do most men. It made him something more.

"Can I not be contemplative without being accused of being a drunkard?"

Nica threw a hand out to the side impatiently. "Are you going to let me see my daughter or not?"

It was silent.

"Not." He took a deep breath. "That's what I came to tell you. You won't see me again. I know you won't want to. I thought, well, it doesn't matter. Have a nice life, Nica."

But that was three dead guards ago. And this was now.

Chapter 39

Yaniqui
The Akar Provenance

It was true. They were in the brain and heart of the ship. Screens, computers, and holos flickered to life. The overhead lights flashed at full force. With the returning machine hum, Yaniqui realized suddenly how quiet everything had been before.

It had all been turned off. That's why they didn't see any blinking lights or whirling servers. It had all been turned off to lure them in. Even the oxygenator. It was hot in the room, but now a vent began filtering in breathable air. They were on a craft as good as dead. The realization of the dangerous nature of the situation came flooding into Yaniqui's head. If they had stormed the area and killed the wrong person, hit the wrong equipment, would they have been able to turn the craft back on in the dark?

But it had been worth the risk to Akar. Guards surrounded them. A scatting of Akar employees stood behind and around Savini. The man who had helped them reach the control bay left Yaniqui's group and went to stand by his coworkers. No shame on his face.

Charla snarled.

"That man"—Savini pointed at Adam—"needs to put his gun down and then you all will be taken back into captivity, but you will be alive. If you continue to fight, you will merely die."

Yaniqui's legs were about to give out, but Mr. Savini was as unruffled as ever. *This isn't the first uprising he's seen.*

Savini nodded at floor-to-ceiling frosted glass windows. "Your mother's in there, Yaniqui. Quell your friends and I'll let you see her one last time."

"M-maemi's here?" she stuttered.

An immense thud came from a locked side door. Everyone, foe and friend alike, turned to look at the door. The thud came again, the door bowing slightly this time. Savini motioned to a group of three guards and they raised their weapons. The thud turned into a powerful, sharp crack. There was a pause.

Yaniqui looked at Savini who looked back at her. It was uncanny how she saw her own confusion reflected in his face. Neither was sure who this was good for.

The door burst out of its frame, flew across the room, and onto a console. Someone shrieked as the screens shattered. An immense shelled animoid led the charge through the broken, gaping doorway. D-68 grabbed a guard by the arm and swung them into a wall where they settled at the base, crumpled. Then, the hoard was upon them. Someone grabbed Yaniqui and pulled her back as humanoids and animoids from both sides fled the stampede. Guns went off and captives threw themselves at anyone in a green uniform.

Hloban stepped in front of Yaniqui.

"We have to get to Maemi," she shouted.

A guard in body armor fell at their feet after being thrown across a bay of computers. Hloban pushed Yaniqui toward the frosted glass windows. Someone jerked on the back of her shirt collar, and she cried out when her hair was pulled. A series of blasters went off, but Yaniqui couldn't even spare the time to look where the shooting was. A dog-sized animoid with yellow and black stripes wrested Hloban to the ground and bit at his face, Hloban straining to hold him off. Yaniqui kicked at the being but was manhandled into turning around and facing a guard with auburn hair in a tight bun who was trying to put manacles on Yaniqui's hands.

Yaniqui lunged away and fell to the ground, anything to get closer to Maemi. The woman pulled at Yaniqui's legs as she tried to claw forward. There was a thunder of people all around her and someone pulled the guard off. Yaniqui thrust herself forward on her forearms. She was paces away from the frosted glass when a stray bullet shattered it.

She cried out.

There was nothing inside.

Nothing inside, but the room had gone quiet and Yaniqui couldn't understand why. She turned slowly and made her way in a squat, crouching behind a desk. The huge alien who had broken the door down lay on the ground. Clear blood dribbled from his chest, his armor cracked deep. His muscles and limbs were flaccid. Lozen fell to his side with a scream.

He wasn't the only casualty. Guards and captured beings lay mangled among each other on the floor. The room smelled of sweat and bodies. She glimpsed a dead man with a melted face before she saw what was in Savini's arms.

Maemi. Yaniqui gaped and Maemi, fingers digging into Savini's forearm, looked at her desperately.

Savini held a gun to her head, his other hand wrapped around her mouth.

"Yaniqui, you are *very* valuable. I would like very much to capture you alive. You've nearly escaped twice, but you can't hope to stay free." Perspiration lined his forehead. There was a wild look in his eyes. "Your arrogance has caused all of this. This is *your* doing."

Yaniqui looked in the eyes of the shooters and saw no reluctance. They asked no questions, encapsulated by the large system that protected them. And they needed protection. As long as there was life in the universe, there was risk.

"Put the blaster down, boy."

Yaniqui looked at Adam out of the corner of her eye and shook her head. That would be the end of everything.

"There's always a consequence to our actions, Yaniqui."

Yaniqui took a step forward, hands out. "Please, don't hurt my maemi."

Savini nodded. "There's no need for her to get hurt."

She took another step. There was no more running away. No more fighting. She just had to reach her mother.

She was almost to him. "All I want is to be with my mom."

Hloban's voice came from behind her. "Yani, don't do this," he pleaded.

Savini removed the gun from Nica's temple to train it on her, the one he didn't love.

Yaniqui charged. Genuine surprise crossed Savini's face. He fired instinctively. A bang echoed in Yaniqui's ears. Maemi bit Savini.

Searing energy tore through her right arm. Blood capillaries burst. Her humerus shattered. She screamed and couldn't keep her feet under her.

She was close. So goddammed close. She fell to her knees and reached out her left hand, shaking with all the pain of death but none of the release. She gasped as her hand closed on his ankle, found skin. Her body hummed, ready to heal, but instead she turned to her anger and fear and dread. She took all the good in her, all her ability to knit bone, smooth tendons, and stimulate cells, all her body's willing eagerness to heal her own body and forced it to Savini and exploded his limb. Blood splattered. A bone shard hit her cheek.

The room broke into pandemonium. She heard fighting and shooting behind her but couldn't see anything. Her body was agony. Her senses were failing. She was dying.

She was really dying.

All her power went to destroy her enemy. An action that took away all hope for her own physical redemption.

She had nothing left to save herself with. Blood rushed from her wound. Her body struggled to right itself, put itself back together, but she was growing colder by the minute. Everything was pain.

Yaniqui called out. It was less than a whisper. A plea dying on her very lips.

A hand grasped her hand. Yaniqui didn't feel it. She saw with bleary, fading eyes. That limb was dead and she was next. A hand grasped the base of her neck. It was Adam. Her friend had come, but he couldn't heal her. She was going to die.

Even as her mind was going dark, her thoughts raced. This couldn't be. And yet she had acted. And her actions had consequences.

She wished she was on the beach with Waquas, the glow of a sunset warming them; not as she was, going cold as her own life set. She should have kept walking on the beach that night and never gone back.

"No, Yani," Maemi was pleading. She had made it to her daughter's side. Her hands shook as she tried to find a spot on her daughter's body that she could heal and save her, but it was too late, Maemi was too overdrawn and Yaniqui was too damaged.

Maemi had come too late.

And then she saw why.

D-68 rampaged the room, smashing a guard against the wall and swiping away a gun that dared turn on him. The sheen of blood dried across his torso. The tide had turned when Maemi healed him.

"Oh, Yani, I'm so sorry. I'm so, so sorry." Maemi sobbed, holding her daughter tight against her. She wrapped her hands around the upper part of Yaniqui's arm, trying to pinch off the arteries, even as her daughter bled out. "No, Yani… Someone help me, please help me—"

Yaniqui breathed slowly but deeply. She had made it back to her maemi.

She had done that at least.

Two Months Later

Chapter 40

Lozen & D-68
The Winslow Space-Earth Station

The wind ripped at her hair as Lozen watched the ship ready on the asphalt.

It was a cold fall, but Lozen had spent much of it indoors at her warm apartment that had a tea and hot cocoa dispenser in the side of the fridge. She didn't feel weather the way she used to at the Catchment. Inside most of the time, she could ignore the fall mood swings between unbearably hot and early snows.

She spent the rest of her time talking in meetings with members of the GIA, rehashing every single moment of her time on the outskirts of the Karmas and working with the agents. At D-68's judicial court days, she spoke venomously against the theft of his life and detailed the difference he made in saving her life and the lives of her friends on the Akar Enterprises ship. She always circled back to Leggs. He was the instigator. She wanted him convicted, but he was missing from the Catchment. Lozen was determined there be enough testimony against him for when or if he was caught. Velazquez had a much more satisfactory ending: a jail sentence. Lozen went back to the Catchment only once. She gave most of her stuff to Marcie's family and said goodbye to Monte, unsure when they would meet again.

Next to her was D-68. He was smaller than when she first saw him, hiding in the forest. He was missing several large platelets, but more than that, he was slowly wasting away. The equivalent food sources on Earth were missing something he needed. He ate enough to keep from dying but not enough to thrive.

He would get on the ship with the promise of home, but not with orders for humans to evacuate his planet or refrain from mining its resources. The taste still felt sour in her mouth. Lozen knew what people could do when they came to your land and stayed.

Even after all this time, D-68's face was unreadable. Everyone preparing the ship gave D-68 a wide berth. He would sleep in confined quarters but have access to water and supplies. Not quite jailed but not trusted either.

When it was time for him to board, Lozen turned toward him. "D-68…"

She didn't know how to say goodbye. He had saved her life, everyone's lives. Thanks to him, Monte, Charla, Jerramy, and the others would, if not prosper, survive alongside their families in the Catchment rather than die alone on a foreign planet earlier than they should.

"Qoan."

"What?"

"Qoan."

"Your name?" Lozen tried "Koawn?"

"Qoan, friend of Lozen." He lay a collection of talons on Lozen's shoulder.

Tears sprang to her eyes.

"Here." He pulled from a small pocket of skin the rose-colored stone and forced it into her hands.

Lozen reached deep into her own pocket and pulled out a flat disc. It was a tiny hologram and the first nonessential item she bought with her stipend once she realized D-68—Qoan—was really going to make it home. She had uploaded a graphic of herself and a graphic of the lake her ancestors once thrived on. Finally, a graphic she surreptitiously copied from an online news outlet that showed the group of Earthlings, foreign humanoids, and animoids, that took down an Akarian ship, Qoan, on one end. He took the disc gingerly between his digits.

"I'll miss you," she said.

"Care," he said simply.

Qoan walked toward the ship and grasped the metal tract to pull himself inside without looking back.

Lozen let out a breath.

Now she just had herself to worry about.

Lozen walked away from the ship. In one of the doorways of the station, she saw a huge, hairy animoid watching the ship Qoan boarded. Once, he would have terrified her, but after Qoan, he was simply another being. She recognized Jeb as one of the witnesses during Qoan's trial. He locked gazes with her and nodded once.

Lozen left the facility and walked for three miles.

Outside the Catchment, she noticed that others didn't walk much. She had a lifetime of miles on her twenty-seven-year-old legs, compared to the wealthy around her in the capital.

It started drizzling and she pulled up her wrap to cover her hair. Within a few minutes it grew damp.

Lozen reached a subway stop. It made her nervous to think of all the dirt and concrete and water pipes above her but not as nervous as the people did. She stood on the platform in warm boots and a beautiful wrap that was softer than the sand on the lake. Underneath, though no one could see, Lozen wore a simple shirt and pants, what she was comfortable in. Even with her disguise, Lozen felt it must be obvious to everyone around her she was an outsider.

Since moving to the capital, Lozen analyzed all her actions continuously and how they would appear to others. She had to.

Lozen lost the first apartment Agent Tril set her up with when the super found out she was fresh from the Catchment. She experienced the passive-aggressive cold shoulder of a few other female students who thought she was a dirty thief, and the overt advances from a teaching aide who thought she'd prostituted her way into a new life, though Lozen could have told him where women who tried that usually ended up, and it wasn't at a government-funded university.

Since she realized how quickly she could lose what she came so recently to possess, Lozen made sure she walked into shops with a vague air of disinterest and never put ground meal loath in her grocery basket, though she craved the staple food of her childhood. She went to great lengths to avoid talking about her past and generally avoided talking except in classes and at Qoan's trials. And now those were done with.

Even on the subway, Lozen avoided looking around too eagerly or striking up a conversation with someone next to her, as she had her very first time.

Lozen didn't have her own communicator and, though she hoped to get a job soon, it was to save up for when the two years' transitional support from the government stopped, not for electronics. She used the computers at school. Her allowance had to go to buy toothpaste and dress-up clothes and all the other things she realized were necessities now that she was living another life. Things that would make it seem like she fit in.

She stayed on the train for eight stops. After the second stop, she scooped up a discarded travel magazine. Lozen was proud she could read fluently now, but she was still building her vocabulary. Yacht. Mooncruise. Carry-on bag. In addition to new things, there were all these new words Lozen needed to learn. Her old words weren't enough on this side of the fence.

She got off the train and walked the mile to her apartment complex. It was a building full of people but better than on the subway where they could look at her. This was everyone's sleeping place and Lozen was used to sleeping among a community. If anything, the building felt austere rather than crowded.

Lozen scanned herself in and tracked rainwater on the gleaming floors. She walked to the elevator. The doors slid open and Lozen startled, certain she'd see Leggs's body crouched on the wall, waiting for her. The elevator was empty so she stepped inside and went up to the fourteenth floor. She worried she'd never stop anticipating his return.

In her own hall, she paused at the dark shape ahead. There was someone sitting in front of her door, back against the woody plastic. Who would sit on the floor of this immaculate apartment building?

Lozen's face broke into a smile for the first time in days and she rushed forward.

"Monte!"

Monte laughed and hugged Lozen.

"I got it yesterday. I went to the mail station and I thought I'd be waiting for nothing again, but there the letter was and I ran to Jerramy's place. By then a whole group had gathered and when he read it out loud I thought my heart would burst."

"But Agent Tril said your papers weren't supposed to come for another month at least. And how did you get here, Monte? How did you even get inside this building?" Lozen stood up, unlocked her door, and pulled Monte in by the hand.

Monte gasped and Lozen smiled again. She only had a mat for sitting and sleeping on and one salvaged shelf she found in a dumpster, but the counters gleamed and the fridge was enormous and there was more than one water tap in the whole place.

"This place is huge. Look at this." Monte ran her hands over the empty counter and then the window caught her eye. She walked over, looked out, and immediately stepped back half a pace. Lozen knew how she felt.

"I knew we were up high, but I had no idea."

"But really, Monte, how did you get here?"

Monte turned to Lozen. "I planned to hitchhike and show my letter around until I found another person who could read and hopefully they'd recognize the address."

"Monte, that would have been a very bad idea."

"Don't worry because while I was making preparations to leave, Waquas showed up. He actually used to live in the Catchment. He had been calling the agency to follow the progress of my papers and he gave me a ride here."

Lozen joined Monte at the window. She ran her fingers up along Monte's scalp. There was a secret stripe of flesh.

"Are you going to let that grow in?"

Monte looked serious. "You and I are out, Lozen, but they need us. Everyone wants a life outside, out here...but that will only happen in ones and twos. What if we made life better inside there?"

"You're such a revolutionary," Lozen said and smiled. She brought up her fingers to cover her mouth, a habit she no longer needed to rely on.

Monte pulled them down.

"So are you."

Chapter 41

Ippa & Adam
New Washington, WI

It came out to only forty thousand gallons of water a day. Though Ippa delighted in thinking of fresh, clean water in terms of gallons, it wasn't enough.

"No, this proposal isn't adequate," she said. "We're going to have 204 communal taps and the multigenerational family houses along the back with their own private supply of water."

"But the cost is so right for the budget," Adam said.

"I know, I know, but I really think we should find somewhere else to save, Adam. Water is one of Gustloaf's four communal guarantees. Let's do it right."

"If that's what Gustloaf says, then sure." He selected a small icon and the previous document appeared. "The bigger system will allow us to provide some security in case of low rainfall."

Ippa flicked her fingers in the aha gesture she used to use at university. "Let's reshape the elderly care program. We can pull funds from that. Instead of hiring workers to visit homes, let's provide a stipend for families that commit to attending training sessions and keeping their elderly in the home."

"We'll try it out," Adam said. "But we're going to have to make it a pilot program to test the model. I can think of a dozen things that could go wrong."

"Hmm," Ippa said, slightly dissatisfied that her solution wasn't an immediate winner. "You know them best, I would defer to your judgment."

"They're—we're—really not that different."

Ippa felt they were shifting into one of those conversations that was more philosophical than practical and though she was itching to get back to work, she didn't mind it too much because it helped her learn. Adam was the Earthling Ippa knew best, but she still learned something every time they talked.

"*My* parents were furious when they found out what transpired with Akar. Your mom came to help you," Ippa said.

Adam laughed, slightly high for his voice range. Ippa cataloged that away in her head.

"I think since Yani came to Earth, my mom knew something like that would happen sooner or later."

"But even that," Ippa said. "If that happened on my planet, everything would have been shut down. We would have gone into a monthlong dormancy mode while our politicians researched the possibilities and repercussions for war while our defenders prepared their remarks for the Joint Council."

"Earth still doesn't have the voice of a mouse on the Council, so it wouldn't have mattered if we did."

"We never would have provided refuge to the people on the ship. It would have been too risky," Ippa said.

"Well, it's clear Earth didn't have all good intentions."

Ippa nodded, remembering the original plan of simply demolishing the forest next to the Catchment.

"Which is why Loera helped get us hired. Which brings us back to…what's next?"

Ippa waved her hand in front of the hologram monitor switching between screens, pulling up her agenda for the meeting. She remembered what was next, but she felt like Adam didn't like it when she rolled through things too quickly. "Yep, the education building needs to be reworked for the library now that we've decided to combine the buildings."

Adam stretched. "Sure, we can work on that, but before we do, we have to go outside."

Ippa looked up. "Adam, I'm not playing that game with the ball again during a workday. It's not good for our subordinates to see us goofing off." Ippa looked around the facility, to see if anyone noticed her talking about the lighthearted basketball game Adam had convinced her to take one lunch break.

"I promise, this is important. And no one's going to be cheering me on this time." When she didn't relent, he added, "It'll be five minutes."

Ippa sighed and remembered that short, small breaks

were good to keep productivity going. She even said so at a training session two weeks ago. She followed Adam through the workspace. She, Adam, and the rest of the team worked across two floors of an older skyscraper that also housed capital administrative offices, convenient for popping up to ask about permits.

At the moment, only a few of them were in the space. A group was with the refugees from the *Akar Provenance* performing assessments and another group was in the Catchment filling out records. A minkin lay curled up in a patch of sunlight, blue fur shimmering.

They rode down the elevator in silence while Adam did something on his communicator and then she followed him out on the street.

She wondered what they were doing out there when Adam spoke, "Sorry, it's going to take longer than five minutes. More like an hour."

Ippa was furious. He had gone too far this time, disrespecting the work schedule. "I can't believe—"

Adam cut across her, "There's this thing on Earth called *putting your foot in your mouth* and I'm trying to save you from doing that. Let me talk."

Ippa was confused and mad now. What did her foot have to do with her mouth? She couldn't think of any culture that put the two together. Except for weird sex things on certain planets, she remembered. *Oh, crisping papers.*

"Follow me, we're going to the Grand Hotel."

Ippa stopped. "Adam, our work agreement requires me to inform you that this is inappropriate. Plus, on a personal level—"

"We're going to be late, Ippa. You can tell me whatever weird alien thing you're thinking of later. You have an interview with the U.N. Secretary-General."

Ippa gasped.

In the weeks after the attack, she had thrown herself into her research. Then, once she was hired as a codirector of the Catchment, she put the research project aside. She was sad but too engrossed in her work to continue researching. Ippa remembered telling Adam that if she ever got an interview with the secretary-general of the United Nations, it was going to be the crown jewel of her book.

"Thank you, thank you." Ippa leaped and threw her hands out, spinning in the street.

Chapter 42

Hloban
Winslow Space-Earth Station

Hloban hugged Obani's neck. He smelled so, so sweet in a stinky kid way. It was the smell of fresh dirt and doughnuts with the underlying hint of uncontrollable vomit if you spun too much on a hot day.

"You're such a strong, caring little man. Take good care of your grandparents. Listen to what they tell you to do."

The little boy sniffed.

"Follow along on the calendar I made you. Mommy and I will be back before New Year's."

Hloban passed the fragile little boy to Loera. She rocked him back and forth in her arms and whispered. He giggled.

"He'll be fine. We'll take good care of him. I'll make sure he doesn't eat sweets before preschool. Except on Fridays." Marla smiled. Loera's ever youthful mom looked like she could weather the fall with a four-year-old.

Hloban shook hands with Loera's dad, wondering how much he knew of their personal lives, and then picked up two small bags. Others around them were saying goodbye before boarding the commercial shuttle. Obani sobbed as Loera handed him to his grandparents.

"It's going to be okay, sweetie. We'll be able to call every night."

He sniffed. "Will you bring me back a present?"

"Of course. Two, in fact."

Hloban and Loera walked toward the security checkpoint. When he had gone to go look for Yaniqui, Hloban knew that Obani would have at least one parent if anything happened to him. With both Loera and him traveling…

His heart pained him all too much these days.

Hloban wondered what thoughts filled Loera's head but didn't want to start a conversation while going through the boarding procedures. Loera was ready, dressed for space travel in pale khaki pants and a long-sleeve blue shirt that would fit well under her jumpsuit. There were no tears in her eyes, but he saw a firmly set mouth.

Loera was a little clumsy going through the launch center. She didn't quite know where to go and took a long time organizing her paperwork and scratching her elbow so she could discern what direction to go in next without looking like she was looking. It would be Loera's first time in space, and Hloban wondered how she would do. He was nervous for her.

But there was no need. She took charge of the situations around her, molding them as she wanted.

A woman with blond ringlet hair helped them get strapped in on the craft. It was a cramped commercial model. He felt a pang for his own ship, gone forever. Hloban still had to pay off the fine for leaving wreckage in space as well as pay fines for "borrowing" the government craft—he thought that was unfair as ultimately Eeriva returned it.

"You doing all right?" It was the first thing he said to Loera since asking her to hand him his voucher at the boarding station.

It was her idea to go to space together. When Loera suggested they fill in on a consulting mission to the Jupiter Station, he knew immediately that it was more.

"I want those experiences too," she said. "You've had adventures in space, but I've never been."

"You've done a lot and built an amazing company—"

Loera cut him off. "I don't feel bad about my decisions and I know my worth."

Hloban knew she did. It was the only thing holding them together.

"But while you traveled across the galaxy, twice, I was taking care of things. I was finishing school and setting up myself to financially take care of my family and then I was taking care of Obani and my lab." Anger seeped into her voice.

"I know and I'm sorry," Hloban said.

Loera took a deep breath. "That's not where I'm going. That's not what I'm trying to say." Loera looked away from him and stretched her neck and shoulders while thinking.

"This can be a start for both of us. You need some perspective. To recover. And I want to push myself in a new area."

"What about Obani?" Hloban asked.

That's when Loera's face quivered. "I'm going to miss him a lot." She adjusted her glasses. "But this is for him too. I want to show him how much we can do. How much his family can do. But it's not just for me and for him. This is for us. You have this entire, wow, literally this entire world, that I don't know about. All our shared experiences are on Earth, but that's not what your life has been and maybe that's not what our future is going to be. I think there's been a disconnect since we got married. We need a bridge."

The ship rumbled to life and Hloban reached over and squeezed Loera's hand.

Chapter 43

Yaniqui
Earth

Her arm ached. It was an ugly blistering stump. Well, to be honest, it had a lot of problems, but no blisters. It just felt that way. It ached with disuse, throbbing when forced to shrug or when she pushed it through a shirt sleeve.

The existing arm was nearly as bad as the absent one. It was a shell of her dominant hand. It sucked at buttoning shirts and buttering her pancakes and was a continual reminder of her loss.

Yaniqui threw her journal across the room. It landed with a dull thud. No one else was home to hear. It would be the last firsthand account of Wea Saa ever written. Yaniqui knew Ippa was eager to probe each little sentence for information about the forgotten planet and send a copy to the Shou University archives. But now Yaniqui could hardly write.

She was getting faster at typing one-handed and didn't have to deal with her atrocious handwriting then, but Yaniqui wanted to finish things properly in the journal she had started after her arrival.

It took an hour to write even a few pages, and then she was mentally exhausted. She felt trapped again, like she had so many times before. It was frustrating but at least not scary, she reminded herself. Yaniqui rubbed her stump with her only hand and then stopped. She was conscious of the movement and was trying to break the habit.

Yaniqui fell backward onto her bed and regretted the action. The flop hurt her stump and getting up was difficult. Yaniqui had a hard time sitting straight up, always having relied on her hands to push her up and now only had her ab strength and maybe an elbow if the spare hand wasn't occupied with something else.

The house was quiet since Hloban and Loera left for their work trip and Obani had gone with his grandparents.

When Yaniqui was brought off the *Akar Provenance*, she was transported directly to a hospital in New Washington, WI. Within the first day, Yaniqui could feel her body stabilizing, adjusting to this new existence without an arm but that didn't mean her mind was okay. Physically, she got stronger, but mentally and emotionally, she was barely surviving.

With no medical reason to stay at the hospital, it was decided she would go back to live at Hloban and Loera's home. The third day she asked that Obani go with his grandparents so she could talk with them. Yaniqui dreaded hurting Loera more than she had already been hurt.

"Yaniqui, I agree we need to talk, but this can wait until you're better," Loera had said from a yellow velvet chair in the living room.

"I don't think I will get better until we talk about this," Yaniqui repeated the phrase Waquas used when he gave her the advice to talk with them. "First," Yaniqui started, "I'm so sorry to have brought this danger to your family." She rubbed her hand over her face and then held it up when Loera started to speak. "I know it's not entirely my fault—who knows how Akar found me—but I'm sorry nonetheless."

Loera looked pointedly at Hloban. He sighed. "That's the thing, Yaniqui. It was my fault. When I traded in my blood for the cloaking device, I cemented the connection between your escape and Earth. I couldn't pay back Onlo, so they sold the information to Akar. When they got here, I panicked," Hloban confessed. "I wasn't even going to go rescue you."

Yaniqui was surprised by her lack of anger. No one should have to decide whether to risk themselves to save a family member from slavery.

"But you did come. Thank you," Yaniqui said.

"Loera, uh, encouraged me to go."

Yaniqui paled. That was going to make the next part even harder. "Loera, I have a confession as well. I-I'm really, really sorry about this."

"About what?" Loera asked.

Yaniqui put her hand on the back of her neck. She couldn't look up at either Hloban or Loera. The living room was quiet and she was pretty sure she wasn't the only one crying.

"For trying to divide you and Hloban when I was first on the *Caneille*. For making the past half year so awkward in your house. For bringing all of this to your doorstep."

A shadow moved at the doorway. Maemi, who had clearly been listening, came in. "Yani, you have nothing to apologize for. We each made the best we could out of a terrible, terrible situation."

Loera smiled sadly at Yaniqui. "I agree with your mother. It's not the fault of women that monsters exist and it's better to fight than to be perfect. Could we all have done better?" Loera looked dryly around the room. "Sure. But that doesn't mean we're not worthy of redemption."

When the approval for Hloban and Loera's off-planet job came through, Loera told Yaniqui and Nica they were welcome to stay as long as they wanted while they were gone, but suggested they begin to look for an apartment. Loera offered to pay the rent for a year while Yaniqui and Maemi got settled. She made it absolutely clear—no one could be more direct than Loera—that they were still family and the move wasn't because of a personal matter regarding Yaniqui and Hloban, or Yaniqui and herself, but a personal matter regarding Hloban and herself.

It was a kind offer and a necessary one. Hloban was a part of Yaniqui's past and would continue to be a part of her life, but there was no mistaking that the fates had shifted. The connection between Yaniqui and Hloban was severed. He was not her future.

Yaniqui wrested herself up off her bed and sat to catch her breath. On her dresser was the paperwork she was supposed to send back. That, she couldn't type. It had to be filled out by hand, but she was in no mood to deal with that either.

Earth made Yaniqui, Maemi, Keyad, and Hloban citizens, and she and her mother diplomats of the planet. It was a quickly made decision, and not without inspiring protest in New Washington. But it was the only way to remove once and for all the possibilities of being legally acquired by Akar Enterprises.

Still, Yaniqui remembered pledging her allegiance to the planet in a wave of emotions. They stood in front of the world flag with the U.N. leader herself leading them through the words to become citizens. At first Yaniqui was nervous that holding her left hand over her heart muscle would be seen as a slight, but halfway through the verses, Yaniqui was overcome with the sense of having a home at last. She was afraid she was going to cry. The one who cried though was Adam, who received a Global Citizen Award, reflecting that his home loved him as much as he loved it.

It was an incredible gesture. It also pushed Earth into the spotlight of the galaxy newsfeed, much to the secretary-general's pleasure. A remote planet with relatively new ties to the interconnected galaxy system gets all six Wea Saavians in one swoop.

Yaniqui and the others—minus Obani who would decide for himself when he came of age—agreed to give two blood samples each: one for Earth's researchers and one to the Galaxy Health Panel. However, Yaniqui also knew that Onlo had a sample from Hloban and not all the blood samples were recovered from the Akar craft. Ippa speculated that Adam's donation of a blood sample to the

U.N. would be the most telling; what differences were there in his DNA versus Yaniqui, Keyad, and Hloban?

And, as a new homeowner of sorts, Yaniqui made the decision to work with what was supposed to be a neutral agency inside the U.N. to heal her new planetwomen and men. There were so many ethical questions to answer, so many angles to consider, so many people in need, that Yaniqui insisted she would only start by healing terminally ill children on a lottery basis.

Yaniqui poured herself some cereal for lunch—it required the least amount of cooking one-handed. She crunched along while watching a graphic comic holo. Yaniqui turned it off when she finished. She should put the bowl in the dishwasher and run it. That was easy enough. The problem was, Yaniqui didn't have much will to do anything. The house was a mess. She vowed she'd clean it up before Loera got back.

The front door opened, and Maemi came in, wearing a ridiculous exercise outfit of Loera's.

"Maemi! When did you start baring your navel?"

Maemi laughed like a child. "It feels good, doesn't it? Now, what are we going to do about this house?"

Yaniqui shrugged, jokes out of mind. "Sorry, I just don't feel like I have the energy for anything."

Maemi came and sat at the table. She smelled of sunscreen and eyed the cereal disapprovingly before turning her gaze on her daughter. "You've experienced a terrible loss. We all have. But right when I thought my life was over, you gave me a fresh start. One where I am not used. Not in pain. And with you. What a gift." She sighed the mom sigh. "I know it's hard to see, but you are healing and you are going to keep healing."

Yaniqui fingered her spoon. "I know."

Maemi touched her forlorn upper arm. "That's what life is. A chance to keep healing."

Later that afternoon, her phone beeped. Yaniqui ran to it.

Yes, it was Waquas. She didn't expect to hear from him until that evening.

I'm done. Will you please come over early? Whenever you're available?

Yaniqui smiled. Waquas never took meeting up for granted and was always grateful when she made time in her life for him. She wrote back.

I'm already here, look behind you...

Yaniqui paused, imagining him looking around.

Kidding.

Yaniqui saw he was typing.

I'm actually glad you're not here yet because I am going to finish this ice cream before you get here.

Yaniqui smiled and grabbed the keys. Yaniqui started Loera's car and hummed along quietly. Driving was one of the things that was still physically easy. She could sit, so there were no balance issues. Her left arm got tired holding on to the wheel and she spent a fair amount of time driving hands-free as she tried to adjust music or scratch her nose, but those minor issues were a relief compared to the simple act of trying to wash her hair or cut vegetables for dinner.

It was a nice day, a sunny and warm burst for the lateness of the season. The day before had been cold and rainy but things dried in the sunshine. Yaniqui drove out of the city limits. The storefronts and houses spread out.

Green crept in. She took a familiar set of turns and drove along the edge of a large forest. In the wide openings, Yaniqui saw Waquas's property.

She enjoyed being there. In the dirt, there were no shapes to draw or write, nothing to button or fold or cut. Just the joining of Earth and plant, perfect in its ability to be without perfection.

Yaniqui pulled up to the overhang on the side of the house and went inside without knocking.

"Hi," she breathed.

"I'm glad you're here." Waquas smoothed her curls back.

She grabbed another spoon from the drawer and turned to the kitchen counter.

Yaniqui stopped. Inside the container was one bite of vanilla ice cream with no cookie dough or fudge or *anything* delicious.

"What is this?" Yaniqui demanded.

Waquas smiled sheepishly. "I was originally joking, but I pulled this out when I figured you were almost here and I couldn't help but get started. It was so good. I'm sorry. I'll buy some more in a few days."

"Waquas," Yaniqui whined. She was madder than she cared to admit. "I can't believe you ate it all. You knew I was on my way."

Waquas looked surprised. "I—"

"No, you should have waited for me."

Waquas took her by the hand and led her to the porch. There were two bowls full of cookie dough ice cream with a chocolate wafer sticking out of each.

"Oh my gosh. I'm sorry, Waquas. I totally believed

you." She started cracking up. "It's hard," she said through her laughter, "everything is so hard these days." The laughter dissolved into tears.

Waquas held Yaniqui and she breathed in the scent of his sweat.

"I know." Waquas held her face gently in his hands. "But it's going to get easier."

They sat down and licked the ice cream. Yaniqui's foot rested on Waquas's knees. It was hard balancing the small bowl without a second hand to provide counterpressure when she scooped.

"How do you know?" Yaniqui asked at last.

"That it's going to get better?" Waquas set his bowl down.

"Yeah." Yaniqui felt another tear slip down her cheek.

Waquas reached out with his finger and wiped the tear away.

"Because you decide your own fate."

Acknowledgements

The Displacement Duology has lived with me for over a decade, and I'm so glad to be able to finish telling Yaniqui's story. I wrote this series largely for myself, but if there has been a reader over my shoulder, it is my book coach, Nicole Van Den Eng. Her absolute taste is my measure and her footprints lie in the best parts of this book.

I appreciate the editing support of Lynnette Kopetsky and Anne-Marie Rutella, as well as the design support of Andrew Davis which allowed me to take this project from an idea to a professional level.

Special thanks to Beth Stevens for sharing her name with me via the named character competition—know she is kinder than her namesake.

More than any of my books, my kids have taken an interest in this one. Madeline and Pierce are not only older and more aware, but I'm finally at the point in my writing journey where I have physical products to share and hence they finally believe I'm doing something with all that time in my office. They are the quickest to celebrate me, commiserate when writing is hard, and provide endless ideas through their antics.

This is the third finished book my husband has held my hand through. Even as I ask for daily strategy sessions (and validation), Oliver always encourages me to ask for more, both of myself and of the world.

Acknowledgements

About the Author

Rebecca M. Zornow is the author of *It's Over or It's Eden, Dangerous to Heal,* and *Negotiated Fate*. She is a Hal Prize winner, a full member of the Science Fiction and Fantasy Writers Association, and has written for numerous print and digital publications.

Rebecca is an alumna of Lawrence University. After graduation, she served in the Peace Corps where she started school libraries and an art club in rural eSwatini. Rebecca is also a board member of the Caneille Regional Development Fund which works in rural Haiti. She is a former magazine editor-in-chief and runs the book coaching business Conquer Books with writer and book coach Nicole Van Den Eng.

Learn more about Rebecca and sign up for her monthly newsletter at www.RebeccaMZornow.com.